Ballroom Forever

by

Natalie Cross

A Dancesport Mystery, Book 3

Ballroom Forever

Contact Information: info@thewildrosepress.com

Cover Art by *Diana Carlile*

The Wild Rose Press, Inc.
PO Box 708
Adams Basin, NY 14410-0708
Visit us at www.thewildrosepress.com

Publishing History
First Edition, 2024
Trade Paperback ISBN 978-1-5092-5504-7
Digital ISBN 978-1-5092-5505-4

Dancesport Mystery Series
Published in the United States of America

Dedication

For my mom, who always believes in me, and shared with me her love of British procedurals.

Also By Natalie Cross

Ballroom Blitz
Ballroom Fever

Prologue

Who did they think they were?

International superstar Tom Havens, no matter what *they* thought, stumbled into the alley behind the rubbish "world-famous" ballroom for a smoke. Bloody closed-minded arsheholes. So what if he had a bevvie now and then? He needed it, working out of this shithole excuse for a town. He couldn't wait to get back to Toronto.

It was dark in the alley, but noise from the nearby clubs filtered down the street past the dumpsters. He kicked at a pile of wadded-up trash, enjoying the way it felt to impose a little more chaos into this wretched place.

A bachelorette party trio careened into the alley as he took a drag on his ciggie. They caught sight of him and tittered like drunken schoolgirls before falling over themselves to head back to whatever dive bar they'd crawled out of. They deserved smoke rings, nothing more. There were easier pickings tonight, far more up to his standard. That was the only bloody perk of working for those wankers.

Tom cracked his world-famous smile, the one that was going to make him bigger than bloody Ryan Seacrest, the tosser. *Dance with Me* was his show. He'd fought tooth and nail, literally, for this job, and those rich-as-fuck daft gobbies could shove their opinions where the sun does not shine.

Tucking his cigarette between his second and third knuckles, he pulled a silver flask imprinted with his headshot from his pocket.

How dare they? Fire him? Hah. He *was Dance with Me*. He was the one who had resurrected it for a new season. Not Jackson Alder. Not Laurie Donovan, that high-brow bitch. Not the bloody bossmen, with their so-called secrets. Tom's face crinkled with disgust, and he took another pull from his flask. How dare they threaten what he had built? They owed *him*, not the other way around.

That thought made him pause as nothing else had. He set the end of the cigarette between his lips and rolled it around, thinking.

He knew what they were hiding. That was the key. They thought he wouldn't use it because it might bring him down as well, but their gullibility wasn't his mistake. He could hide his own involvement.

Flipping the cigarette butt onto the wet pavement, he ground it into the tarmac with his toe, enjoying the feeling of it crumpling beneath his Italian leather brogue. Like the carapace of an insect, crispy on the outside, juicy in the middle. He pictured the fat fingers of that posh faker instead of the ciggie.

Revenge. Tom Havens was very, very good at revenge. They'd regret threatening to fire him.

Chapter One

The train rumbled and swayed through the English countryside, past row houses with the day's washing hanging on lines in postcard-sized backyards.

In his lap, Patrick O'Leary's phone buzzed with the reminder that he was now using his international data plan, and all the tension in his body eased. Away. He was finally geographically away from his mom. Her prison cell was across an entire ocean, and he had two weeks in the frigid north of England with his fiancée and about a thousand other ballroom dancers. If she piled up the phone calls from prison while he was in Blackstone, he did not even have to think about it.

Glory Britannia, and all that.

Speaking of glory, his supermodel-gorgeous fiancée sat beside him. Anita's blonde head lolled onto his shoulder as she released an enormous snore.

She was absolutely adorable. Patrick snugged an arm around her and squeezed her against his side. This was going to be a great trip. Jet lag and the northern wind aside, both he and Anita desperately needed not to be in Lewis, Pennsylvania. Ever since his injury and the giant revelatory shitshow that had happened with his mom and Anita's dad the previous fall, things had been tense.

But now they were in England for the Blackstone Dance Festival, invited to dance in the fabled Team

Match of all honors, and Patrick was certain life had to get better.

It certainly couldn't be worse.

With the arm not surrounding Anita, Patrick fitted his earphones into his ears and turned on his Blackstone playlist. He focused on the scenery outside the window while listening to Sergio Mendes and mentally running through their choreography.

Drizzle misted against the sides of the train as they passed through English countryside. Under his arm, Anita stirred and yawned in an endearingly feline way. She blinked her eyes open. "Did I fall asleep?"

"You need to rest." He pressed a kiss to the top of her head, which still smelled of grapefruit and hibiscus, even after the six-hour flight from Philadelphia to Heathrow. "Jet lag is a beast."

She groaned slightly and righted herself, pulling her long, thick black cardigan closer around her body. Patrick had laid her rainbow swirl patterned raincoat over her lap as a blanket, and she readjusted it so it didn't fall at their feet.

Anita yawned again and he turned off his music. Anita deserved every inch of his focus.

"Is anyone else on the train?" she asked.

Patrick scanned the immediate area of their train car. "No one I can see. Lucy and her parents arrived yesterday so they should already be at the house. I'm surprised we haven't run into any other competitors we know."

Anita nodded, sniffing. He was pretty sure she only asked because jet lag had sapped her memory. Before they'd left, she had made at least three detailed checklists of everything they needed for this trip. It had been far too long since they'd traveled for an international competition, and they both wanted this to be a successful trip. For many reasons.

One of which, if Patrick were honest, was because maybe then Anita would finally agree to set a wedding date.

But that was a quandary for a non-travel day. The only thing he should decide today was whether to indulge in fish and chips, a sausage roll, or have the grilled chicken and vegetables that was his usual pre-competition nutrition. An athlete was only as good as what went into his body.

Patrick frowned slightly. That meant all that delicious British beer was off the table. Boo.

Anita poked him in the side. "You have that look on your face like you're ruing the fact that we're here to compete and you can't try all of the local microbrews."

He chortle-snorted and tried in vain to hide it behind his hand. "I didn't realize I was so predictable."

She yawned again and stretched her neck. "Only to me. That's the downside of having met in high school."

He kissed the top of her head again. If only he'd been brave enough in high school to tell her how he felt, maybe…

But there were roads that were foolish to travel, so many years later. Everything they had been through had brought him and Anita closer together, and he should be grateful for it.

And therapy. He was definitely grateful for therapy.

"How are you feeling?" Anita asked, straightening and taking her phone from her pocket.

She could mean absolutely anything by it, but

Patrick knew what she intended. Was he still having panic attacks? Did he feel strong enough to compete? Was he mentally screaming at his mom every chance he got?

"Fine, Anita. Everything's going great."

Chapter Two

The train pulled into the station at Blackstone a few hours and two trips to the tiny train bathroom later. Anita slung her carry-on duffel over one arm while Patrick hefted their two over-packed suitcases from the storage area and off the train car. They'd have to find a taxi to take them to their vacation rental. There was no way she was going to roll those suitcases through the rainy, windy streets of Blackstone. Well, she would because she was not one to forego hard work, but she would definitely prefer a dry car ride.

"Does it feel good to be back?" Patrick asked, following her through the train station toward the cab stand.

Anita shrugged. "I don't know. It's been years since I was here." The last time had been with her former partner and good-riddance ex-boyfriend Mikhail, and they had barely made it past the first round. Which he had subsequently blamed on her. Not her fondest memory.

A thrill of annoyance ran down her spine, but she tried to pass it off with a smile. "It's great to be here with you," she said. She should be happy. She was here with Patrick. This was her first paid international coaching gig. They had been invited to compete not only in the open professional Latin championships, but in the Team Match as part of Team Americas. This was the dream, right?

So, she was languishing. She was going through the motions and barely anything brought her joy anymore. She could get over it.

If she didn't, the next week was going to be torture.

"It's so cool to be here," Patrick said. They'd reached the cab stand and stood in line in the frigid rain with far too many other people, all likely on their way to the exact same competition Anita and Patrick were attending. Crowds and rain. It was almost June, for the love of Springsteen. Why could this damn north country not behave like it?

Anita tamped down the underlying current of irritation running through her bloodstream. Patrick had never been to Blackstone. He'd done other international competitions, but certainly not this one, the most prestigious in the world. She needed to make this a good experience for him, even if she would prefer lying in bed with a pile of covers over her head. "It is, isn't it?" She forced excitement into her tone. "We're going to do great. I just know it."

He linked his fingers with hers and squeezed. "Totally. Nothing's going to go wrong."

The irritation she had tamped down now flared with trepidation. The rose-gold band with the diamond setting weighed heavily on the fourth finger of her left hand. So much had already happened in their relationship, but this was a ballroom competition. They finally approached the end of the cab stand where, blissfully, a black hackney cab waited. She breathed deeply. Nothing worse than torn gowns and blisters was going to happen. "Of course. It's just dancing. What could possibly go wrong?"

****

The cab zipped through the crowded streets from the train station and down the stormy coast toward the small neighboring town of Lythe, where they were staying. And thank goodness. The last time Anita had attended Blackstone, she had narrowly avoided being pissed on by a drunk pensioner outside their apartment rental.

The dark gray sea churned to one side of them, while on the other the more industrial makeup of Blackstone slowly morphed into a picturesque British town.

She definitely owed Lucy's parents, the Knights, for treating them to a luxury rental.

"Whoa," Patrick said as they turned into the drive of the rental property.

"Whoa indeed."

Set a little away from the street, behind black-and-ivory stone gates that rolled open like this was some Hollywood high noir version of her life, Gryphon Manor could be called anything other than usual. It was not a tall building, but instead sprawled like an octopus spreading her tentacles across the lush, manicured green lawn. Box hedges stood at exactly the right intervals, like the entire design had been recreated from a book of Regency British landscaping. The house itself was red brick with black-lined windows that glimmered with lights that looked more like candles. It was Gothic and imposing and the most spectacular house she had ever seen. She practically expected Elizabeth Bennett to appear in the driveway.

"I should style my hair like Veronica Lake while we're here," she said to Patrick, partly to allay her own anxiety.

"She stayed here." The cab driver parked in the spacious brick roundabout before the massive front door of the place and left the car running. "In the forties, during a film premiere." His accent was thick and lush. For the first time since they had started planning this trip, Anita's heart thrilled with a little excitement.

"Wow, Veronica Lake." Patrick whistled a low, impressed tune. "These are some fancy digs the Knights are treating us to."

As if on cue, the front door opened with an eerie groan and seventeen-year-old Lucy Knight, in jeans and a faded gray concert T-shirt, raced across the driveway.

"Hey!" Lucy cried, leaping into the air. Her long black ponytail followed her movement.

Anita's heart thawed another three degrees. She suspected Patrick felt the same, but Lucy was one of her favorite students.

Lucy threw herself into Anita's arms before Anita could even get out of the car. "Hi, Lucy."

"Thank goodness you guys finally got here." Lucy rolled her eyes. "I cannot take this much together time with my parents." She said it in a way that implied that she really liked spending time with her folks but knew it was outré to say such things.

Anita could relate. Or she used to be able to, before her father had torpedoed their entire family in spectacular fashion.

Yup, irritability had returned.

"I've got to get back to the station," the cabbie said. He had unloaded their suitcases from the trunk and now slid back into the driver's seat.

"Oh, right, sorry." Anita hastily clambered away from the car and stood on the brick driveway. Patrick followed suit after paying the man.

Lucy bounced up and down in her black sneakers that she had decorated with graffiti style art. "Come on inside. There's an actual, like, butler here, and he *insists* on giving everyone the full tour. Isn't this place creepy? I'll bet it's rife with paranormal activity. Last night I swear I heard someone crying."

Anita caught Patrick's gaze, and his eyes widened with hers. They rolled their suitcases with a minimum of difficulty across the driveway. Anita had expected the bricks to be more like cobblestones, but her suitcase wheels glided like they were dancing across ice. One of many surprises here at Gryphon House.

"Are you excited for the competition?" Patrick asked.

"I suppose." Lucy shrugged as she pushed the massive front door open with a heralding groan. "Careful. This door swings shut all on its own for, like, no reason at all. Yesterday we came back from dinner and it had locked itself."

Eek. Anita did not particularly like anything not naturally possessing neurons which moved of its own volition.

They stepped into the foyer and the first unwelcome thought that popped into Anita's head was that her father would love this place, with its masculine wood overtones. The second was that her mom would probably hate it. Then she would make something delicious and the entire house would smell like cinnamon and citrus and allspice and the entire thing would be wonderful.

Sorrow pricked at the backs of her eyes, but like every emotion this trip, Anita tamped it down. She was here as a professional. There was no room in Blackstone for the grim demise of her nuclear family unit.

A gentleman who could have been ordered from a catalog of "men who look like butlers" appeared wearing a dark suit and a grim scowl. Once he spoke, it was apparent that this encompassed his entire personality. "Hello. I assume you are Ms. Anita Goodman and Mr. Patrick O'Leary? Guests of the Knights? Welcome to Gryphon House."

"Thank you." Anita nodded her head, unsure whether to offer to shake his hand or curtsy. The head-nodding thing was somewhere in between.

"Hello," Patrick said, bending slightly as though he, too, were caught in some weird time warp where they had to bow. Lucy stifled a chuckle behind a cough.

The butler sniffed as though a skunk had sprayed inside his beloved home. His gray-brown eyes narrowed. "Very well. I am Mr. Butler. You may call me such."

That seemed on the nose. The languishing, self-pitying part of Anita wanted to ask but she wasn't the paying guest here and thought it better to play as though this wasn't an episode of "Upstairs, Downstairs."

Mr. Butler sniffed again, the small gesture barely moving a single gray-brown strand of the hair that had been shellacked to his head. "If you would care to follow me, I will give you the grand tour. Ms. Knight, of course you are welcome to join again, if you wish to pay more attention than you did yesterday."

Lucy brushed his comment off her shoulder like it

was a piece of lint.

"Very well." Mr. Butler led them from the spacious foyer into the main room, which was dominated by a sturdy and imposing black-brick fireplace. The furnishings had been done in a subtle color of chintz that seemed to match the heavy, dark colors of the wood. "Gryphon House was originally built in 1734 as a church and served the Church of England faithfully for over two hundred years, before it was purchased by the Grantward family."

"Local bigwigs," Lucy whispered, loud enough that it could really only be considered a whisper in a room full of people shouting. Mr. Butler shot her a quelling look, and Lucy responded by popping the gum in her mouth.

Anita turned in place, taking in the mahogany floors, the dark-wood walls set with hunting pictures. Why people had such a fascination with hunting pictures, she would never know. Guns were never her favorite. Tasers, though, she could be persuaded.

"As I was saying," Mr. Butler said, his BBC-perfect accent clipped. "The Grantward family purchased the property in 1937, and converted it into a family home, which they maintained for their progeny until approximately five years ago."

Lucy coughed and leaned toward Anita. "That's when the reigning Grantward lost all his money backing a failed oil scheme, and—"

Mr. Butler loudly cleared his throat. "And at that time, the property was converted into a holiday house." The acidic tone he used clearly conveyed his feelings on the matter.

Patrick inspected a curio cabinet filled with china

boxes that looked too similar to coffins for Anita's taste. "It's a cool place," he said.

"We have have climate control here." Mr. Butler waved dismissively at a small box showing the current inner temperature in degrees Centigrade. "Still, we are on the sea and quite far north. It is not unusual to have drafts."

Patrick's eyes lit up like he was electrified. "Is that from the Blackstone ghost?"

Mr. Butler's eyeroll was the most epic one Anita had ever had the fortune to see. "There is absolutely no such thing as the Blackstone ghost. Now, if you will follow me through to the kitchens."

They trailed after him as a trio.

"He wouldn't tell me yesterday, either," Lucy said, clearly undisturbed by this reticence. "But I looked it all up online. Every year, particularly around the competition, women disappear. They say the Blackstone ghost takes them for his own pleasure. *Phantom of the Opera*-style."

Anita felt an odd twinge of sympathy for Mr. Butler. "There is no ghost. I've been here twice before, and nothing has happened except for falls, sprains, and a lot of hairspray and tears."

"Anita," Patrick said, in a mockingly chiding tone. "Just because you haven't seen it, doesn't mean it isn't real."

He and Lucy exchanged a quiet high five.

This was going to be the longest working vacation of Anita's life.

Chapter Three

Patrick could tell the jet lag was catching up to him when every single soft surface he saw in that pompous mausoleum of a house started to resemble a bed.

They'd already visited the gym and spa, both of which Mr. Butler not-so-subtly derided in his fan-of-preserving-history way, as well as the kitchen, complete with restored Aga, and several other random rooms. A glass-domed conservatory, which seemed to be an indoor garden. A music room with, for some reason, light blue wallpaper entirely covered in various British songbirds. Several small bathrooms, alternatively dubbed by Mr. Butler as either water closets or washrooms.

Patrick had no idea of the distinction and cared even less. If there was no bed, he had lost interest.

Anita lagged slightly behind him, the desire for sleep clearly evident on her face as well.

"I feel like we're in a game of Clue," he said, taking her hand in his.

"OMG, totally," Lucy replied from beside them. She was examining something on her phone. "I haven't played that game in ages, but this house one hundred percent reminds me of it."

"Here concludes the tour," the spindly and prickly Mr. Butler said, stopping outside yet another closed door. "Ms. Goodman and Mr. O'Leary, this will be your accommodation. My associate has already brought your luggage upstairs. If you need assistance unpacking, please advise. Tonight we will provide your meal, but unless you require us to cook, you are on your own. The shops are nearby. If you'll excuse me, I must ensure that supper has been started by my nephew. You'll have time to rest and refresh before the meal this evening. The Knights are anxious to speak with you."

"Bye, Butler!" Lucy called, waving her fingers at the man's retreating back. "See? This place is wild, isn't it?"

"It's certainly something," Patrick said, turning the knob. To his immense relief, the furnishings of the bedroom they had been assigned were nowhere near as anachronistic as the rest of the house, which seemed caught in a war between medieval, country hunting lodge, and 1980s San Diego chic. This room was far more simply furnished. There was a king-sized bed made with a down comforter and a handmade quilt, a small bathroom, and a functional set of drawers. Their extra-large, overstuffed suitcases sat beside the closet.

It looked a lot like heaven.

"You two must need to rest," Lucy said, nevertheless snooping around their room before making her way back to the door. "I know when we got in yesterday, I wanted to sleep like the dead. See you at dinner. It's at seven." She closed the door with a far too hearty *thunk*, and Patrick and Anita were finally, blissfully alone.

"This place is something," Patrick said, sitting on the edge of the bed. This was an immediate mistake, as it was even more comfortable than it looked, and he realized he was sinking straight into it. "And the butler

Butler?"

"I just want to sleep." Anita slipped off her fleece-lined soft boots and crawled on top of the comforter.

"I'll set the alarm." But he might have forgotten because the very instant he closed his eyes, he was dead asleep.

****

A bee buzzed near Anita's ear, and she swatted it with a limp hand. She had been having such a nice dream. Such comforting quiet.

The buzzing stopped, then started again.

Her eyes fluttered open reluctantly, jet lag and ennui weighing her muscles down. She wanted to sleep for another hour. Or maybe ten more years. Wait, how many had Rip Van Winkle had? Maybe that would be long enough.

Patrick shifted in his sleep, moaning and curling into a fetal position. His dark brown hair flopped over his forehead in a curly tangle. Anita wrapped her body around his. His nightmares had improved over the last few months but hadn't completely resolved. Even through her languishing, she wished she knew what to do to help him.

He stilled in her arms, pressing his back closer to her, like she was the one thing warming him.

A small twang pulsed through her heart. At least she had Patrick. She didn't need a resolution to her family issues, not while she had him and he needed her.

The buzzing sounded again, like something skipping across a hard surface. Anita winced. It was her phone, of course. Keeping her body in as much contact as possible with Patrick, so he could rest, but contorting to pick up the phone from the nightstand behind her, was a Herculean feat.

Still, she managed it. Bleary-eyed, she glanced at the lock screen notification and grimaced. Her mom again. A simple *good luck* text this time. She'd been texting more and more often, like the less Anita responded, the more her mom tried. Her stomach twisted into knots. Great.

Then Anita saw the local time at the top of the screen and her entire body reacted.

"Patrick. Patrick, wake up. We overslept."

He grumbled and shifted in his sleep, turning and wrapping an arm around her waist.

Despite her newfound urgency to force herself awake, she felt her body sink into his embrace. Was this how it would always be? Even when they were old and gray? They wouldn't get there unless she got her head out of her ass and set a wedding date.

"Patrick." She nudged his shoulder with her hand, his strong muscles unyielding beneath her touch. "Patrick. Wake up. We have to go down to dinner."

His eyes opened briefly then shut again and he released a low snore.

More drastic measures were clearly necessary. Anita slipped out of bed and stood over him, shaking him a little more violently. "Wake up, sleepy butt."

"You're a sleepy butt," he said, eyes still closed. They fluttered open. "I'm sorry. You have a really nice butt."

She shoved him playfully beneath the covers. "You, too. But we're working and we're late for dinner. Let's get up and thank our hosts."

He groaned and rolled over on his back. "Jet lag sucks."

“So does adulting.” Anita tossed a pillow at him, knowing it wouldn’t hurt but would likely wake him up a bit more. “Get up and wash your face. I love you, but you smell like airplane chicken salad.”

Chapter Four

They made it down to the formal dining room—separate from the kitchen dining area that Mr. Butler had indicated earlier on their tour—with mere moments to spare. Lucy was already seated at the table that would easily hold sixteen, with her parents on either side of her. There were ceramic bowls full of pink and red peonies interspersed between the silver candlesticks, and so much glassware it practically lit the room by itself.

The Knights fit right in to this highly polished scene. Cassandra Knight was a petite woman with pale skin whose presence and command of attention more than made up for her stature. Tonight she was dressed in a gorgeous, silky blue-and-black printed wrap dress, her smooth black hair perfectly coiffed, like she hadn't fought a battle with the north winds and lost. Anita touched the end of her blonde ponytail, wishing for a moment she had taken a few extra minutes to brush the bedhead out of her own hair. Maybe she really should invest in one of those facial rollers that kept popping up in the dance studio's social media ads. They clearly worked.

Jason Knight sat at least a foot taller than his wife but was distracted by the cell phone glued to his hand. He had kind, wide-set eyes that seemed simultaneously to see everything and nothing all at once. His suit probably cost the same as the studio's rent. Or maybe it was his similarities to her own father that irked her, but she was far too jet-lagged for such self-reflection at the moment.

Anita pulled limply at the bottom of her wrinkled silk blouse, wishing she had brought fancier clothes. As always, Patrick looked perfect, dark brown hair messy-sexy and dark blue eyes sparkling. At least after washing the airplane off himself.

Lucy gave them both a shy wave.

"Thank you so much for hosting us, Mr. and Mrs. Knight," Anita said, resting her hands on the back of a chair across from the family. "It's so generous of you."

Cassandra waved a hand in the air as if conjuring magic. "Of course, of course. We were very lucky to find this place on such short notice. And you are helping us by finding a new partner for our Lucy." She smiled fondly at her daughter, her berry-red lips pulled into a maternal smile. A pang of homesickness rocked Anita. Of all things, did she really miss her mom? "Please, sit. Dinner is ready."

Patrick pulled out Anita's chair for her, because of course he did, and then took his own seat beside her.

The table was set with fine bone-white china, inlaid with a pattern of gold filigree. The dining room itself was dominated by a massive crystal chandelier above the table, its arms wiry and elegant, like it danced at night when no was watching. As seemed to be the case everywhere but in their own bedroom, the walls were dominated by hunting prints.

"The Grantwards must be huge hunters," Patrick said, following her gaze. "I've never seen so many paintings of people on horseback chasing a furry fox."

Jason Knight glanced around then turned back to his glass of red wine and his phone. "I suppose I haven't noticed."

At that moment, Mr. Butler appeared, carrying a large ceramic soup tureen. Behind him was a good-looking young man with dark brown hair, closer to Lucy's age, holding a wooden tray filled with bread rolls.

Anita's stomach turned with hunger, and she salivated. Had she eaten anything that day? She'd had breakfast, which felt like eleven thousand hours before, and a fruit cup at the airport in Philadelphia, but she hadn't been hungry on the plane. Particularly not for the generic cold sandwich they had served where the meat looked more gray than edible.

Mr. Butler served Mrs. Knight first, ladling soup into the bowl waiting before her. "Tonight we have cress soup. It is watercress served with a traditional mixture of cream and spices." It looked green and tantalizing, though Anita might have eaten anything at that moment. Mr. Butler gestured at his young associate, who was offering the bread tray to Lucy like he was serving the very queen of England. "This is James Barrow. He is my nephew and assistant here. He's helping me out for now, and then he's off to university after the summer."

James nodded slightly, but his attention was wholly fixed on Lucy, who couldn't really be bothered. Aww. Someone had a crush. It was a good thing James wasn't in charge of the soup or it would have been all over Cassandra's dress.

Anita thanked both Mr. Butler as he ladled and James as he handed her a whole grain roll.

"Would you care for another?" James turned again to Lucy, tongs in hand and bread brandished before him like a tray of diamonds.

Lucy's gaze flicked to him then back to her parents. "Nope. I'm great. Thank you for asking." The slightest flush rose up the back of her spray-tanned neck.

Okay, way too cute.

"James." The single word was Mr. Butler's command, and the pair of them left the dining room, Lucy surreptitiously staring at James's departing back.

The Knights picked up their soup spoons en masse, like this was a practiced ritual.

"How was your flight?" Cassandra asked, dabbing at the corners of her mouth with her linen napkin. "We flew to Manchester, which I think was better. A much shorter train ride than the one from London."

It had felt a little like six hours of a far too long movie from the 1970s. At least no one had been murdered on the train. "It was fine, thank you," Anita said, soup spoon halfway to her mouth. "We flew into Heathrow, but fortunately the train was running on time."

Jason Knight said nothing and proceeded to demolish his soup.

Patrick buttered his roll. "Are you ready for the Juniors competition, Lucy?"

Lucy shrugged as she shredded her roll into thin strips. "I suppose. It's weird, to think this is the last time I'll dance with Henry."

She and Henry Kim had been dancing together for the past six months, but while they had a lot of potential, he was graduating high school in a few weeks, then heading to California. The Knights had been very clear about their expectations for a new partner for their only daughter.

Cassandra covered Lucy's hand. "Henry is a wonderful dancer. But we'll find you someone even better. Right, Anita?" She glanced over at her, like Anita had all the answers.

If only. "After the Juniors competition, we have a number of auditions lined up for Lucy. We will find her someone perfect." Anita had spent hours trawling through dance message boards and contacting every other coach she knew, searching for potential partners. They'd auditioned a few locals in Pennsylvania, but so far no one had suited Lucy.

For an easygoing seventeen-year-old, she was remarkably difficult to please in this respect.

"Good." Jason Knight set his soup spoon beside his empty bowl and picked up his cell phone again. "Lucy needs to start competing in higher level competitions, more like Blackstone here. It will set her apart from the other Ivy League hopefuls."

Anita saw the subtle stoniness settle into Lucy's shoulders, and she sent her a mental wave of sympathy. If anyone understood parental pressures, it was Anita. "Of course. Blackstone will be quite the feather in her cap. Just by being here, she and Henry are setting themselves apart."

Lucy sent her a grateful look as she dabbed a fragment of roll into her soup.

"Is there anything else you hope to do while you're here?" Patrick asked.

Anita used the moment to devour her soup, which was delicious. She was also near-starving and anything would taste delicious, but still.

Jason tapped the edge of his wedding ring against his wine glass. "We have to go to Manchester for Cassandra's business after the Juniors competition. Of course, in between auditions for a new partner, Lucy has her schoolwork to catch up on. You cannot slack junior year of high school."

Lucy tore a tiny shred of bread in half and worked it under her nails. "Even if there's only two weeks left of school," she muttered.

Cassandra smiled, clearly the most dazzling object in the room. "Finals matter, honey. Of course this is important, too." She turned her full wattage on Anita, and she blinked in the great effort not to freeze under her attention. "We also have Team Knight jackets for everyone to wear, during auditions and the Juniors competition. I've heard Blackstone this year is looking for standouts." She accompanied this statement with a flourish of her long, red-polished nails. "Teams that go the extra mile, who will photograph well. Maybe we will even catch the attention of Tom Havens."

"I don't really think you want Lucy catching Tom Havens's attention." Patrick spoke slowly, like he was choosing his words carefully. Anita was grateful he'd come up with a tactful way to say that the gossip about Tom Havens was not to be taken lightly. The former boy band star, now host of the reignited reality TV hit *Dance with Me*, apparently fully lived up to his reputation.

Cassandra's expression barely dulled, still celebrity-dazzled. "No matter. I'm sure Anita and Patrick will watch out for you, Lucy."

Anita nodded as Mr. Butler and James re-entered,

now carrying some sort of roast meat and veg, like this was a Dickens novel. Lucy did not need babysitting, and from her glowering expression she definitely felt the same way, but it was one more thing to add to her to-do list.

"Are there bogs around here?" Lucy directed the question to James, effectively shifting the direction of conversation away from Things Anita Now Had to Manage.

"Bogs?" He raised one eyebrow and a smile played around his lips. "Why would you be interested in bogs, miss?"

"Bog bodies," Patrick said, a little too loudly.

Lucy's eyes twinkled. "Exactly. What kind of awesome stuff have they found in the bogs?"

James served Anita some of the roasted vegetables while Mr. Butler sliced pieces of meat that no longer appealed to her. The thought of bog bodies certainly killed her appetite.

"They've found quite a few things in Chat Moss," James said, serving Patrick but keeping his eyes on Lucy. A dormant matchmaker urge curled inside Anita's belly. "That's the nearest. It's outside Manchester. I have a friend, he's studying them at uni there."

Lucy's eyes gleamed with excitement and what was likely to be a highly-detailed plan on how to escape the dance competition and run away to explore this Chat Moss. From the way James was looking at her, he'd go anywhere she asked.

Uh-oh.

"Bogs are not appropriate dinner conversation," Cassandra pronounced, and Lucy clapped her mouth shut, whatever question she was about to ask dead on her lips. “After dinner, I’m certain everyone needs to get ready for tomorrow. I’ve already spoken to Mr. Butler, and either he or James will drive you all to the competition and back each evening. If you wish to find alternative transportation, simply let him know.”

“Wonderful. Thank you so much.” Anita sliced her roasted carrot into eight teeny bits, her mind still full of bog bodies. Blergh. Talk about nightmares.

“Excellent.” Cassandra clapped her hands together, the sound reverberating against the overly floral wallpaper. “This is certainly going to be a Blackstone Dance Festival for the ages.”

Chapter Five

Thank everything holy that Patrick and Anita had had the presence of mind to pack their competition suitcase before they'd gone to bed the night before, because the pair of them woke up way too late the next morning to do anything short of change clothes, brush teeth, and meet Lucy downstairs.

Cassandra and Jason stood in their robes beside Lucy, whose long black hair was piled on her head in a messy knot. "Anita? Will you do Lucy's hair for the competition? You're so good with all of the styles," Cassandra asked.

"Of course!" Anita chirped.

Patrick heard the too-bright twinge in her voice. Anita must be as tired as he was.

"Excellent." Cassandra hugged her daughter tightly, her pale arms stark against Lucy's dark green *Team Knight* jacket. "Patrick? Do you have your Team Knight attire?"

Patrick pulled the dark green jacket with the silver screen-printed cartoon knight over his fleece. "I'm on board. Go Team Knight." He neglected to add how they really ought to have added Henry's name.

"Wonderful. We will see you all at the ballrooms in a few hours. Oh, this is so exciting. Jason, take a picture." Cassandra nudged her husband with her hip, and he hastily pulled out his phone to take a few snapshots.

Of what, Patrick wasn't entirely certain. None of them looked their best yet. He and Anita were still at least four spray-tanning sessions away from competition readiness. At least, as coaches, they didn't need to be as presentable today as Lucy did. Still, he posed and smiled.

When Cassandra clucked approvingly and showed them the photo on the screen, Patrick couldn't entirely convince himself that it was a trick of the light and not a real, live ghost floating at the back of the open hallway closet behind them.

No. That couldn't be it.

****

Mr. Butler wordlessly chauffeured them in an electric SUV back up the coast from Gryphon House to Blackstone. In between cliffs, flashes of blue-gray ocean appeared, but the color darkened as they neared Blackstone.

"The river here runs through the peat moss, and it darkens the sea when it drains there," Mr. Butler said, in his ever-present monotone.

"Bog bodies," Lucy said under her breath.

Anita shuddered beside Patrick. "Please. No more talk of bog bodies. I have to get my head in glam mode, not preserved carcass mode."

"Ew." Patrick kissed her cheek. He loved it when she played along. Besides, it was easier to focus on that than the possibility of a ghost in the picture Mr. Knight had taken. It had to have been a trick of the lighting, or jet lag.

Mr. Butler let them out in front of the Crystal Gardens Ballroom, where approximately eight million hopeful competitors and their respective entourages poured through the storied glass doors. It was an explosion of color and chatter and garment bags overstuffed with costumes. If anything could erase the thought of that weird photo, this was it.

Patrick peered up at the white-and-gold Baroque architecture of the ballroom. Even his jaded heart could appreciate the history here. Every great ballroom couple had competed here. Riccardo and Yulia, Troels and Ina, Donnie and Gaynor. He'd probably remember more if he wasn't so exhausted.

Mr. Butler removed the competition suitcase from the boot of the SUV and handed it unceremoniously to Patrick. "I'll return around four o'clock. If I'm needed earlier, just ring." With that encouragement, or lack thereof, he slipped back into the driver's seat and pulled away, letting a black hackney cab take his parking space.

"Ready to go?" he asked Lucy. Anita fidgeted with her own Team Knight jacket so the image featured more prominently, though as he could attest, its warmth did nothing against the strong north wind.

Lucy crossed her arms over her chest, her expression blank. "I suppose we might as well."

"That's the spirit." Patrick nudged her forward, not thinking at all about spectral presences in closets, and they entered the Crystal Gardens Ballroom.

Chapter Six

Anita made a beeline for the check-in queue while Patrick steered Lucy to the green room preparation area in hopes of securing even an inch of precious table space. He'd done enough European competitions during his amateur days to remember what it was like. As in, very similar to a horde of hungry wildebeests on their way to a drying-up water hole.

Sidestepping children, teenagers, and adults in various stages of makeup and spray tan, Patrick scored a single square of green room and maintained his land-ownership with a derisive stare, honed by years of practice.

Lucy snorted. "I've never seen you look like that before."

Patrick glowered at a couple from Spain who had been trying to spread a towel a mite too close to their space. "It's all about the killer side eye. Space is at a premium here, and you need to defend what you have like it's the last can of baked beans and you're in a zombie apocalypse."

Lucy laughed softly as she unzipped the enormous garment bag containing her Standard dress. That was good. She'd seemed so morose lately.

He elbowed her gently. "Hey, remember this is a competition and smiling is mandatory."

Lucy rolled her eyes at him. "Sure, Coach. If I

don't feel like smiling, I'll just put Vaseline on my teeth."

He shrugged and removed a battery-operated hair crimper, a hairnet, an enormous can of hairspray, and approximately seven thousand hairpins. Anita was like a ballroom fairy with her supplies. "Let's get started on your hair and makeup. Anita can help with the finishing touches, and then maybe you and Henry can warm up a bit."

"Do they do the Latin heats first?" Lucy released her long black hair from its messy bun and ran her fingers through it to loosen the tangles.

"Yeah." He handed her a comb. "First Latin heats, then Standard, then the Latin quarter and semifinals, then the Standard, yada-yada. It's a long day." He presented her with a large refillable water bottle. "Hydrate."

Lucy took a sip, then flipped her hair over her head and back-combed for volume.

Across the crowded green room, Patrick spied Henry and his parents picking their way balefully through the crowd. Patrick waved enthusiastically, because that was likely the only way to catch their attention. Henry's mom's shoulders relaxed in relief when she saw him, and rushed to their small patch of prep space.

"Thank goodness you got here early," Mrs. Kim said, handing him a garment bag and a large duffel. "We had *no* idea it would be so busy. We thought we'd have time to get coffee, maybe see some of the other heats or something."

Patrick had prepared Mrs. Kim for the crowds, but he knew even the best preparation sometimes didn't help. Blackstone was a class unto itself, even without a literal specter in the ballroom. Or closet. Nope, not thinking about it. "No problem. Anita will be here in a moment. She's checking them in and getting their numbers. We'll help Henry get ready."

"Hi, Lucy." Henry nodded toward her Medusa headdress of back-combed hair. He had already shellacked his black hair with blond highlights and had not skimped on the spray tan. Good guy.

Mrs. Kim held a hand over her heart and leaned toward Patrick in a conspiratorial manner. "Did you hear? Tom Havens was supposed to be here, but so far he's a no show."

"Oh." Patrick could think of no situation in which this information applied to him but thought it best to play along for his students' benefit. "That's awful. But he's not supposed to judge until the Team Match, right?"

Mrs. Kim clucked. "It just seems fitting with his reputation. At least my Henry isn't like that."

This was true. Henry Kim was, in Patrick's opinion, an awesome kid. He showed up, understood the coaching, asked appropriate and relevant questions, and toned down some of Lucy's rambunctiousness. He was in every way far superior to what Patrick had heard about Tom Havens.

The problem was that Henry Kim was graduating in a few weeks and heading almost immediately for sunny California.

"We're going to get coffee." Mrs. Kim took her husband's hand and leaned over to kiss Henry's cheek. "We'll see you soon. You two will be so wonderful."

Patrick cracked his neck. This was his job. To help

these two kids through their first international competition. Why neither set of parents had wanted to try a smaller one first was beyond him, but he could do this. At least he could with Anita on his side. Unless she got taken by the Blackstone ghost.

In which case, he would need to google how to make an EMF meter out of whatever he could find at Tesco.

Chapter Seven

Anita crawled infinitesimally along in the registration line, checking her phone repeatedly for the time. She really shouldn't do that. Ten more seconds only ever looked like the time barely moved. Besides, texts from her parents kept popping up like irritating garden gnomes.

She wasn't quite sure why she was so anxious, apart from the fact that Lucy and Henry were the first students she had ever brought to Blackstone. One of the many reasons she had ended up going professional after her fairly successful amateur career was to help couples like them excel.

Maybe it was that being here reminded her so much of every mistake she had ever made. Never once had she come here before with Patrick. Never once had she made it past the quarter final round. Never once had her parents ever attended. Not that this trip was going to fix that one.

Now she was here, as a teacher and professional, about to compete in three days in the Latin Team Match and then a few days later in the professional open Latin championship. With Patrick. Wonderful Patrick. Supportive Patrick. Drop dead sexy Patrick, particularly in his costumes that lined his muscles. She really should just set a wedding date and lock it down.

A yawn caught her by surprise, and she stifled it

behind her hand. That ate up ten more seconds and another step closer in line.

"Anita?" A soft, Scottish burr greeted her.

Anita turned to see Evelyn Zhao, world champion ballroom dancer and an old friend. Evelyn pulled her into a much-needed hug. "Evelyn? It's been way too long. You look amazing."

She wore a fitted black athletic suit with rainbow patches on the shoulders. Her dark hair was down in soft, dark waves, and her brown eyes twinkled like someone who was in love. Rumor said she was, too, not that Anita liked engaging in gossip.

"I feel amazing." Evelyn linked arms with Anita and waited beside her in line. "Love will do that to you."

Rumors confirmed. "Really? You and Jackson Alder?"

Evelyn sighed dramatically, like they were in a Regency-era movie of their lives, taking a turn around the room in bonnets and Empire-waist dresses.

Which, upon reflection, sounded kind of awesome. Anita did have a major soft spot for historical romances.

"Jackson's fab," Evelyn said, unable to keep the smile from lighting her entire face. "I've never been with someone who just makes things…fun. Even the dreary bits are rather enjoyable. And I rather think since he moved *DanceSportTV* to Scotland, the ratings have improved."

"I'm sure it's easier for Jackson to get the footage he needs if he has you as a carrot," Anita teased, her mood already lighter. Waiting in line beside Evelyn seemed far less like the purgatory of waiting at the

DMV.

"It's mutual. So what are you here for? Are you dancing pro/am before the Team Match?" Evelyn tossed a lock of hair over her shoulder with an ease Anita longed to replicate. "Also, Team UK is going to kick the Americans' arses this year. FYI."

Anita laughed, and the release felt too good, too needed. What had she been doing, not talking every day to old friends like Evelyn? Oh right. Stewing in family drama and trying not to be unalived. "Patrick and I coach a couple in the Juniors Standard competition. It's their first year together, but they've already gotten a few titles stateside." She ticked off items on her fingers. "Then new partner auditions for Lucy, since Henry's off to college, and Patrick and I will be attempting to find even ten minutes for practice and workouts."

"Tell me about it," Evelyn replied. Thankfully, they were almost at the registration desk. "My partner Alexei's running about like a hen without a head, he's got so many students here. It's easier for them to travel down from Scotland, though. Everyone wants a shot at the famous Blackstone luck."

Only one registrant in front of them. "At least you're talking about the Blackstone luck," Anita said. "Patrick has been talking nonstop about the Blackstone ghost."

"Oh, but the ghost is real!" Evelyn turned her twinkling gaze on Anita. "Every year, something awful happens, or some ingenue 'disappears,' and the ghost takes the blame."

"You need to meet Patrick and Lucy. You would all fit together." Anita shook her head and approached the registration desk, giving them Lucy and Henry's names and World Dancesport Federation registration information. When she turned around, number and info packet in hand, Evelyn was signing autographs for two teen girls both dressed in bright pink Standard gowns dripping with glitter and marabou.

Evelyn turned back to her. "All right then? If you'd like, I could maybe give your two students a little help before their heats."

Anita stopped in the middle of the crowded walkway, anxious parents and coaches sidestepping her like she had the plague. "Are you kidding?"

"No, of course not." Evelyn linked arms with her again and steered them both toward the green room. "Why do you ask?"

"Because you're Evelyn Zhao." Anita had long ago rid herself of any resentment toward her friends who had made it higher in the rankings than herself. She competed for the love of it and was incredibly pleased to see her friends succeed. That didn't mean she was incapable of being starstruck. "You and Alexei are ranked, what, second in the world?"

Evelyn shrugged. "Well, third, but who's counting? Hopefully first after this week. Come on. Let's give them a quick tutorial and a fright."

Anita tagged along in her wake. Anything really could happen at Blackstone.

Chapter Eight

Patrick O'Leary was many good things, a rarity in adults of Lucy's experience, but he was complete shit at doing competition hair.

Currently, he frowned at her head like she'd sprouted a second one. She wouldn't have minded. It would help to keep everything in her life separate. The Lucy Knight her parents wanted her to be, and the Lucy Knight she secretly nurtured after her homework was done.

"Maybe try pulling it up like this?" Her coach gestured uselessly at the side of her head. Henry, tying his bow tie because men had all the luck, was clearly holding back laughter.

"When is Anita coming?" Lucy hated the frustration in her voice, but seriously, what did they expect of her? She'd flown halfway around the world to dance in this super-crowded competition, and how on earth were she and Henry supposed to stand out? How were they supposed to be Team Knight?

In all fairness, Lucy had lobbied extensively for team Knight/Kim, because not only did it include Henry but also sounded like a badass time travel superhero, but her parents had roundly rebuffed her.

"Hopefully soon." Patrick tried to stuff Lucy's crimped locks into a hairnet.

"I think you need to put it in a ponytail or a bun

first," Henry said. Of course Henry conciliated. He was a mastermind peacekeeper. Why did he have to go to Stanford? She had zero desire to start this whole process over with someone new. Not that she would ever say that to her parents.

"Hey!" Anita Goodman wound her way through the crowd, waving broadly.

Lucy's entire body relaxed.

"I've got your numbers and information." Anita handed a stack of paperwork to Patrick and then turned to Lucy, hands on the hips of her ubiquitous black leggings. "All right. Perfect. Lucy, you look amazing. Just give me ten minutes for your hair."

****

It took fifteen, but even without looking, Lucy could tell the hairstyle was going to kill. With the efficiency of a surgeon, Anita had taken her wild lion's mane and styled it into a chic chignon affixed to Lucy's head with a river of crystals and accented with a blue peacock feather that matched her gown.

"Thank you so much," she said under her breath to Anita as her teacher applied the contouring makeup.

"Any time." Anita smiled at her, her brush strokes light across Lucy's skin. It was oddly mesmerizing, to be painted this way. "You and Henry are going to be awesome. Just keep breathing and trust each other."

Lucy released a tense bark of laughter that she hadn't realized she had been holding in. "I'm beginning to wish I could vanish like Tom Havens."

Anita frowned slightly as she darkened the liner under Lucy's eyes. "I'm sure he hasn't vanished. Don't listen to idle green room gossip. He's not even supposed to be here today."

"Maybe he's—"

Anita paused, holding the makeup brush before her like a nun with a ruler. "If you say anything about bog bodies, I won't tell you about your surprise."

"Ooh, a surprise?" Lucy promptly forgot the extensive lecture she had lurking on the plethora of things found in peat bogs. "What is it? Does Henry get one, too?" Not that she would admit it, but she would miss Henry. Ever since she had broken up with her boyfriend and former partner the past fall, she and Henry had been in complete sync. Not, like, romantic sync, obviously, because Henry had a girlfriend and was *not* Lucy's type. But they had become really good, solid platonic friends. In Lucy's humble opinion, people needed more solid platonic friends. Who else would she ride or die with in the zombie apocalypse?

Anita checked her watch, nodded, and removed a container of false eyelashes. "Let's finish getting ready and I'll show you both. Open your eyes wide. The glue on these is tricky."

****

A few minutes later, changed in a makeshift room created by Patrick and Anita and Henry holding up towels like this was some beach bathing club instead of a ballroom competition, Lucy was finally ready. Packed and shimmied into a peacock blue and green gown with feathery fringe and long sleeves that made her arms look toned.

Okay, Lucy could admit that it was the hours she spent in the gym, rocking out to the Clash, that made her arms look toned, but attire always helped.

Anita and Patrick led her and Henry out of the green room and through a twisting series of corridors before arriving at what was the Holy Grail of this competition: an empty hallway.

And in that empty hallway, to Lucy's celebrity crush delight, was Evelyn Zhao.

She was a little taller in person, but no less athletic and kickass gorgeous. Henry halted beside Lucy, equally starstruck.

"Hello," Evelyn said, her Scottish accent both endearing and posh. "I'm Evelyn Zhao."

"Holy shit, yes, you are," Lucy said in a gush, then clamped her mouth shut. "Sorry, I'm sure it's not cool to fangirl."

Evelyn shrugged. "Fangirl away. My friend Anita said you two are competing shortly. I thought maybe I'd give you a few last-minute pointers."

Henry exhaled loudly. "I can die happy now. Evelyn Zhao just said she'd give me pointers."

Lucy elbowed him playfully in the ribs. "You can take that with you to the Stanford ballroom dance club."

"Don't think I won't," he replied, brown eyes wide.

For the next twenty minutes, Lucy and Henry ran through their Standard choreography in the empty hallway. Evelyn made slight adjustments to their posture, a few tweaks here and there to their lines, but in general, she was the coolest person Lucy had ever met.

"Lovely," Evelyn said, clapping her hands together. "You two will be smashing. Just try to find your space, that's the hardest part of Blackstone. I'll send Patrick the info on the Standard pyramid, too. There are a few videos online that Alexei and I use for our students. We'll remove the paywall for you."

"Why don't you dance Latin?" Lucy asked. For the

first time since she had arrived in England, she felt alive. Aware and in touch with her body. Maybe she and Henry really could move past the first round, and this wasn't merely a way of making a giant ass of herself just to please her parents.

Evelyn shrugged. "It's not my passion. Life is too short not to follow your passions."

Lucy was definitely silk screening that on a T-shirt.

Anita clucked through her teeth, checking her watch for the eight bajillionth time. "No pressure, but it's time to go. They're about to start the Standard heats."

A hot thrill of excitement mixed with possible gastroenteritis whirled in Lucy's belly. It also was maybe making her delirious, because as she followed Henry and their coaches down to the ballroom, she couldn't be entirely sure that she didn't see Mr. Butler standing in the shadows and watching them.

Chapter Nine

"Tell the truth," Patrick whispered in her ear as they anxiously waited for the announcement of which Juniors couples would be called to the next round. "Are you more nervous for them or for us?"

"One thousand percent." Anita would have spoken up more, but her mouth was currently occupied by chewing the inside of her cheek. Arms crossed over their Team Knight jackets, she and Patrick stood like twin statues beside Henry and Lucy and their families. She could *not* fuck this up. Henry and Lucy seemed to understand that they might not make it, but their parents were another story.

The main judge, Horace Brixley—who, to everyone's disappointment, looked nothing like Tom Havens and more closely resembled an inebriated bloodhound—stepped to the podium and every hopeful contender and their entourage held their collective breath. Brixley's reputation as a womanizing sot did not endear him to Anita's anxiety at the moment. She'd heard that last year, during the competition she had missed, he'd been found *in flagrante* with a young hopeful a quarter of his age. And still got called back this year to judge. Toxic masculinity, ruining the party yet again. She'd throw up if she didn't have to appear professional.

"Called to the next round," the bloodhound Brixley

stated in a perfunctory tone. He proceeded to list several numbers, all in rapid procession, which probably would have been better were he not slurring. To Anita's jet lagged brain, and the worried parents surrounding her, it all resembled so much gobbledegook.

Then she heard Lucy and Henry's number called out, crystal clear and ringing in her head.

"Congratulations, now go stand in the on-deck area for when they call you." With very little additional prompting, Anita pushed Henry and Lucy in the proper direction and resumed her position beside Patrick, chewing her nails.

"Relax, they're doing great. They found space in the first round. After this, they're golden." Patrick slid his arm around her, but it didn't help relieve her nerves.

Maybe it would help if her parents stopped texting her. She had told them she was overseas and working, but it hadn't paused their incessant questions. *—Can we talk? Anita, please.—* And, of course, from her dad. —*You're being childish.—*

How was she being childish if she was leading young minds to ballroom victory?

Okay, that was probably an overestimation of her skills, but she needed the feeling of a win. She hadn't eaten enough breakfast. Horace Brixley's lecherous bloodhound face begged for a punch, which was likely a poor decision. And she was loath to leave the ballroom in case Henry and Lucy needed her. If she couldn't pull herself together, there was no way she would have the winner's mindset she'd need for her own performances.

Mrs. Kim squeezed her elbow, and Anita turned on

her full professional smile. “Thank you so much, Anita. Henry has made such wonderful improvements since you and Patrick started coaching him. We never thought he’d be here at Blackstone.”

Right. Instructor mode time. Anita tightened her ponytail. “Henry is wonderful, Mrs. Kim. Thank you for letting me teach him.”

This conversation was a distraction she did not need or want at the moment. *Play along*. That was the goal. If Henry and Lucy did well, if their parents were pleased, it meant longevity for the dance studio.

The first couples called back were now returning to the dance floor in a flurry of color and feathers and glitter. Henry and Lucy weren’t among them.

Behind her, she heard Mrs. Kim and Cassandra Knight discussing something in low tones. Were they critiquing her teaching skills? She focused a little more on eavesdropping.

“Are you hungry?” Patrick asked.

“Famished.”

“No worries. I’ll run out and pick up something after Lucy and Henry dance.”

She nodded, still attuned to the parents’ whispers.

“Did you hear Tom Havens is missing?”

“Such a shame. That man is too handsome for his own good.”

“I heard one mom in the bathroom talking. They said they saw him last night at one of the bars along the pier.”

“The bars here, really. It’s like spring break. I haven’t let Henry leave the hotel.”

At least they weren’t critiquing her team management skills. Why did everyone care where Tom

Havens was? He was likely holed up in a decent hotel miles away from here with whatever he wanted, because he was a goddamn celebrity.

Henry and Lucy danced next, and though Anita thought they had presented well, she wasn't quite sure they had stood out enough. Which was fine, because the minute Lucy returned to Anita's side, she said, "I can die happy now, Anita. A private lesson with Evelyn Zhao and we got past round one at Blackstone."

Anita hugged her tightly, though careful not to muss her hair. "Never count anything out. You're doing wonderfully."

Henry was panting, and Patrick seemed to be holding him upright while pouring water down his throat.

"You need to sit. Why don't you two go back to the green room and rest on the suitcases?" Anita gestured. "Patrick's going to get food."

Henry nodded gratefully and left for the green room, buttressed by his beaming parents.

"Well done, sweetheart," Cassandra said to her daughter, wrapping her in a brief hug. "We are so proud of you."

"Let's get you something to eat," Jason said. He slipped a Team Knight jacket over Lucy's slim shoulders. "We will be back."

"Great." Anita gave them a thumbs up and immediately regretted it.

Patrick kissed her cheek and disappeared in search of sustenance, leaving her alone. Alone with at least twenty unanswered text messages from her parents.

Anita sighed and fought her way through the crowd at the edge of the ballroom. She just needed a breath of fresh air. The overpowering scent of spray tan was getting to her.

She headed toward the front entrance but could see through the theater's enormous glass display windows the rain pouring down outside in great, thick sheets. Perfect. Nothing like weather to match her mood.

Pulling her thin jacket tighter around her body in preparation for the biting, wet north wind, she stepped outside and clung to the side of the building underneath the faint shelter of the marquee. Not that she wasn't grateful to Lucy's parents, but would it have killed them to pick fleeces?

Her phone buzzed again in the pocket of her leggings. Sighing, she removed it. She would have to face her own music at some point.

To her immense relief, it was not yet another pleading text from her parents. This was instead from Hanna Pascal, another old friend and one of her teammates for the upcoming Americas Latin Team Match.

Hanna: *—impromptu team mtg tonight??? Big news…—*

Anita's stomach turned at the lopsided grin emoji. That couldn't be good.

Anita: —Sure. What's going on.—

Hanna: —Tell you tonight. Good luck with your juniors. Don't freak out—

What was it about someone telling her not to freak out that immediately made Anita slide into panic mode?

She tugged her ponytail just as a whip of freezing rain lashed against her. Shivering uncontrollably, she bit her lip. Now she definitely wasn't ready to deal with family drama.

As she bounced up and down on her toes, forcing feeling back into their almost-frostbitten state, she saw a sleek black sedan parked illegally in the roundabout before the ballroom. No one else was outdoors at the moment, apart from a few people scurrying with umbrellas and carrying bags of food or other necessities.

What was going on in this car?

As surreptitiously as she could, she turned and held her phone in front of her, the camera facing toward her, but she adjusted it so she could see what was transpiring in the car behind her. Nothing to see here, just Anita taking a selfie in front of the Crystal Gardens ballroom.

In the car, two figures seemed to be arguing, one with long, wavy hair, and one with shorter hair. It was impossible to tell anything else from this vantage. Hand gestures flew wildly and with abandon. That couldn't be safe in such a confined space.

Though Anita usually tried to tamp down her natural curiosity, she couldn't help but keep watching. She could chalk it up to stress if anyone asked.

One of the figures emerged from the car, slamming the door shut before the sedan pulled out into the rainy afternoon.

Anita recoiled slightly, the recognition hitting her like a punch in the gut. She slid her phone back into the pocket of her leggings and turned, smiling. "Mr. Butler. What a surprise."

He frowned intensely at her. "Ms. Goodman. It is far too cold to be lingering out of doors."

An interesting response. "I needed some air. I'll head inside in a moment. I thought, hey, it's almost

June, it should be warmer." Was there a good way to ask who the red-haired woman he'd been arguing with was? Probably not.

"Welcome to Blackstone, Ms. Goodman." And with that, he brushed directly past her and into the theater.

Anita paused, tugging repeatedly on the end of her ponytail as she did rélevés in place to keep her blood pumping. What had that been about and why was Mr. Butler here instead of at Gryphon House? Had the Knights called him? And what on earth had he been arguing about and with whom?

She wasn't given much time to muse as Patrick returned, panting and damp despite his rain jacket, plastic carrier bags over both arms. "What are you doing out here? It's fucking freezing. Come on, let's go inside."

Chapter Ten

Nothing made Patrick feel more valuable than delivering sandwiches and fruit salad to starving competitors.

Well, nothing except being with Anita, helping make the studio a success, and finding joy in his own writing. He had sold his influencer blog, PhillyProud, to a local start up two months ago, and even with the bit of newfound financial freedom, he still liked to take the odd freelance writing job now and again. His friends kept telling him to start a podcast.

Anita elbowed him gently. “What are you thinking about?”

Patrick finished chewing the apple he’d devoured. “Starting a podcast.”

“You should. Maybe with you and John and Will.”

Patrick grinned and chucked the apple core into an empty carrier bag. “In all of our copious free time? Will’s in full wedding planning mode, and John and Katie are busy nesting.” Lucky assholes, all of his friends. At least John and Will had the tact not to ask when Patrick’s own wedding was going to happen. At the moment, it seemed like never.

The crowd in the green room had thinned slightly, since some competitors had left after being cut in the first round. That didn’t mean there was substantially more breathing room.

Anita checked her phone and a furrow appeared between her brows. “They’re announcing who made it into the quarterfinals. Are you two ready?”

Henry and Lucy, both with more color in their cheeks than before lunch, nodded.

Patrick and Anita led them out to the ballroom floor, where they waited with the other couples and their eager entourages. As they read out number upon number, none of which were theirs, Patrick could see the relief seep into Lucy’s posture. Hadn’t she wanted to win?

When the judge had finished reading off the numbers, Patrick and Anita gathered Henry and Lucy. “How are you guys doing?”

Even Patrick could see the lightness on Lucy’s face. “Great. We did great, right, Henry? And now I can finally take out these hair pins. My head is killing me.”

At least she was taking it well. So was Henry. “I’m fine, just a weird mix of wired and exhausted. Can I go back to the hotel with my parents?” he said.

Patrick and Anita exchanged a look. “Really, it would benefit both of you to stay to watch the couples who advanced to the quarterfinal,” Anita said, arms crossed in that adorably stern posture Patrick adored. “It’s a good way to learn. Lucy, some of the boys who are auditioning for your new partner are competing. You could get an advance idea of how they dance.”

Lucy’s posture stiffened in resignation, and Patrick’s heart twinged. He caught Anita’s sympathetic gaze.

“Of course, if your parents say it’s okay, you two can do whatever you think is best,” Anita said.

“Awesome.” Lucy immediately relaxed and

grabbed Henry's hand. "I'm going to change and then see if my parents can take me to the peat bogs for a tour."

She left without another word, Henry in tow.

Anita shook her head, but she was smiling in a tolerant way. "I don't understand the bog thing."

Patrick looped an arm around her shoulders and pulled her close. "Come on. I'll explain it to you."

"We should practice, or exercise, or something." Anita slipped out of his grasp, and he felt the loss of her touch like the Earth turning away from the sun. "There's a team meeting tonight, too. At seven. Maybe we should stay here in Blackstone."

"Okay." He knew his role here. "Whatever you want. I'm in." Who was he kidding? He would follow her anywhere. He didn't need the marriage license to prove it.

Though it would be nice to have.

Chapter Eleven

It was an immense relief to pull the pins and crystals from her hair. It was far too shellacked with hairspray to comb out, so Lucy left it as it lay and changed as swiftly as she could into her leggings and sweatshirt. No Team Knight for her right now. Not just because it was ridiculous and an affront to Henry, but because the lining was scratchy. She should have known her dad would skimp on the quality and tell her mom it was prime.

None of it mattered. Henry's parents had coerced him into staying to watch the quarterfinal, but Lucy was more than certain she could finagle her mom and dad to let her out. After a whole day of preening and dancing, Lucy desperately, desperately needed to get out.

"There you are, sweetheart," her mom said, greeting her with a proud smile. "Are you sure you don't want to stay? We really should watch the other dancers and hone your technique."

Lucy forced a tense smile. "I get that. But I, um, really need to get some—" Shit, she needed to think of an excuse. Any excuse. "—research done for my paper." Genius. Blame schoolwork. Her parents would lap it up like a starving person with a never-ending bowl of pasta. "That's right. I have to do a paper for, um, science class."

Her mom arched one perfectly tweezed eyebrow.

"Science class?"

"Yes! Science class." *Stall, stall, stall.* "I told my teacher that, um, in lieu of doing labs while we're here, I'd…do research." She knew she shouldn't have opened up her mouth, but she couldn't stop now, not while the slew of lies paraded forth. "On the effect of climate change on England's famed peat bogs."

At least that had a ring of truth, not that Lucy's science teacher gave two shits about reading any paper. He was more of the hiding-vodka-in-his-reusable-water-bottle-and-giving-arbitrary-A's kind of teacher. But her parents didn't know that.

She supposed she should feel guilty about lying, but it came pretty easily to her after all this time. What else was she meant to do in a house where her parents' eagerness to please made her desperate to reciprocate? Disappointing them might as well be a stake through her heart.

Her mom typed on her phone and frowned, a slight furrow between her eyes. "Oh, dear. Mr. Butler says he's not available to drive you. He'll have to send James. Jason? Are we all right with James driving Lucy?"

Her dad looked up from his phone. To Lucy's shock, he never quite developed the kyphosis she thought he deserved after spending all day crouched over the device. "I'm sure whatever you think is fine, dear."

Her mom chewed the inside of her cheek. Lately, Lucy had realized she did something similar and had done everything in her power to correct the tic. "I suppose it's fine. Is it all right if we stay for a while? Anita said we could check out some of your potential partners."

"Of course." Lucy forced another tight smile, knowing she would shortly be free of this conversation. Her parents had chosen her first and only boyfriend. They had picked out Henry for her. Might as well choose her next ball and chain. Metaphor optional.

****

James pulled up in the turnaround in the front of Crystal Gardens five minutes later. Lucy wasn't terribly familiar, for obvious reasons, with the geography around Blackstone, but she'd already seen enough traffic to be surprised by his punctuality.

"Thanks for driving me," she said, sliding into the passenger seat beside him. It would help her immensely if James didn't smell so good, like fresh linens with a hint of sandalwood underneath. Lucy didn't have a ton of experience with crushes, or almost zero, really. She didn't need one now. Why couldn't fate have made him look more like a crushed apple instead of a Hemsworth?

James eyed her as he turned the car into traffic. He had the hottest golden flecks in those hazel eyes. Blergh. "You don't want to sit in the back? You could be chauffeured like in *Downton Abbey*."

Lucy crossed her arms over her chest and stared out the window at the city misted in rain. "*Downton Abbey* bored me. Give me *Luther* any day of the week."

She didn't turn but could hear the smile in his voice. "Right on. Have you seen *Appropriate Adult*? It's one of my favorites, but I'll watch anything with Emily Watson. She's a bloody genius."

This turned Lucy's head. Any fan of true crime dramatizations, well, it was simply a case of like calling like. Without any actually *liking* going on. For sure. "I like the angle they took with the Fred and Rosemary West story. What about *Des*?"

He chuckled, a low sound that rumbled through her in a way she didn't care for. She wasn't sure if he was trying to be charming or trick her, and she immediately decided she didn't care for either event. "I liked *Des*. But I mean, if you're going to talk David Tennant, you can't neglect *Broadchurch*."

She tilted her head to the side, considering. "Fair enough. *Broadchurch* wins. So sad, though."

"They're all sad." James turned the car onto a larger motorway, the buildings getting older and more dilapidated as they left the city proper. "I like stories that focus more on who the victims were, typically. They deserve to be remembered for how they lived, not how they died."

Lucy traced the droplets of mist against the pane of her window. "I totally get what you mean."

She felt his gaze on her even though she knew he was watching the road, weaving around traffic. She'd found if she didn't pay any attention to which side they were on, the switch in sides of the road didn't disconcert her.

What did was his eerie way of saying exactly what she thought.

"My mum's house is over there." He gestured vaguely toward a patch of farmland. "Do you mind if we stop and pick up my dog?"

Lucy's eyes widened despite her innate cynicism. "You have a dog?"

"Of course. It's almost a necessity here in the, what do you Americans call it?" He tilted his head in a frankly endearing way that made Lucy simultaneously want to vomit and also wrap him in layers and layers of hand-knitted scarves. "The boonies." He elongated the O's and Lucy swooned a little inside.

Pull it together.

"This hardly looks like the boonies. There's shops and houses and everything. In Pennsylvania, the true boondocks are where there's nothing but forest for miles. Acres and acres of pine trees, packed so tightly it's like the sun never sees the ground." Lucy wrapped her arms across her chest, wishing she'd brought a sweater.

James turned onto the off ramp, reached behind her seat, and handed her a wool blanket speckled with dog hair. "That sounds spooky. It won't take long. River needs a bit of a run, and the bogs are a good place for her."

"So this is River's hair." Lucy plucked a clump of fur from the blanket and snuggled deeper into its warmth. "What kind of dog is she? Besides a furball."

James shrugged. They were on a country road now, surrounded by patches of flat farmland and green stretching to the horizon. In the distance, she saw the cut of a black river through the landscape. "She's one hundred percent cuddly mutt. She's a good dog. Don't be frightened by her size. She wouldn't hurt a gnat."

They sat in silence for a few more minutes, passing small green lawns and rows upon rows of red brick houses with sharp angles. After a few more moments, James pulled the car into a parking lot and shut off the engine, tapping on the wheel.

Lucy couldn't see why he was nervous. She'd seen photos of council housing in the UK before, and this development fit most of the specifics. Red brick row homes, small gardens, a few trees, a well-loved play set in a central yard. "Is this where your mom lives? It's nice. It must be awesome to have other people around." Her house was set far away from any others, so if she ever wanted to visit friends, it was at least a ten-minute drive. Don't even get her started on being snowed in.

"I suppose." He ran his hand through his shaggy brown hair, no longer so neat and kempt as he was when he was at Gryphon House. It looked really good on him. "We're lucky to have this place." He cast her a worried glance, then redirected it to the brick buildings before him. "Mum has COPD."

"Oh. Wow." Not that Lucy knew much about it, but her father worked with a lung doctor at his hospital and was always talking about the variations in COPD. In all fairness, Lucy usually tuned him out. Her dad worked hospital administration, which in her opinion was the most boring job imaginable.

"She's all right." He unclipped his seatbelt and stared at her, gamely. "Well, come on in, if you'd like. Mum will probably foist a cup of tea and some biscuits on you."

"I like your mom already." Mood already improved at the prospect of hot drinks and sugar, Lucy unclipped her own seatbelt and popped from the car, bouncing on her toes. "Do you have chocolate ones?"

James laughed, a low, soft sound that was barely more than a whisper of emotion. "I'm sure we can accommodate you, Ms. Knight."

"Ugh, if you call me Ms. Knight, I'm definitely stealing all the biscuits and running for the hills." Lucy followed James through the cold May mist. "So, explain Garibaldi biscuits to me."

Now the laugh sounded genuine. "You're a different hen, aren't you?"

Lucy shrugged beside him. "I've seen a lot of *Bake Off*. It's a whole thing."

James took a large brass key from his pocket and fitted it in the lock. "I'm never sure if that show has done us more harm or good. Mum! It's me. I've got a friend."

Despite her earlier reluctance, Lucy's spine thrilled a bit with the friend moniker. Not that she wanted to be friends with James. Of course not. She was only here in England for, like, less than a hot minute, and during that time needed to attend remote classes, find a new partner who would magically make her some kind of ballroom champion and, most importantly, manage her parents' expectations. A friend only led to complications.

Complications that were entirely mitigated by the arrival of his freakin' adorable sock moppet of a dog.

River clearly liked Lucy, as she approached her almost as soon as James had dropped a single pet to the soft, overgrown hair on her head. River then turned her massive sixty pounds of love on Lucy. She was as big as a standard poodle but with long, silky black and white fur and a head the size of a bear that she dug into Lucy's side, demanding rubs.

It was love at first sight.

"Jay? Is that you, Jay?" A pretty blonde woman with pale skin and a nasal cannula entered the living room. "Oh, you've brought a friend." She said it in a kind way, not a how-dare-you-bring-this-stranger-into-my-house way, and there was something about James's mom that radiated welcome. Something about the house, too, called to Lucy. The furniture was well-loved, everything was clean and smelled faintly of lemon soap and cinnamon. In her house, there was an entire room where Lucy hadn't been allowed until she turned sixteen and proved she wouldn't spill grape juice all over the fluffy white carpet.

"Hi, Mum." James crossed the room and kissed his mother's cheek. "This is Lucy Knight. We're off to the peat bogs."

"Whatever for? There's nothing there but grass and the stench of decay." James's mom coughed several times into a hastily-procured handkerchief, James rubbing her back.

Lucy hugged River one more time around her huge, furry neck and stood. "Hi, Mrs. Barrow. Sorry to barge in like this. Also, I *love* your T-shirt." Which was one hundred percent true. Beneath the beige wool cardigan, Mrs. Barrow had on a faded black concert tee from a K-pop band Lucy loved.

James's mother straightened, beaming. "You like them, too? Good on you. Oh, and it's no missus. Miss is fine for me. Can I fix you some tea and biscuits?"

"Do we have time, James?" Lucy asked.

He shrugged. "It's not too far from here to the bogs. Sure."

Miss Barrow walked over and wrapped an arm around Lucy's shoulder. "Perfect timing. You come help me set up the tea things and tell me which song is your favorite."

****

After fifteen minutes of tea, chocolate-covered biscuits from a purple packet that Lucy knew she was going to buy a case of before returning to the United States, and talking about pop music with James's super cool mom, Lucy had almost forgotten why they were there in the first place.

Almost.

"So, you're off to the bogs? You'll not likely find anything." Miss Barrow dipped a biscuit into her milky tea. Lucy preferred hers dairy-free, but neither James nor his mom had commented. "People are always out there, looking for buried treasure or whatnot. They never find anything except their wellies stuck in the mud."

"Not never," James said. He'd already finished his tea and Lucy felt his gaze on her again. This made her feel unsettled and in definite need of more chocolate biscuits. "Remember last year? During Blackstone? They found that tourist's luggage, all in a weird fairy circle."

"Ooh, maybe it was the Blackstone ghost!" Lucy said. She was pretty sure her eyes were bright and she was speaking a little too loud. Chocolate always gave her a bit of a high.

James laughed, shaking his head. "There is no Blackstone ghost."

Miss Barrow slapped his hand playfully. "James Barrow, how dare you tell this girl lies? Of course there's a ghost. I've seen it myself, wandering the beach and pleasure park." She turned to Lucy, a smile playing around her lips, her gray-blue eyes narrowed but sparkling. "Once, I saw it strung up on top of Blackstone Tower, hanging by its neck from a rope."

"So cool." Lucy's entire body thrilled. "What's the story? Who is the ghost?"

Miss Barrow shrugged, her body language still playful. “No one really knows. Some say it’s an ancestor of the Grantward family, a young woman who got into trouble and her family disowned her. She wandered off in the middle of the night to have her babe and die alone in the woods. But that’s always been a bit too Thomas Hardy for me, and not the hot actor, neither.”

“Mum!” James said.

Lucy shrugged. “Don’t take it personally. Tom Hardy is a god among men. Are there any other theories?”

“Loads.” Miss Barrow coughed again, and James’s face twisted with concern, even as his mother shrugged it away. “Gryphon House used to be a church. A safe haven for some, but hell for others. I’ve heard all sorts of tales about the attics, but the Grantwards discouraged all that kind of talk, and I suppose boarded them all up.”

“Okay, wait,” Lucy said. “Gryphon House is haunted by the Blackstone ghost?”

“I don’t know. They’re mere fairy stories, Lucy. But there are loads of ghosts up here in the north, if you know where to look for them.” Miss Barrow coughed once and rubbed James’s cheek, which was etched with concern. “You two had best be getting on. River needs a walk, and you don’t have much daylight left.”

Chapter Twelve

James was silent during the drive to the peat bogs, which suited Lucy just fine, since River, despite being in the back seat, had laid her enormous head on Lucy's shoulder.

"Your mom is awesome," Lucy said, scratching the space on River's nose between her eyes. The dog practically purred. "I like your dog, too."

"She likes you," he said without looking at her. "Thanks for being nice to my mum."

"What are you talking about? She's so cool. I want to be her when I get older. And, she's the one who explained Garibaldi biscuits to me, because you wouldn't." She poked James playfully in the deltoid, trying not to appreciate the firmness of his shoulder muscles. This wasn't her. She didn't faint at the sight of a good-looking man with a decent physique and an awesome dog. Not that she had noticed James was hot.

She'd better look out the window instead of continuing along this derailed train of thought.

James sighed and kept his gaze on the road stretching ahead of them. They'd entered more country now. Lucy noted fewer gas stations and shops, more farmhouses, sheep, and cows. Bucolic. She had gone to Lancaster County in Pennsylvania plenty of times with her family and on school field trips, and it reminded her a lot of here. "Do they have shoofly pie here?" she asked.

In response, James laughed. "What goes on in that mind of yours? You skip from topic to topic like you're playing bloody leapfrog."

"It's not my fault. I'm just curious." She scratched River's soft doggy head. Her mom might be pissed at the dog slobber on her Team Knight jacket, but Lucy couldn't care less.

"That you are. Thanks for saying that about my mum. She is the best. But she's been through a lot in her life. She deserves a rest after everything."

His voice was stern and full of conviction. Lucy tilted her head. "Why are you going away for school? Wouldn't it be better to stay around here, since you're worried about her?"

James's face tensed. Even the corners of his eyes narrowed. "I wanted to stay here and take courses in Manchester. Going away was my uncle's idea, and once he got it into Mum's head, she couldn't let it go. When I got the full scholarship, she made it impossible for me to refuse."

While on one hand Lucy noted the casual reference to the full scholarship, which meant James was extraordinary, she also caught and felt kinship toward his reluctance in following what his parent wanted. "I get that feeling. My, um, mom and dad have a lot of plans for me, too. It's difficult sometimes to say no to them."

"Is that why you're at Blackstone? Because they wanted you to compete?"

Lucy sighed and buried her face atop River's. "Yes and no. First off, I desperately wanted to come to England. Who wouldn't rather have a field trip than actually deal with high school? And I love dancing. I really do. It's fun and elegant and the costumes are gorgeous. But I'm not like my coach, Anita. She told me once how much she gave up to follow her dreams, and I respect her. But it's not for me. I want a life outside of dancing. I'm not destined for the big leagues, and I'm cool with that." River had terrible breath but was an excellent comfort pillow, so Lucy didn't care too much. "But my parents see any possible hobby as something that should be pursued until the bitter end. Once when I was ten and going through a *Hunger Games* phase, I asked for a play archery kit. You know, a little plastic, princessy one that was pink and purple and the arrow barely flies farther than a paper airplane? Well, my parents instead found me a coach, signed me up for twice weekly archery classes, and bought me two different weights of bows." Lucy sighed. "They're still in a closet somewhere in our house. It's sweet in some ways. Like a super aggressive support system. In other ways, it's a bit…"

"Stifling," James said.

Lucy caught his gaze as he stared over at her. For a moment, their eyes met, and Lucy felt something completely unexpected. A spark, deep in her belly, crawling along her lower spine.

James broke contact first, leaving Lucy a little unmoored. What was going on with her?

"We're here," he said, turning the car down a lane into a little empty parking lot. "Welcome to the moss."

Chapter Thirteen

Anita sat high in the mezzanine, her Team Knight jacket folded under her butt as a cushion against the hard surface. It wasn't easy assessing future partners for Lucy, particularly when the choices seemed slim. As she watched the couples in the quarterfinals, she could hear Lucy's teenaged voice in her head like the world's most irritating gnat.

That one was too short. That one was too tall. That one didn't have enough presence in the Paso Doble. That one gave off creepy Paso presence. How had that one gotten into the quarterfinals with those chainé turns? At least Henry Kim could spot.

In her head, Lucy was a very demanding Goldilocks, but Anita got it. The kid deserved someone worthy of her. Anita herself had wasted far too much time without her perfect partner.

So engrossed was she with analyzing the quarterfinal couples, she completely missed the fact that there was a well-dressed man in a bespoke Savile Row suit with artfully styled salt-and-pepper hair beside her. She might have ignored him completely if the scent of his strong, spicy musk cologne hadn't engulfed her like a mist of poison gas.

"Miss Goodman," he said, his voice clipped and elegant.

Anita tried not to cough. There was something

familiar about him, but for the life of her, she couldn't remember his name. Probably best not to bring that up since he seemed to know her.

"Hello," she said. Opting for inane replies seemed a wise decision. "Are you enjoying the competition?"

He sniffed loudly and slipped his hands into the pockets of his trousers. "I suppose it's all right. My son is clearly the best of the bunch, as you can see for yourself." He nodded toward the open seat beside her and didn't wait for her assent before sliding next to her. Great. Now she would probably reek like his expensive cologne. She preferred Patrick's more woodsy scent.

He was also clearly waiting for her agreement, though she had no idea who his son was, nor why she should care. "Yes, absolutely. He's killing it out there."

"Exactly." The man's quotidian-handsome features settled into a snarky grin. "His partner is subpar, though. She's holding him back."

"Hmm." Anita could list at least five couples that fit that bill, gender-swapped and not.

"I'm very much looking forward to him meeting Lucy tomorrow. Though, perhaps now that you've seen him, you agree that they would suit? Auditioning is so exhausting."

She heard the cajole in his tone, the expectation that she would agree. Why? Because he was a privileged white man? Hardly. The asshole wouldn't even deign to identify himself. "Lucy knows what she needs. I'm not going to deny her the chance to find out for herself."

His features hardened and there was a distinct drop in temperature in the room. "You know, Miss Goodman, I am one of the organizers this year. I was instrumental in bringing you and Mr. O'Leary here. Did you really think your erratic performance schedule of the last year was enough to earn your spot?" His voice chilled her to the bone, but she kept her composure, firming her posture and maintaining cool eye contact. "I invited you because of your social media presence and also for what we could be to each other."

Ew. That was a creepy left turn.

His gaze tilted southward over her body, and she did everything in her power not to recoil. It was a good thing the Team Knight jacket was roomy. Common sense still had her shifting away from him.

His lip curved into a sort of sneer. "See you tomorrow, Miss Goodman. Don't disappoint me."

With that, he stood and left.

"Asshole should have a long, curly mustache he can twirl," Anita muttered, mostly to calm her racing heart and trilling nerves.

Lucian Chatelaine. That was his name. It hit her all of a sudden like a burst sewage pipe.

"What's up with you?" Patrick asked, handing her a mug of steaming green tea, which she used to warm her hands. He sat down beside her and immediately wrinkled his nose in disgust. "Ugh. Who sat here? The posh ghost of someone with anosmia?"

Anita chuckled and leaned against him, his solid frame restoring some part of her that she'd lost. "It was Lucian Chatelaine."

"The TV producer?" Patrick sipped his coffee.

"He's a TV producer? I thought he was some sort of private-jet-CEO-type. Like a venture capitalist." Anita had no idea what a venture capitalist did, but it sounded like it would fit Lucian Chatelaine.

"He produces the new *Dance with Me,*" Patrick said. "Not the early seasons, which are the only ones worth watching. Tom Havens is no Jackson Alder."

"True." Back during the first two seasons, she used to watch religiously as amateur dancers paired with professionals and competed each week for the chance at a dance scholarship or to work in a Hollywood movie. Since it had returned, the very sight of Tom Havens made it unpalatable. She supposed he appealed to some audience, or at least had a lot of inside intel that made him impossible to fire.

"What did he want?"

"His son is auditioning to be Lucy's partner." Anita sighed and blew some of the steam from her cup. "And he wasted no time in telling me that he's the reason we're even here."

"Oh, please. Pure egotistic crap." He nudged her in the side. "Plus, how hypocritical is he? Most organizers try to remain neutral so as not to rig the competition for their family members. Blackstone must have been hard up for cash if they let riffraff like that in."

"I know." Anita scratched at the cardboard teacup with one long fingernail. She needed to paint them before the Team Match. Team colors, obviously. "It's one thing, though, to feel something inside, and completely another to have a stranger validate your own sense of inadequacy."

Patrick kissed the top of her head. "There is literally nothing inadequate about you, Anita."

A kernel of warmth bloomed along her spine, and she linked her elbow with his, leaning her head on his perfect Patrick shoulder. "You're the best person in the entire world. Do you know that?"

"I do. It's part of my awesome future husband powers."

Anita twirled the engagement ring on her finger. She'd successfully avoided her parents and any talk of marriage for the better part of the day. "I will set a date some time. I'm sorry to keep you waiting."

Patrick removed his arm from her elbow and instead looped it around her shoulder, pulling her close. "I waited over ten years for you, Anita. I'd wait a thousand more. Take your time."

It would be better if she felt that this would be true. Even Patrick, king of patience, had to have a limit. And she didn't want to find out what happened when he reached it.

Chapter Fourteen

The peat bog was not what Lucy had expected. She had visited national parks back home, some for research and poorly thought-out school field trips, but this was literally an expanse of various types of green and brown mosses stretching to the misty horizon. There was only one battered heavy-duty truck parked in the small lot, with a russet-headed young man beside it, who could only be a researcher based on his tall rubber boots and full yellow rain suit.

James raised a hand toward him. "Hey, Pete."

Lucy held back the snicker. Pete worked in the peat bogs. He probably got that all the time.

Pete nodded at both of them but came over to say hello properly to River. "Hey there, River girl. How've you been?"

James hooked a thumb at Pete. "Pete works on the peatlands preservation. You can't just visit, typically. People have died in here, getting sucked into the bogs. Like that old movie, what was it?"

Lucy cleared her throat. "*The Neverending Story*?"

Pete snapped his fingers and grinned at her, a smile that creased his face nearly in half. "That's it. I love the dragon in that movie. Reminds me a bit of River here. So you want to be careful out in the bogs. I'll show you the path I take, which is relatively stable. I haven't been out yet today. Had lectures down in Manchester, so I've only just arrived myself."

A twinge of fear curled in Lucy's spine. "Should we be worried about River?"

James shook his head. "She's smart and light on her feet. She won't go too far ahead or around, but it's a good chance to stretch the old girl's legs."

Pete pointed at Lucy's practical sneakers. "You need better footwear. I've got an extra pair in the trunk. What about you, James?"

"It's all right. I brought my mum's wellies for Lucy." James went around the back of the car and removed two pairs of tall black waterproof boots. "What do you think, Lucy? You up for a ramble?"

Lucy glanced between the boots and the miles and miles of peat bog surrounding them. Without another moment of hesitation, she took the boots in her hand. "Definitely."

****

There was something oddly satisfying about walking through the bogs. They stepped mostly on firm hillocks of soft brown-and-green moss, but there was a pleasant swish of plant against boot that spoke to Lucy's need for ASMR.

"It's called sphagnum moss," Pete explained, leading the way by using a tall walking stick to probe the ground in front of him. "It helps protect the wetlands and hold the moisture in underneath. They can hold up to twenty times their weight in water. Isn't that incredible?"

James nudged Lucy's side with his walking stick and said in a loud stage whisper, "Pete is studying British botany."

"That is so cool." Lucy particularly liked the little

wispy tufts of cotton grass dotting the landscape. They looked like little clouds or fairies perched on thin reeds. It had stopped misting finally, and a hint of sun peeked through the clouds above. The air smelled clean and moist, like it was holding on to this ancient moment in time. "So, Pete, what's the coolest thing you've ever found here?"

Pete crossed a gully with a trickle of water running through it and dark, drying-out peat on either side. "That's a good question. Last year I was out here with my da and we came across some folks who had tried to camp out here. Their tent was almost half sunk in the bog. It took all of us just to yank it free." Pete shook his head. "People amaze me. Plants make more sense."

River barked ahead of them, wagging her long, fluffy tail, now streaked brown from the peat all around them. When they moved toward her, she turned and ran to a spot not much farther on before burying her nose deep into the side of a gulley.

James shook his head. "Mum's going to have a fit. We'll have to give her a bath before we bring her inside."

Though it wasn't quite the true crime exposé she had expected, Lucy found she rather liked this excursion. It felt good to be outside, hiking in this strange, otherworldly place with only the three of them and River. The ground was spongy and made eerie splooshing splashing sounds, but the path Pete took kept them from sinking in too deep.

"Are you enjoying yourself?" James asked, waiting for her to join him. Of course she was the one faffing about and bringing up the rear.

"Definitely. But don't think I've lost hope of

finding anything buried in here. Even a keychain or really cool skipping stone would work."

James laughed, his voice rising to the sky. "I'm sure Pete will see what he can do."

"Did you call him?" It seemed odd otherwise that they had all arrived simultaneously.

"Yes. Otherwise I don't really like walking out here. As he said, people have gotten hurt or even died, and their bodies won't be found for ages. Not even by an intrepid explorer like you." He flashed her a smile that did something nuclear to her insides, making them all warm and melty. She looked ahead toward River, who was now digging with her paws into the side of the gulley.

"So, what exactly does peat bog restoration look like?"

James sighed. "Pete's the expert, he really should explain it. Pete! Slow up and give Lucy your spiel."

"Really?" Pete turned, his face bright and eager above the neon blue of his rain jacket. "Normally I can't tell anyone before we're three pints in. Are you sure you want to know?"

Lucy shrugged. "I'd also kind of like a pint, but I'm seventeen and my mom would literally kill me. Sure. I'd love to know." Plus she had to reinforce the lie she had told her mom earlier, about the paper on the effects of climate change. Might as well have hard data that wasn't easily searchable. Her mom had been checking her research papers since her second grade presentation on horses.

"It's wicked." Pete joined them and, as they walked, spoke with grand gestures. "So, the peat bogs have been here in the UK forever. And people have long used them to burn for fuel or for compost, because they hold on really well to carbon."

"Like carbon dioxide?"

"Exactly! But with erosion, and overuse of peat farming, the bogs are now releasing a lot of their carbon into the atmosphere."

A lightbulb clicked in Lucy's brain. "Oh, I see. So, like, with the gullies, the peat that's drying out is adding carbon dioxide to the atmosphere?"

"Exactly!" Pete looked like he might kiss her, and Lucy subtly dodged behind James, who snickered because men sucked. "Some people never get it. You're amazing, Lucy. Anyway, the goal is to cover the areas that have been exposed and restore the peat bogs. We bring in diggers and more moss to cover them."

"That's why there are a bunch of construction vehicles over there." Lucy pointed to a spot in the distance where there were two yellow-orange excavators.

"Pete won't let me drive one," James said, a laugh playing around his eyes. Of all the boys Lucy had ever met, James did have one of the most expressive faces. It was disconcerting.

"You don't have a license," Pete replied.

The two boys devolved into some sort of masculine playground argument, and Lucy rapidly lost interest. She reached down to touch one of the soft tufts of the cotton grass, liking the way the tendrils slipped against her fingertips. They had gotten closer to River's gulley, where she was still digging.

Using the walking stick Pete had given her, Lucy made her way over the little mossy hillocks toward River. "What did you find, girl? Miss Barrow is going to be *pissed* when she sees how muddy you are. Hopefully James has a towel in his trunk or something or you are going to get mud all over his car."

The walking stick plunged into a soft piece of moss, sinking lower than she had expected, and upsetting her balance. Of all the things in the world, she did not want to fall, not here, not in front of two local boys who would probably laugh and laugh at the stupid American who wanted to explore a peat bog in the northern part of the United Kingdom.

She righted herself, yanking her walking stick free from the moss with a splodgey, unpleasant sort of sound, and took another path to River.

Then stopped still.

Not because River was now staring at her, wagging her tail, happy to see Lucy and proud to show off her discovery.

It was because of the expensive Italian leather loafer River had unearthed beneath a thin layer of peat. And the foot that was still in it.

Chapter Fifteen

After the quarterfinals, Patrick convinced Anita to decamp to the pub where they were going to meet their fellow contenders on the Americas Team. She hadn't really perked up after her visit from Douchey, Lord of Dickhead, but some time with her friends might cheer her. More than he could, at any rate.

Blackstone seemed comprised primarily of seedy bars with people in oddly fitted clothing using most every surface as makeshift urinals, dance clubs which may or may not be strip clubs, and graffitied takeaway joints, none of which seemed crowded at the early hour. Patrick had a feeling, though, they truly came alive after midnight to feed the super-drunk and nearly comatose crowd.

Not that he minded people enjoying themselves and a good drink. He sidestepped a couple making out horizontally on a bus stop bench. It was more that he had left his wild spring break days in the never-happened bin. Apart from one time in Tokyo when he got a little too friendly with sake, he'd generally managed to enjoy himself without committing a crime. He didn't particularly have a desire to see a bunch of drunk people take off their tops in the middle of the street.

Unless that someone was Anita, but that was also firmly in the never-happen bin.

"Jeez, it's like some misogynist *Girls Gone Wild* shit," Anita said, dodging a very tall man dressed incongruously in a purple-and-yellow jersey and a *Groom to Be* shot-glass necklace swinging around his neck.

Privately, he agreed, but he was still in cheering-up-Anita mode. "The pub we're meeting at is just ahead. We'll call a cab from there and avoid this whole mess on the way back to the house."

"Thanks." Anita pulled her hood over her head as another sprinkle of frigid, rain-soaked wind sliced through them. "I swear Blackstone's gotten worse since the last time I was here."

"I was listening to this podcast, and they said Blackstone's basically ground zero for every possible crime." In retrospect, that was probably not the way to cheer up Anita.

Fortunately, they'd finally reached the shelter of the pub. To his immense relief, it was a much nicer—and safer—sort of pub than the ones they'd passed. This one had a long, polished wood bar with gold-plated draft handles dominating the center, and red leatherette booths and the odd four-top table lined the sides. In one far corner, near the sign for the bathrooms, was a decent-sized fireplace, complete with roaring fire and mantel over which hung various photos of bygone Blackstone Dance Festivals.

"Thank goodness, not a single bachelorette party," Anita said, removing the hood of her rain jacket and shaking rain from her blonde ponytail.

Patrick scanned the crowd for their friends. "I think we're early. Do you want a drink?"

"Definitely. I'll get a booth."

She went off in search of an unoccupied booth, which wasn't challenging at that hour. Unlike the seedier places, this pub seemed to cater to more of an older crowd who might drink a bit later.

Patrick ordered a white wine and a lager from the young, curly-haired bartender who could double as a young Albert Finney.

The comparison left him a bit cold. His mom had made him watch the original *Tom Jones* every single time it came on PBS when he was young. It wasn't Albert Finney's fault that Patrick practically hated the story.

The bartender slid his drinks across the polished bar, and Patrick handed him a twenty-pound note. He liked how easy it felt, slipping back into International Travel Patrick. The last year of college and for a few years afterward, he and Anita and their dance partners had spanned the globe in search of amateur dance championships.

He hadn't realized how much he had missed it over the last five years of adulting stateside. Why had he given it all up?

"What are you thinking about?" she asked as he slipped into the booth directly across from her. She took the wine he gave her and wrapped her fingers around the sturdy glass base.

"That this is perfect." He sipped his beer, practically swooning at the malty, sultry taste. He smacked his lips to rid himself of the foam mustache he was sure he sported. "This beer is perfect."

She smiled, but her shoulders were still tense. "This is what you wanted, right? A beer and a pub."

"No, not really. I wanted to spend time with you."

She rolled her blue eyes, which finally had a bit of their brightness back. "You are completely ridiculous."

"Ridiculously in love with you."

She laughed more at that, rocking back and forth slightly in her seat. The sound filled the nearly-empty pub, reverberating around the glassware.

A shadow crossed their table, and for a moment, Patrick wasn't sure if Death had stopped by to suck all the joy from the room.

He glanced up at the shadow creature and his heart sank. The person wasn't quite as futile as Death, but equally unwelcome. "Hello, Mikhail."

Anita's ex. The douchebag king of Doucherton, who had dumped Anita right before Keystone last year, giving Patrick his one shot at showing her how he felt—

That didn't mean he liked the guy. And he refused to feel any sense of gratitude, particularly toward this asshole with his stupid hair.

Who also was one of those people who insisted on squeezing into a booth, thereby crushing Patrick against the wood-edged window frame and forcing him to squish his elbow against his side.

At least the lager he was drinking mitigated his displeasure. Slightly.

Patrick recognized the woman he had arrived with as the dancer Laurie Donovan. She was the one bright spot of the new *Dance with Me*.

"Hi," she said jovially. "I'm Laurie."

"Anita. And this is Patrick."

Laurie squeezed in beside Anita, which still left Patrick rammed into the corner.

"So…" Mikhail said, his voice as thick and greasy

as the pomade he used in his hair. "You two made it into the Team Match? Excuse me, but you've never competed before at Blackstone, and now you are in one of the highest-watched performances?" He sucked his teeth and tapped the heavy metal of his thumb ring against his cocktail glass.

"Mikhail, no." Laurie shut him down flat, earning Patrick's undying appreciation. She shook her head, her long, pretty locs swaying. "They're doing something different this year. It's no longer the top-ranked couples, but the most popular. I've seen your videos, Anita, and they're fab." She elbowed Mikhail in a pointed fashion, brightly colored rings flashing against her dark brown skin. "We wouldn't have made it either, if I weren't on the show. We almost didn't. Sorry if we're a last-minute surprise."

Anita blushed and clinked her glass with Laurie's in thanks. "You are amazing on that show, BTW. *Dance with Me* is lucky to have you."

"Thanks." Laurie straightened, pleasure radiating from her. Why on earth she was with Mikhail completed eluded Patrick. Not only was she far prettier than he was, both in personality and looks, but Patrick couldn't see how she tolerated listening to him.

Mikhail grunted and drained his glass in one swallow.

"So, what's Tom Havens really like?" Anita asked. Patrick had a feeling she didn't genuinely care, but she was not interested in engaging Mikhail in any sort of conversation.

Laurie rolled her dark brown eyes and uttered a sound best characterized as complete disgust. "Everything you've heard. Honestly, I'm not sure why they're keeping him on the show. Don't tell anyone, but half the time we can't find him, and the other half he's drunk and hitting on nineteen-year-olds." She sighed and twirled her white wine glass between her long fingers. "The other women and I do our best to protect them."

"It's good you're there," Anita said, her voice quiet.

Clearly miffed at being left out of the conversation, lack-of-talent Mikhail segued dramatically. "Who else is on the team? Are we certain everyone's outfits coordinate? Is anyone doing Standard as well, or are we just the Latin team?"

Patrick swallowed his anger with a gulp of his beer. If he didn't slow down, it would soon be gone.

Laurie placed a calming hand on Mikhail's arm. "Chill out and get us some more drinks. Lemonade for me, please."

Mikhail huffed like the toddler he was but did as she asked.

Patrick's entire body relaxed the moment Mikhail was gone.

"Look, I know he's an ass," Laurie said, her voice low and meant only for the three of them. "But he is trying. Lord knows my girlfriend keeps telling me I should find a new partner, but he suits what I need right now. I'm just sorry you all have to deal with him."

"We did think we were free once he moved to Toronto." Patrick drained his beer. "But he couldn't have found a better partner. You deserve better."

"Thank you." Laurie grinned, her smile accentuating her high cheekbones. "Now let's talk tactics while we wait for the others."

****

Losing Mikhail in the crush of bar patrons that had arrived turned out to be the very best part of Patrick's day. He hadn't spent much time with Laurie before, but after ten minutes, he and Anita had invited her and her girlfriend to spend time with them in Pennsylvania, and they were planning a possible couples' trip to the Finger Lakes in the autumn.

Then Hanna and Markus Pascal arrived, slightly frazzled, but their arrival managed to delay Mikhail's return even further, since it was far easier for him to collect the entire round of drinks rather than having new people wait.

All in all, Patrick was in a far better mood even without a second pint in front of him.

"So?" Hanna raised her eyebrows at the group of them, Team Americas. "Are we all ready for the match? Anyone have questions?"

As the only couple who had previously danced in the Team Match, Hanna and Markus were the resident experts and de facto team captains.

Anita finally drank the last of the white wine she'd been nursing. "So we dance all five on the floor together with the rest of the teams?"

"Yes." Hanna nodded as Mikhail returned, his expression delightfully mutinous when he realized his previous seat had been taken by Markus. He disappeared to find himself an empty chair. Patrick wanted to hum but thought his companions might find it odd. "Then they tally the total points per team and the winner gets…well, mostly recognition. I understand you've all already met Mikhail and Laurie. We're so grateful you could be here." She directed this comment toward Laurie, holding her pint glass in one hand.

"Works for me. Anything we should look out for?" Laurie held her bottle of lemonade tightly, the only thing that belied her inner nervousness.

Markus shrugged. "The new organizers want everything flashy and film-able this year. Whatever will hit on social media and draw attention, they want it and they want it now."

Mikhail finally returned and set his chair down hard on the floor of the pub. "It's a travesty," he said. "It's like they have no respect anymore for Dancesport. They cannot maintain the beauty and elegance of the event."

Laurie shook her head. "They respect it, and know they need cash to keep it going. It's a business, Mikhail, like everything else."

"It's foolish. Just as foolish as this bloody Blackstone ghost everyone keeps going on about." Mikhail downed his second cocktail, likely just to be dramatic. It was his own fault, in Patrick's opinion, if he had to go back to the bar.

Hanna arched an eyebrow. "Hey, the Blackstone ghost is real. I've been in the ballroom when it's quiet, a miracle in and of itself, and I swear I've heard crying and screaming before. Or wait, what is it called?" She looked to Markus, who shrugged, not following her train of thought. "Wailing. That's what I've heard. Wailing. Isn't that a ghost thing?"

A wailing ghost in the basement of the famed ballroom. It sounded a little too maudlin and cinematic.

Patrick stared out the frosted window at his side. The sun was still low in the sky, not yet evening, not still day. Almost twilight. Didn't ghosts prefer twilight?

A shiver ran down his spine, which was only compounded when his phone rang loudly in his pocket.

He jumped a little, hoping no one saw, and glanced at the text message, his blood slowly turning to ice.

Lucy: —911. Come now. Sending you pinned location—

"Anita," he said, standing and impatiently waiting for his friends to leave the booth. "We have to go now. It's Lucy."

Chapter Sixteen

While this was not Lucy's first foray into crime scene investigation, this was the most useless she had ever felt. Over her last winter and spring breaks, she had interned with the local police department, and her mentor, interim Sheriff John Flaherty, had treated her almost as an equal.

Within reason, of course.

Now, though, standing at the edge of the peat bog with River on one side of her, James and Pete on the other, and the evening rapidly approaching, Lucy felt superfluous. And she *hated* feeling superfluous.

She hadn't watched enough British crime procedurals to distinguish the officer who approached her, but he was a good-looking, lean man with light brown skin and soft eyes. She would say one thing for the British police, and that was that their interrogations sounded far more polite with a BBC accent than a Philly one.

"Ms. Knight, Mr. Barrow, and Mr. Fletchender," the officer said, glancing down at his notes. "Can I ask you a few more questions?"

In the US, she would require a chaperone because of her age, but apparently that wasn't a thing here, or maybe they didn't care.

"We've already answered a lot," James said. "Look, I'm sorry, but Lucy's not from here. Her parents are going to be beside themselves. Can I please take her home?"

A thrill coursed through her. Not at the thought of her parents worrying. They probably didn't expect her home until eight or nine at the earliest. But the thrill came from the realization that James was trying to protect her. She'd never had that before. Odd that she kind of liked it.

"It won't take long," the officer said. She tried to read his name tag, but her eyelashes were dewy from the rain, and the jet lag and events of the day must be catching up with her because everything seemed fuzzy. "Did any of you know or recognize the victim?"

"It's Tom Havens," Pete said. He'd stood stock still the entire time, which had been almost an hour and a half so far. "From *Dance with Me*. My mum and sister like him. Blimey if I know why."

"Have any of you met Mr. Havens before?"

"No," Lucy replied. "Though I was at the Blackstone Dance Festival this morning, and people kept talking about how he was missing."

The officer ticked back through his notes. "Yes. You mentioned that you overheard several conversations where people said he was last seen yesterday evening."

Lucy shrugged. "I didn't see him personally, but I think that's what they said."

The officer looked her directly in the eye, but she could tell from his posture he didn't really consider her a suspect. Or at least she hoped that was the correct interpretation of his body language. "And last night? You were…"

"I was at the house with my parents and my dance

teachers. We had dinner. James and his uncle, Mr. Butler, were there as well."

The officer turned his gaze to James, and his eyes narrowed slightly. Hmm. He couldn't think James a suspect, could he? Not that she knew him all that well, but he didn't appear to be a murderer who would take her out to the scene of the crime. River seemed to share her opinion, as she rubbed her head against James's leg, as though in solidarity. "Mr. Barrow. What time did you leave Gryphon House yesterday evening?"

James rubbed River's soft head. "I don't remember exactly. I think around ten or so. After we'd cleaned up the dishes and whatnot, my uncle dropped me at home."

The officer made some notations. "And your whereabouts today?"

James's face went slightly paler, though perhaps it was Lucy's imagination. "This morning I was working at Gryphon House. Then they called for me to pick up Lucy, so I went straightaway to the Crystal Gardens ballroom."

A tingle niggled at the back of Lucy's mind. He had arrived awfully fast from the time when her parents had initially summoned him. Had he really driven from Lythe to Blackstone in such a short time?

"And you, Ms. Knight?" The officer asked.

"I was competing in the Juniors competition at the dance festival," Lucy said, shoving the kernels of doubt down into her subconscious where she could later analyze them. "My partner, Henry, and I were cut after the second round, but we were there until about two this afternoon."

"Very well. Mr. Fletchender?" The officer now addressed Pete, whose stony expression had barely changed.

"I had classes this morning in Manchester. Then I drove up here this afternoon when James called me. I suppose I arrived here around half past three or so."

Lucy's phone buzzed in her pocket, and a mixture of relief and apprehension filled her gut. Patrick and Anita had gotten her text and were on their way. Better them than her parents. She still hadn't figured out what, if anything, she should tell them. After all, they were leaving for business meetings in a different city in the morning. She'd be lying if she didn't admit how grateful she was they'd be gone while she went through auditions.

So maybe they didn't need to know about her finding a dead body. Not yet. Or ever, preferably. One decisive way to kill her dreams of being a criminologist was to tell her parents she had been actively involved in a case. She hadn't even told them the full extent of her extracurricular job with the sheriff's department.

It wasn't that they didn't support her and her dreams. Lucy knew that. It was more that they worried almost too much about her safety. Anything was better than having to explain herself to her parents.

"May I get each of your directions, please?" the officer asked, going around them in a circle and collecting phone numbers. "We will be in touch if we have further questions. Thank you."

For some reason she couldn't identify and didn't particularly care to, Lucy felt a little bereft. Tears pricked at the backs of her eyes but she sniffed them away. She wished she remembered the officer's name. She wished she were at home, cozy under the thick bedspread at Gryphon House, watching movies on her laptop. Maybe James would let her borrow River for the night.

"All right, then, Lucy?" James asked. His voice was soft, not at all patronizing, more laced with concern. She turned to him, her inner resolve softening slightly. He was pretty cute, for a boy she shouldn't have anything to do with. And nice, and funny.

But none of those were things she ought to be thinking at that moment. If John Flaherty were here, he would trust her to ask the right questions, do the right thing. He wasn't here, though, and for the first time in a while, Lucy didn't know what to do.

It sucked.

"I'm fine. Thanks." She knelt beside River and buried her inner turmoil by thoroughly scratching the dog's head. "You're such a smart girl, aren't you, River?"

River responded with a chuff and dug her scalp into Lucy's side.

"I've got to get home. My mum's going to light into me if she finds out about this," Pete said.

Lucy's stomach felt like a pit of boiling acid. James touched her arm, so gently it was more like a nudge from a butterfly, and a thrill of electric pleasure coursed through her. She'd have to shut that down right quick. "We'd best be getting on, too."

Lucy nodded, following him to the car. She couldn't help but take one last look over the moss, the landscape hillocked and pockmarked. In the distance, where River had found Tom Havens, bright portable arc lights lit the site, which was cordoned off with yellow police tape.

Damn it, her spidey sense wouldn't let her go. She

opened the passenger door of James's car and leaned on the hood, River buffing her side for more rubs. "James?"

"Yeah?" He stood before his own open door, his posture easy and relaxed.

Great, now she had to be the questioning asshole. Oh well. "It's just, um, when I called for a ride, it took you, like, zero time to get to the ballroom."

He shifted his weight slightly. "I suppose."

Asshole, asshole, she was an asshole. "Did you really come from Lythe?"

He wouldn't meet her gaze. Shit, the first cute guy she'd ever liked and he was a murderer. Perfect. Great taste, Lucy. "All right, no. No, I was already at the ballroom."

At least he was an honest murderer. Lucy resisted rubbing River again, despite what the dog demanded. "Why?"

He laughed a little and ran a hand through his hair. There was a flush rising up his neck. "I like to watch the dancers. All right, look, it's not the whole truth. I, um, went today because I wanted to see you dance." His gaze flicked to hers and held it, and liquid warmth trickled through her bloodstream. "You're a grand dancer, Lucy."

"Oh. So, like, not a murderer then?" Foot, meet mouth.

His mouth curled up one side. "Not today. Can I take you home?"

If he insisted.

Chapter Seventeen

It took far too long to find a ride share, so by the time Anita and Patrick found one, they'd already heard from Lucy to meet them at Gryphon House instead of the bog.

Anita didn't voice her relief, but the gnawing pit of worry at actually seeing a body eased.

When they arrived at the estate, none of the Knights were present. Anita was full of nervous pixie energy, and she had a feeling she was driving Patrick bananas by fluttering around the house, making tea, opening and closing the refrigerator, and doing jumping jacks in the middle of the foyer.

While she was in the kitchen, pouring hot water into a mug of herbal tea, the pantry door slammed closed behind her. She leapt into the air like she was more ballerina than ballroom dancer. "Holy hell!" She clasped her heart over her chest like she clutched a string of pearls.

Mr. Butler stood beside the closed pantry door, scowling. "Ms. Goodman. You've returned from the dance festival?"

Clearly. Her heart still raced, but she was able to speak. How in the world had he gotten there? "Um, yes. Patrick and I just got back a few minutes ago." More like twenty, but who was counting?

"And the Knights? Are they with you?"

That didn't sound right. Wasn't he supposed to be driving Lucy's parents? Anita had zero idea what a butler's actual responsibilities were. Besides, it was absolutely none of her business, and there was also no way she was going to tell Mr. Butler about the discovery of Tom Havens's dead bog body. She shuddered involuntarily. "No. Your nephew, James, picked Lucy up a while ago for some sightseeing." She was pretty proud of herself for coming up with that excuse. "I'm not sure where her parents are."

"Very good." It didn't seem like he believed that, though. Not with his downturned expression and steel gaze. "Your tea is ready. Would you care for anything else?"

"No, I'm good. I can get things myself."

He made some noncommittal noise, then disappeared from the kitchen.

Anita threw out the tea bag, the short encounter rattling her almost as much as the news of the murder. But definitely the murder took precedence. Had he been hiding in the pantry the entire time? Why on earth would someone do that?

To allay her curiosity as much as settle her mind, she opened the pantry door herself and inspected the contents. Nothing out of order. Boxes of tea, pasta, jars of sauces, bags of rice, cans of fruits and beans and vegetables.

"I'm losing my mind," she whispered to herself.

She promptly shut the pantry door, arming herself with her herbal tea.

This was not a mystery for her to solve. Mr. Butler had every right to be in the house, doing whatever it was he had been doing. That was his job. Probably.

Either way, it was absolutely none of her business.

****

Patrick wasn't one to bite his nails, particularly in the days leading up to the most major competition of his life, but if Lucy didn't show up soon, he might start gnawing them down to the knuckle.

"Are you okay?" Anita handed him a mug of herbal tea, something that smelled like cinnamon and apples and autumn. At least she knew what to do to make him feel better.

"I'm worried about Lucy." He sipped the tea and coughed. Jeez, it was hot. He'd be shocked if he had any tongue left.

"Me too. But she'll be okay. She's a lot tougher than we give her credit for." Anita sipped her own tea, completely stone-faced. Maybe her drink was cooler than his.

Patrick sank onto the couch in the drawing room, but found it was less comfortable and more posture-improving than he had anticipated. "I know." He shifted his butt around on the cushions until he could find a slightly better position, which was turning out to be a Sisyphean task. "John trusts her a lot, too. He says he's going to write her a recommendation for whatever college she wants. He told me he likes her better than Curtis."

Anita smiled, but it was a tad half-hearted. "Poor Curtis. He's a decent deputy, just green. We all deserve a chance to grow into ourselves."

Patrick tilted his head, examining her. "What do you mean? You're pretty full-grown, Anita."

"I don't know." She sighed and blew away some of the steam from her mug. "Sometimes I wish there was someone around who would just tell me exactly what to do."

"Ditto."

At that moment, the front door creaked open with a gaping sort of crunch. Those hinges were in dire need of oil, but that wasn't a task Patrick was going to undertake.

"Mom? Dad?" Lucy called from the foyer, in a voice that clearly said, "Please don't let my parents be here."

"Lucy." As one, he and Anita dashed toward the foyer.

Lucy looked a little bedraggled, her dark hair plastered to her forehead from the mist and rain, and her clothes streaked with a mixture of green and dark brown slime. But her eyes were bright and curious. "Oh my God, can you believe I actually found a body?" she said.

Standing beside her, James Barrow hovered over Lucy in a protective manner. Aww. "Do you need anything, Lucy? I've got to get River home, and get my mum something to eat."

"I'm fine. Really." She reached out to touch his arm but withdrew it at the last moment. "Thanks, James. For everything."

"Of course." His face softened into a smile, and something deep and protective within Patrick reared its head. He crossed his arms over his chest and glared at James. Hah, he stumbled. Teenagers. "I'd best be on my way."

"Did you want to talk to your uncle?" Anita asked.

James's face creased in question. "My uncle? Is he here? I hadn't thought he would be. We weren't supposed to cook tonight."

"Oh." Anita flushed slightly. "It might be jet lag hallucinations. I thought I saw him in the kitchen earlier."

"Hmph." James took out his phone and checked through his screen. Likely looking at messages. "I'll check with him when I get home. Good evening."

"Good evening," Patrick replied, keeping the steel in his voice. Lucy's dad might not be home, but he could look out for her and Anita.

"Right." James turned and left.

Anita elbowed him in the ribs. "Ow!" He rubbed at the spot. Hopefully she had packed the arnica. Of course she had; she prepared for everything.

"Drop the tough guy act, Patrick. Lucy is fine. James brought her safely home." Anita shook her head. "I'll get you a towel, Lucy."

"It's okay." Lucy removed her sodden rain jacket and hung it in the cavernous hall closet. Seriously, Patrick had hung up his coat earlier and thought he might emerge in Narnia. "I'm going to take a hot shower, and then can we eat? I'll fill you in on everything that happened."

"Perfect," Anita said.

****

"So, then the officer told us we could go." Lucy shrugged, picking up a spear of roasted broccoli between her fingers and snapping off the top with her teeth.

"I think we should call John," Patrick said. Anita arched her eyebrow toward him. Even she knew that was futile. "Okay, I know. He doesn't have any jurisdiction here. But it's a knee-jerk response." She could respect that. John always did feel like the adult in the room.

Lucy tapped her fork against the side of her plate. Besides the broccoli, she had barely touched the cauliflower-and-lentil cottage pie Anita had made. Which was a shame. Though Anita was not the best cook, this was one of her recently concocted specialties, and it was more than edible.

“What do you want to do?” Anita directed her question toward Lucy, who shrugged in response.

“I definitely don’t want my parents to know. They have to travel for work this week, and I don’t want anything to get in the way of that. My mom’s working on a big merger.” Lucy suddenly looked much younger than her seventeen years.

“We promise we won’t say anything,” Anita said, her voice poised and conciliatory. “But it might make you feel better if you do. Secrets only give you wrinkles.” To which she could attest, after staring at her own nascent crow’s feet for at least ten minutes the other day.

Her phone with its unanswered texts from her parents weighed heavily in her pocket.

Lucy shook her head decisively. “No. It’s better they don’t find out.” She picked at the mashed cauliflower on her cottage pie. “It’s better just to keep doing what we were planning. Go through the auditions, you guys practice and perform, and everything will be fine.”

Anita narrowed her eyes. She had known Lucy long enough to realize when the girl was full of shit. “Lucy. You absolutely, positively cannot go investigating this thing on your own in a foreign country when your parents are out of town. There are like eight thousand things wrong with that."

Lucy dropped her fork, indignant. "I would—"

Patrick shook his head. "You absolutely would. Keep it to armchair sleuthing."

Dropping back in her chair, Lucy crossed her arms over her chest and harrumphed like a grumpy ancient mariner. "But that's boring."

"It's also safe," Anita said. "Your parents aren't here, and Patrick and I have a lot of obligations on our time. It may not be the most exciting thing to stay home on your laptop instead of, I don't know, tramping about the moors with a cute guy in a parka, but you're seventeen. You are not a police officer. No one's criticizing your intelligence or abilities, but seriously, Lucy."

Lucy frowned deeply, staring at the marled wood of the kitchen table. "He's not that cute."

So Anita's first instinct about James's interest had been spot on. She gave her inner matchmaker a little pat on the back. "It's late. Today has been eight hundred years long. Let's clean up, go to bed, and start fresh tomorrow."

"Good idea." Patrick scraped the last of his cottage pie from his plate and drank an entire glass of water.

In the distant foyer, the front door opened with a loud creak.

"Lucy?" Cassandra called, her voice echoing along the stones of the hallway. "Are you here?"

Lucy turned a murderous look at them. "Not a word. Please."

Anita crossed her fingers over her heart but caught Patrick's warning glare. "Promise."

Chapter Eighteen

Patrick woke with a jolt and a taste in his mouth that reminded him of old socks and rotten banana peels.

That thought alone made his stomach heave. Combining it with the thought of Tom Havens's dead body stuffed in a bog?

He gulped several times and sat upright in bed, the covers pooling in a little puddle around his waist. Wait, if the covers were pooling, where was Anita? She was typically the hoggiest of cover hogs.

Blinking several times to rid himself of both the horrible dreams and the remaining sleep in his eyes, his unfocused gaze swept the room.

There she was. On a yoga mat in tree pose, eyes closed, right foot poised just so on her left thigh, palms pressed together.

Patrick's breathing eased. She hadn't noticed him or his nightmare. He'd been trying his best to hide them from her. She didn't need the memories any more than he did. Even if his therapist kept telling him to open up to her about his experience, there was still that niggling sense in the back of his head that maybe if he did, if he confessed to her all his fears and every single awful repressed thing about his childhood, that she wouldn't like it. And therefore, by extension, him.

Anita exhaled and opened her eyes, her face lighting up when she saw him. That look was enough to banish the rest of the rotten banana peel dreams. "You're up. Did you sleep okay?"

"Great," he lied. "You're up early."

"Jet lag and nerves." She rolled down into a forward fold, then lifted halfway before bending again. She looped her elbows together and swayed, head down.

Patrick reached for the glass of water on his bedside table and took a deep drink. "Are the nerves about finding a partner for Lucy or competing tomorrow night? Ugh, or about stupid-hair Mikhail?" He grimaced at the memory of it.

"Seeing him was definitely a downer. I like Laurie, though." She paused at the top of her mat in triangle pose. "It's a combination of things. Lucy finds a dead body, we can't talk about it, she has at least four auditions today." She moved from triangle pose into warrior one, then opened out to warrior two. "Not to mention Mikhail, the upcoming Team Match that we've widely been accused of not qualifying for, oh, and my parents won't stop texting me." She sighed and bent into a crescent lunge.

Patrick twirled the glass of water between his fingers. "What do you mean we're widely accused of not qualifying for the Team Match?"

Anita rolled her eyes and a small laugh escaped her as she ended in a seated position, eyes closed. "Out of all of that, that's what you're upset about?"

"I mean, I like to know when someone's throwing shade so I can toss it right back."

She laughed louder now, then stifled it, seeming to remember they were in a very echoey house with three other people present, and it was the wee hours of the morning. "You're ridiculous."

Patrick stood from bed, stretching into a back bend. "That's why you love me."

She tilted her head, pensive. "Part of the reason. Not all. Want to go for a run?"

"If we go for a run, will you tell me more about your parents?"

Her face shuttered. He'd known it was taking a bit of a risk, but he had to try, regardless.

"It's okay," he said. "Let's just get our endorphins pumping." He accented his statement by flexing his biceps, and Anita snorted with laughter. "OMG, stop, you're going to wake our hosts."

"You stop, you ridiculous man."

He approached her, hands innocuously tucked behind his back. Okay, so yes, he knew he looked pretty good in his black boxer shorts. Months of physical therapy and competition prep had honed his abs and he was nearly romance-novel-cover-worthy.

He mostly had done it for that glint of pleasure and lust in Anita's eyes. "Seriously, Patrick, stop," she said, wrapping her arms around his waist. "We're guests."

"I'm not doing anything." He bent down and kissed her lips gently, teasing, feeling her body against his. This was simply the best possible way to wake up in the morning.

****

As a longtime Pennsylvanian, Patrick thought his home town was one of the most beautiful places in the world, but even he had to give credit to the coastal hamlet of Lythe. The town itself was the very definition of quaint. Green and brown window boxes overflowed with a riot of colorful blooms. The cafes had white awnings and small iron-work tables and chairs on their cobblestone patios. People walked their dogs around the street in mackintoshes, both canine and human ones.

The sunrise over the beach took first prize, though. The oranges and reds and purples cut through the clouds, breaking into shards of brilliant color that painted the shoreline.

“Umm, this is idyllic,” Patrick said, keeping stride beside Anita. “We should move here.”

Anita shook her head. She was barely breaking a sweat, a queen in her slim-fitted neon-pink-and-black running gear. “Like you will ever move out of Pennsylvania.”

“That’s true. Though at some point, we might need a bigger house.”

Her expression dulled and she ran slightly ahead of him. “Thinking about where to put your boat?”

He was tired of running from this conversation, literally and metaphorically speaking. “Anita, come on.” He slowed to a halt and stared at her back, hands on his hips.

She kept jogging for a few paces before seeming to realize he was no longer following her, and she turned back to him, blonde ponytail swishing in the heavy breeze off the ocean. “What?”

It was ridiculous that he was going to have this conversation here, but it needed to be said, and he needed to have the courage to have it. “We have to talk about our future.”

“Like, our immediate future?” She gestured down the running path. “Because we need to finish our run, then head to the dance studio we contracted for Lucy’s auditions.”

"No." He shoved his hands through his sticky, sweaty hair, and it did not make him feel better about himself. "Like our *future* future. Kids and puppies and…and boats and houses and everything. Look, all of our friends pretty much have that now. Will and Bobby are getting married in a few weeks. Katie and John are settled." He and his therapist had discussed often that part of his need to set the wedding date stemmed from the lack of relationship with his mom. Which made total sense, but he also didn't want to put all of that baggage at Anita's feet. "Okay, look. I love you. I think you love me. We're good together." He sighed, knowing he was about to throw even more shit onto the manure heap of this conversation. Anita stood with her arms crossed over her chest, staring out at the ocean. Great to have her attention. "Don't think I haven't noticed the three bridal magazine subscriptions that your mom sent to the studio. Or the text messages every time *Say Yes to the Dress* comes on, which is all the time, by the way. Or the flower arrangement or cake samples that have mysteriously appeared in our apartment. Are you living with a secret wedding gnome or is your mom also trying to talk to you about this?"

She huffed slightly, her breath condensing in the crisp fog of morning. "I just can't deal with it right now. Not here. We have a job to do. Can we finish that and then talk about this later?"

He was about to cave, really he was. It was how he always dealt with this argument, which his therapist was quick to point out also stemmed from his mommy issues. He didn't want his entire life reduced to that woman's bad choices. "I really want to talk about it now. Please. It's important to me, to feel…secure."

Her expression shifted to one of empathic concern, and she rested a hand on his arm, her touch burning through the thin, moisture-wicking fabric. "Patrick—"

"Anita! Patrick!" A few paces down the road ran Evelyn Zhao, her boyfriend Jackson Alder panting just behind. "Good morning! Fancy meeting you here." She pulled up beside them, her face shiny and bright with exertion, though she had barely broken a sweat.

Jackson, on the other hand, looked a little more worse for wear. He doubled over, his brown hair streaked with sweat, his breath heaving.

Evelyn patted his back. "Poor Jackson. He's still getting back into shape."

"I'm fine," Jackson said, though it could also have been, "Mmphf hfpgmhf." He took in a few deep breaths, then straightened and forced a smile. "Hey. Long time, no see."

"Hi." Anita nodded to both of them.

Patrick released the choke hold he had on his tongue. They'd have to pick this argument up later. "Hi, Jackson. Evelyn. You guys enjoying your run?" They'd met Jackson once before, in a professional capacity, when he had interviewed them after the events that happened at Keystone. Patrick remembered him as affable and funny, someone he had always sort of wished could be his friend.

"Enjoying is such a strong word." Jackson stretched to his left side, releasing an audible pop from just below his ribs. "For the love of Giselle, why does it take so much longer to get back into shape when you're in your thirties?"

Evelyn reached up on the tiptoes of her sneakers and kissed his cheek. "You're killing it, love. You'll be back in no time." She turned to Anita and Patrick. "So you two are in Lythe as well? Good on you. Blackstone's gotten way too seedy over the last few years. I ran into a girl I'd met at a master class a few years ago, and she said she got jumped on her way back from the grocer's the other day. Lucky she's fit and there was a police officer nearby." She shook her head, the shaggy bun of black hair flopping atop her scalp. "If it keeps up, they're going to have to move the dance festival. No one will come otherwise."

"Well, and then there's Tom Havens." Jackson seemed to have regained his breath. "Did you guys hear about that?"

Patrick swallowed. "Oh, yeah. They found his body?"

Evelyn nodded. "Aye. In the bog, of all things. They said some teenagers found the body. Can you imagine?"

"In high school, Patrick wished he could find a dead body," Anita said.

"That was a long time ago." Before he'd survived two attempts on his life. The idea had since lost its appeal.

"They called Jackson last night, to see if he could step in for the judging," Evelyn said, looping her arm through Jackson's.

This came as a surprise. "Weren't you a ballet dancer?" Patrick asked. "I know you judged the first two seasons of *Dance with Me*, but that was as contemporary, right?"

"Yes." Jackson nodded, pursing his lips. "Which is why I initially told them no. Then Lucian Chatelaine and Horace Brixley cornered me and said if I didn't do it, they'd pull the permits for *DanceSportTV* so we can't film the pro/am or professional finals. What was I supposed to say?"

Patrick arched an eyebrow. "They cornered you? They came to your house?"

A faint blush rose on Jackson's cheeks. "It was a video call ambush. I'm not very good on the phone, particularly not with two people staring down my camera. They're very intimidating."

"At least Bollocks Brixley spared you his bad breath." Evelyn kissed his cheek again. "You'll be all right, Jackson. This dance festival is already a bit bonkers. You'll be grand."

An alarm chirped on Anita's phone, and she glanced at the time, frowning. "Sorry. We have to get back. Will we see you later?"

"Absolutely. Ice skating movie marathon? Promise?" Evelyn pointed a single finger between the two of them. "After Team Match, let's do it. Popcorn, snacks, the whole enchilada, as you Americans say."

"Evie, no one says that anymore." Jackson stared at his girlfriend with a fond, devoted sort of expression.

She shrugged. "Doesn't matter. Enchiladas are delicious and I stand by my statement. Come on, old man. Let's keep going."

With a few groans and protests, Jackson followed Evelyn farther down the path.

Anita opened her mouth, as if to say something, then closed it again. "We do need to get back. Do you want to get anything on the way?"

Remembering their earlier conversation or Tom Havens's dead body did not improve his appetite. "No, thanks. Let's go."

They set back at a reasonable jog, enough to keep their muscles warm for a mile or two before they could walk the rest of the way.

Patrick searched for a conversation topic that he didn't have a personal stake in. It was nearly impossible. "Who's Horace Brixley?"

Anita glanced at him before returning her gaze to the road. "He's the emcee and one of the organizers for the dance festival. Didn't you see him yesterday? Bloodhound face and bulbous nose? He's an earl or something, I think. He's always droning on about the House of Lords and how backward America is. It's a shock we're even invited into the Team Match."

"Probably about money," Patrick said.

"Isn't everything?"

Was the reason she wasn't setting a wedding date about money? That was a futile question for another week.

So instead of asking, he jogged beside her back to Gryphon House, where they showered, ate, and pretended they had never fought at all.

Chapter Nineteen

Lucy crossed her arms over her chest and eyed the sign above the door. If anyone asked, she was one hundred percent justified in her suspicion. "Anita, I'm not trying to question your judgment, but this does *not* seem like the place for dance auditions."

Beside her, Anita frowned up at the sign. "Just think of it as a British thing."

James, who had driven the three of them to Blackstone this morning, snorted and then tried to hide it by coughing. Ineffectively. At least this was a distraction from staring at him, which Lucy had been doing all morning like she was in some moony-eyed melodrama. Even now, her gaze kept shifting to him, not too tall and not too short, wearing a maroon crewneck sweater that made his eyes smolder.

No. No smoldering. Focus on the inappropriate signage.

"Um, I'm not one to double-check, but are you sure, Anita?" Even Patrick looked skeptical. "Pleasure Palace Dance Hall?"

Anita sighed. "This is not Vegas. This is a dance studio. Why does no one trust me?"

"I do trust you. Completely." Patrick slipped an arm around his girlfriend, and for a moment, just a moment, Lucy wished she had someone like that. Someone to ground her, someone to steady her. Her gaze involuntarily flicked to James again, and then she shook herself out of her sentimentality. It was because her parents had left this morning for Manchester, and she missed them. That's all. They'd found out that Tom Havens was dead but were none the wiser that she had discovered the body.

So she was justified in feeling sentimental. Plus, she had to be on her best, most dateable behavior for the next few hours, and the prospect of it was beyond exhausting.

Anita sighed loudly. "Everyone, just…stop. Come on." She pulled open one of the double glass doors overlaid with fading gold metalwork designs.

The inside was far less sketchy than the outside. There was a simple check-in desk, then a ballroom lined with red velvet curtains around it. It was freezing, but Lucy hadn't felt warm the entire time she had been in the UK so far. They should change the city's slogan to "Come Here and Freeze."

And fine, maybe she had barely slept the night before, but it was *not* because she was bothered by any of the events of the previous day or her parents leaving. She was seventeen and old enough to make her own damn decisions, thank you very much.

"Are you okay, Lucy?" Patrick asked, his eyebrows raised.

"I'm fine." She pulled her sweater more tightly around her body, and looked for James, even though there wasn't a reason to do so, and she knew that. Absolutely.

But James wasn't looking at her. He was staring at the receptionist talking to Anita.

A kernel of irritation bloomed in her gut, making

her want to scream and gnash her teeth and generally behave badly. Then she saw the receptionist and totally understood where he was coming from.

She was the type of woman who would command any room. Her long, perfectly curled auburn hair was the color of a rich sunset. Her blue eyes sparkled like the Caribbean Sea. Her face was…Lucy couldn't come up with any more inane similes, but the woman was freaking gorgeous.

Apparently Lucy had her attention. Something in her stomach turned over, and the oatmeal and banana she'd eaten for breakfast rose in her gullet. Having someone that pretty focus on you was like staring too close at the sun.

The secretary's smile was kind, and her accent American. Southern. "You're here for the auditions? Best of luck to you. Restrooms are toward the rear. You can change back there." Now she turned back to Anita, who was the most composed of their entire group. Even Patrick looked a little dazzled by the receptionist, and he was more whipped than Lucy's dad. "If you need anything else, please don't hesitate to ask."

"Thank you so much, Miranda." Anita picked up her enormous duffel bag, carrying who knew what. Probably supplies in case there was a dance competition in the zombie apocalypse. She raised her arms at the group. "What? Are you guys okay?"

Just starstruck by the most beautiful person Lucy had ever seen. "We're fine. Let's get this over with."

Patrick laughed. "That's the spirit."

****

After an hour and the first two auditions, Lucy's sleepless night was not only catching up to her but threatened to wrap her up in a tight little ball of extreme irritation.

It did not help that James had asked to stay, citing nothing else to do. Would it kill him to have the common decency to involve himself with his phone like a normal person? Instead, he watched every single moment of the two awful auditions, chin propped up on his hand. Like he cared. Not that she cared if he cared. But did he think that she cared if he cared?

It all made Lucy want to scream.

"Great!" Anita clapped her hands together lightly, her voice high-pitched and so grating that Lucy ground her teeth to hold in a retort.

It had not been great. This potential partner, Felix, had the musicality of a tone-deaf giraffe and the handsiness of a rowdy prom date.

His coach, whose name made no difference to Lucy, stood beside Anita, and he was either far too excited about standing beside her or had completely missed the travesty that had just occurred on the dance floor, but he was practically beaming with excitement. "This is such a good match, don't you think, Anita? The two of them are perfect for each other."

Lucy had to physically restrain herself from rolling her eyes. To his credit, Felix looked as dubious about his coach's assessment as she felt. The only potential benefit was that Felix lived in New York City, so it wouldn't be a beast to travel for practice.

Anita was clearly trying not to laugh, but Lucy knew her professionalism would win out. "Sure. Yes. We will definitely be in contact."

When Felix and his coach had retreated to the restrooms to change, Patrick made a cutting motion across his neck toward Anita.

Sighing, Anita slumped into a chair beside him. "I know, I know."

Lucy stretched her triceps by arcing her arm behind her shoulder. "We could forget this whole thing and find someone back home."

Anita rubbed a spot over her left temple, like she was getting a migraine. "We promised your parents we would try, Lucy. At least give it a shot."

"I have. I've had two auditions." And the fact that her parents assumed the caliber of potential partners here at Blackstone was superior to the ones at home felt spurious.

"That's not a shot," Patrick said. "That's failing at speed dating."

Lucy bristled. She didn't fail. That was not her M.O. "Whatever. This whole thing is ridiculous."

She moved to the opposite side of the ballroom, away from her supposed coaches, and examined the photos hanging on the wall. They were all black-and-whites of ballroom legends, interspersed with smaller, color photos of more recent couples.

Behind her, she heard footsteps padding across the floor.

"I don't feel like talking about it," she said, picking at a spot on the long sleeve of her ballet-wrap black cardigan. At least her outfit was cute. Since they were dancing Standard per her mother's request, she had on a long black practice skirt that flowed around her like a river and swished pleasantly.

"I'm only here to see the photos," James replied. He had his hands in his pockets, his posture lanky but not arrogant or pressing.

Her stomach exploded into little curling seahorses. Fine. She could still be alone with someone present.

"Do you want a break?" Anita called.

"Obviously," Lucy muttered.

She could practically hear the shake of Anita's head, but the music turned from slow foxtrots and boisterous, big-band-style quicksteps into pop music.

James hummed beside her. "I love this station. I never listen to the radio anymore, though. I'm all streaming now."

She'd thought his humming would annoy the piss out of her, but she grudgingly admitted he had rather a nice tenor to his voice. It wasn't his fault she was here being groped under the pretense of finding a dance partner. Anita had warned her, but there was always a difference between expectation and reality.

"I know what you mean. Radio's peaceful, in a way." Lucy traced the photo outline of Gaynor Fairweather's gown, the folds and flash of her skirt. "There's still spontaneity in it."

She caught the glint of his smile from the periphery of her vision. He did have rather a nice smile, open and guileless. She never felt like he was trying to pick her up when he smiled like that, which stirred all sorts of unwelcome emotions within her.

"Do you want to dance?" He held out his hand to her, palm upward, fingers curled, the way people did in old movies. She half expected Colin Firth to emerge from a pond in a wet shirt somewhere.

"Do you know how to dance?" she asked, settling all her weight on one hip.

He shrugged, his eyes sparking. "I know a bit. I'm not as good as you, but I can move to this."

It was, of all songs, "How Do I Live Without You?" Honestly, with that level of melodrama, what else could she say?

"Fine. We'll see if you can keep up." She slid her hand into his, ignoring the tingling of his palm against hers.

Then he dropped her hand and left her no choice but to laugh like she was in a sitcom audience. For the first few measures, he grooved, he moved, he leaned into the overwhelming over-the-topness of the song, and he leaned into it *hard.*

"For the love of everything holy, stop! Stop!" She waved her arms in front of him as he dropped into a perfect slow-burn version of the worm, then into a stylistic sprinkler move. It was one of the best things she had ever seen. "What on earth are you doing?"

"Making you laugh, obviously," he replied, straightening.

The music stopped and the announcer came on, reciting an advertisement for some sort of Texas-BBQ-and-chippie in a nearby town.

"Aww." Lucy slow-clapped. "You lost your groove."

He shrugged, his expression now playful. "I'll find it again. You were having a bit of fun, too."

She shook her head, too vigorously. "Absolutely not. I never have fun. I'm work, work, work all day."

"I've only known you a few days, and that's definitely not true."

She flushed, the unfamiliar heat rising in her cheeks and spreading down her spine. He was too close to her all of a sudden. She could feel the warmth of him, his clean, welcome scent beside her own. She didn't hate it.

The music clicked over again to a new song, and the famous opening strains to Neil Diamond's "Sweet Caroline" played throughout the ballroom.

James arched an eyebrow. "Neil Diamond?"

Lucy shrugged, helpless to look anywhere but at him. "Be grateful it's not Springsteen. Anita has…interesting taste in music."

He raised his arms into dance position. "How about we dance for real?"

"Will I still have feet afterward?" Why couldn't she move forward? It was like her shoes had been glued to the ground, and she hadn't even castor-oiled them the night before like Anita kept exhorting her to do.

He moved another inch closer to her, taking her right hand in his left, and sliding her left hand over his shoulder. "I'll protect your feet. Promise."

Before she even knew what was happening, he swept her into the foxtrot. Slow and meandering and more fun and rhythmic than any other time that she had ever danced. She thought she knew these steps backward and forward, but with James…everything felt effortless. She melted into him, letting him lead for once. With Henry, she would push as much as he pulled, but there was no need with James.

As Neil Diamond crooned, they slid across the floor. She didn't have time to think or overthink or wonder what would come next. James controlled this show, communicating small movements with a gentle nudge or slight tug, her body reacting to his.

She had never felt so close to someone, not Henry, not her ex-boyfriend. For once in her life, Lucy flew like she was the star princess in her own movie, and she never wanted to hear anything but goddamn beautiful Neil Diamond for the rest of her life.

Of course, she had the worst luck in the world, because the song was only three minutes long. As it ended, James spun her in ever-tighter circles, pulling her closer, lining his body to hers. Was she giggling? She was, and she did not care in the slightest.

He pulled her into a final posture, one where they were wrapped around one another. She felt the rapidity of his heartbeat against hers. If she looked up at him right now, would he kiss her? Because she wanted that. More than she had ever wanted anything, even that junior detective kit when she was eight. What would he taste like? Would his lips be as warm as his body?

Then, to her immense disappointment, their little dance cocoon broke apart with the sound of whoops and applause.

Like a spark from a shotgun, Lucy leapt backward, her heart beating so fast inside her chest that it was practically an arrhythmia. Had she almost kissed James in front of her teachers? Mortification set in faster than a cheetah could sprint.

James stood a few feet away, clearly as dazed as she felt.

The only way to rectify this situation was to play it off, and maybe apologize profusely later in private. Or semi-private, as she wasn't totally sure she could trust herself around him after that dance.

Patrick and Anita stood by the chairs, the two of them beaming like she had climbed Mount Everest or something. Perfect. Even Miranda the stunning receptionist had been watching them.

No matter. She was still Lucy Knight, impervious

to super-romantic gestures. Even if her armor did feel a little cracked. “So.” She clapped her hands together. “Are we done for the day?”

Chapter Twenty

At that moment, because Fate could really be a bitch, the front door opened and Lucian Chatelaine and a young man who could only be his son appeared. “Miranda? What’s going on? We’ve arrived.”

As if everyone should know who he was. Anita *hated* people like that.

Beside her, Miranda stiffened, and the easy joviality of the last few minutes of watching Lucy and James twirl around the floor evaporated like steam off a hot mug of coffee in January. “Hello, Mr. Chatelaine,” Miranda said. “Of course. I believe they’re ready for you.”

Lucian glared down the slope of his patrician nose, nostrils flaring. “Excellent.”

Inwardly, Anita sighed. It was almost a blessing everyone else after the Chatelaines had cancelled. Unusual, since many of them had been eager to audition with Lucy, but a blessing because this interview had barely started and her bullshit tolerance was already at its end.

Chatelaine’s son was an almost exact replica of his father only wearing black dance pants and an expensive windbreaker in lieu of whatever giant-rich-asshole suit Lucian had on.

Anita picked up her now cold mug of green tea and sipped at it. So she was irritable and hadn’t slept well the night before. She had a job to do and she could damn well do it. "Good morning, Mr. Chatelaine. We met yesterday, but this is my partner, Patrick, and our wonderful student, Lucy Knight."

Lucian's eyes fixated on James, who stepped at least six inches farther away from Lucy. Shame that. Anita had all kinds of questions for James after that foxtrot. "Hello. This is my son, Carter." He put a hand on Carter's back and shoved him toward Lucy. Great start to an audition.

"Hello," Carter said, running a hand through his hair before extending it to Lucy.

Inwardly, Anita cringed. Hair gel and handshakes? Ugh, no thank you.

Patrick elbowed her and gave her an expression that clearly told her she wasn't selling this. "Wonderful!" Her voice was too bright, and everyone looked at her as though she were deranged. She softened her tone. "Carter, once you change your shoes, is there a dance you prefer to start with?"

Carter shrugged. "Anything is fine. I pick up choreo very easily."

Something about his manner or accent grated on her insides, like Parmesan over a rasp. "Perfect. Lucy? Preference?"

Lucy watched James, who had retreated to the wall of photographs again. "No. No preference."

This was going to go swimmingly.

****

"He's not that bad," Patrick whispered in her left ear, handing her a fresh mug of green tea.

Carter Chatelaine wasn't, really. He had listened to the choreography, and he was a decent partner.

Technically quite proficient. Not as handsy as the last one.

Still, something was missing. The spark. The joy on Lucy's face, the one she'd had when she danced with James. That was what Anita wanted for her. That was what had been missing from and she had blatantly ignored in her own dance career, until she finally partnered with Patrick. Life was far too short to waste on partnerships that didn't bring you to life.

At the end of the three-dance audition, Lucian clapped precisely five times and stood from his chair. "I think we can all agree that was excellent."

Anita addressed her words to his son. "Carter, you're a wonderful dancer."

He bowed slightly. "Thanks. It was nice to meet you, Lucy."

Now that her job was finished, Lucy kept looking around the ballroom. It only took a moment for Anita to realize what she was searching for. James had left after her and Carter's waltz audition. Anita cleared her throat, catching Lucy's attention.

"Oh," Lucy said. "Thanks, Carter. That was fun."

"Perfect." Lucian said it like it was the very final word and this was a business deal he had crafted. "Carter, I have a meeting. Ms. Goodman, we can speak later to finalize the details of the partnership."

"Wait." The single word she had uttered stopped Lucian in his tracks, and she didn't miss Miranda's flinch, as he stopped directly beside her. Patrick placed his palm against her low back, because of course he knew she needed a bit of courage to stand up to this hateful man. "What do you mean, finalize the partnership? We haven't finished Lucy's auditions, and we need to discuss—"

"I don't see what there is to discuss." Lucian didn't even look at Miranda, but there was the flinch again. Hell, if it had been Anita, she would have shied away faster than a skittish Thoroughbred beside a backfiring truck. "Carter and Lucy are clearly well suited. I've already spoken to her parents about travel arrangements for practices and whatnot."

He might as well have said, "This is what I want and this is what I'm going to have." Though it might be petty, it made Anita want to throw it all right back in his face. Or maybe roundhouse kick him, though that would not be professional. Probably.

Lucy stood in the center of the ballroom, and the shrinking of her posture strengthened Anita's resolve.

"Lucy is my student, and I want what's best for her. You don't want to be late for your meeting, Mr. Chatelaine. I'm sure you have a lot going on today."

His eyes narrowed, as though he had clearly caught her meaning, and when he spoke, the tone of his voice dropped the temperature in the ballroom by at least fifteen degrees. "I see. Good day, Ms. Goodman. Miranda, I'll be in touch with you later."

Miranda's nostrils briefly flared, but then she seemed to relax once Lucian and his son finally left.

Anita couldn't worry about her now. She went to Lucy instead. "Are you okay?"

Lucy sighed and shrugged. "I guess. Where did James go?"

Anita rubbed her back, but Lucy was too tense. "He said he had some errands, but he'd come pick you up once you were finished with your auditions."

"Are we finished?" There was such hope in her

voice Anita would have cancelled everything if it hadn't already happened.

"Yeah. No more today. Look, you don't have to decide on a partner here and now. If none of them really felt right, it isn't worth it." If she loaded her words any more carefully, her sentence would weigh approximately as much as an elephant.

Lucy shrugged in a feigned noncommittal way. "Cool. I'm going to read for a bit while you practice then."

Anita agreed, then watched Lucy retreat to a corner of the room, where she pulled sweatpants on beneath her practice skirt, then removed the long twirly fabric.

"She's a changing in public pro, too," Patrick said.

The front door to the studio opened again, and the atmosphere in the ballroom tensed.

At least until Anita turned and saw who awaited them.

"Is this the greeting I get?" Nigel asked, shaking raindrops from his spiky blond hair. He'd frosted the tips recently. "What's everyone doing, just standing about?"

Anita's muscles filled with relief at the sight of her dance teacher and—why not admit it?—surrogate father figure. Finally. An adult in the room.

Chapter Twenty-One

For the next three hours, Nigel prodded, urged, outright insulted, and finally approved of their planned choreography.

Patrick wiped his brow with a towel. “It’s probably a good thing Lucy got bored enough that she caved and called James for a pick-up. She’d be insufferable if she was sitting here through all of this. Not to mention all the British curse words you fling at us.”

“Fuck you, Patrick,” Nigel said in a light, good-natured tone. He sipped from a massive portable coffee cup. “I’m a bleeding delight.”

“Of course you are.” Anita slumped into a seat, grimacing as she ran a finger around the straps of her practice shoes, loosening them from their tight grip around her ankles.

Patrick wordlessly handed her a blister bandage, then gulped half of his water.

Nigel’s gaze flicked between the two of them. “So what’s with you two? Please don’t tell me it’s about Tom Havens. I hope for your own sakes you didn’t know that arsehole.”

Patrick wasn’t one to speak ill of the dead, but after what he had heard about Tom Havens… it still made him uncomfortable. “It’s just weird, isn’t it? A dead body at a ballroom dance festival. I can’t wrap my head around it.”

"Technically, he was found in a peat bog, or so I heard," Nigel said. He sipped again at his coffee. "If you ask me, this entire dance festival is a shitshow, innit? Neither of you were here last year, but it was almost dull in how routinely things went. None of this bloody confusing mess of arsehole celebrity judges, popularity contests, and organizers with family in the fray."

Anita's face, which had brightened with the exercise, now dulled. "So you don't think we earned our spot in the Team Match either?"

To Patrick's immense relief, Nigel's demeanor changed from surly ballroom majordomo to reassuring parent. "No, of course not, love. You and Patrick are sublime together. Give you another year, and the pair of you will be as famous as Evelyn and Alexei. You're going to crush it tomorrow night." His eyes narrowed. "As long as you two stay away from trouble."

That seemed rather pointed. Patrick held out his hands, conciliatory. "Anita and I do everything in our power to mind our own business."

Nigel rolled his eyes. "You know what I'm saying. Enough rest. Let's go through your jive twice more. It's your final impression with the crowd and judges, and Patrick, don't use your old injury as an excuse. You need those flicks tighter and faster."

Patrick saluted. "Aye, aye, captain."

****

After approximately seven thousand more jive flicks, until Patrick's thigh muscles wobbled like they were made of watermelon jelly, Nigel finally declared the practice session over. "Go do yoga."

Anita excused herself to go to the restroom, leaving

Patrick with Nigel, and Miranda, of course.

"How are you holding up since the divorce?" Patrick asked, changing his dance shoes for his sneakers. Nigel's latest wife had left him three months earlier after finding some suggestive texts from an old flame on his phone.

Nigel shrugged. He'd long since emptied his coffee cup, and now sipped water. The man must have a bladder the size of Texas. "All right. I get on just fine, you know."

Patrick did. Whether it was Nigel's native Liverpool accent, which stubbornly refused to yield to his two decades living in Philadelphia, or the man's bravado, Nigel had never lacked female company. Patrick nodded toward Miranda. "I'm a bit surprised you're not chatting her up." He'd seen Nigel turn on his full wattage for women like Miranda before.

Nigel shook his head. "I don't have a death wish, Patrick."

"A death wish? That seems extreme." Though judging from Miranda's biceps, she could probably bench almost as much as Anita.

"Is it?" Nigel arched an eyebrow. "Do you know who owns this studio and three others like it here in town? Horace Brixley and Lucian Chatelaine." He shook his head, gazing off into the distance. "I'm not getting into any of that."

Patrick opened his mouth to ask more, his curiosity a feral animal, but Anita returned from the restroom at that moment.

"Patrick, are you ready to go?"

Nigel stood and kissed both of her cheeks, then clapped Patrick on the shoulder. "See you tomorrow morning, yeah? We'll do some last-minute prep exercises before the Team Match." With that, he strode out of the dance studio, only pausing to tip his hat toward Miranda.

Patrick watched him go, his brain still swirling with questions. The warmth of Anita's hand on his arm re-directed his attention.

"Everything okay?" she asked, her brow furrowed.

"Yeah." He forced a smile and swung the dance bag over his shoulder. "Of course. Everything's just fine."

Chapter Twenty-Two

After an hour of watching her coaches practice, completely in awe of their skill and ruing her own inadequacy, Lucy caved. Besides, if she watched one more recorded lecture on *Catcher in the Rye*, she was going to write the school board a strongly worded letter on the necessity of decolonizing reading lists.

So she told Patrick and Anita that James was picking her up, but she hadn't called him. He'd left twenty minutes before, but it was cool. No big deal. She could definitely handle herself in the city.

She hadn't expected Blackstone to be so…unpleasant.

Whatever. With her earbuds in place and her favorite true crime comedy podcast on, she walked toward the beach and dodged puddles of suspicious-looking fluid and people who were way too old to be drunk this early in the day.

It was worse than the one time she had gone to Coney Island off-season with her mom. The entire visit, her mom had clutched her hand like she was afraid Lucy might vanish into a storm drain with a killer clown. That was the only thing Blackstone had going for it at the moment—no clowns in sight.

The walk to the beach didn't take too long, but a fine misty rain started as she crossed a boulevard. She pulled the hood of her rain jacket over her head to protect her ear buds. Great, now she was lonely and wet.

No, she wasn't lonely. Of course not. She was fine, totally and completely fine.

The beach itself was mostly deserted, probably because of the rain. Still bored and ignoring the tingles of hunger in her stomach, she walked toward the amusement park, which was a huge mistake because the entire place gave off major Scooby Doo vibes. Despite her inner bravado, Lucy shivered at the garish colors, the ricketing sound of the wooden coaster as it careened around the track. There was a funhouse topped with fading old-school monsters, their fur made of what looked like chipped paint and modeling clay.

"What the hell is wrong with this town?" she muttered. No wonder there was a Blackstone ghost, stealing unsuspecting females.

"Lucy?" A voice said behind her, and to her utter embarrassment, she leapt into the air.

Who would know her here? Her parents were at business meetings. Henry had flown back home with his parents earlier this morning because he'd had graduation prep stuff to do, and Anita and Patrick were still in practice land. Which left only one person whose voice would make her spine tingle.

She turned to see James standing behind her, a slight smile on his face and some sort of pastry wrapped in paper in his hand. The scent of cooked meat and butter wafted toward her through the mist, and her stomach grumbled in response. "That smells so good," she said.

He laughed and extended it toward her. "Are you hungry? You're welcome to it."

Heat rose in her cheeks. Why could she never say the right thing? Not that it mattered, because she wasn't interested in James. She was just hungry, that was all. "Oh, no. I can't take your food."

As if he didn't believe her, he took a small bite. "Are you certain?"

"Of course." Though it did look good, and her stomach was churning at about a five on the Richter scale. "What are you doing here?"

"I came for a snack. I have a friend who works in the shop."

"You have friends all over, don't you?" That came out as far more flirtatious than she had wanted.

He shrugged, looking dashing and far too appealing, with that little lock of damp brown hair falling into his eyes.

Lucy's spine tingled and she shifted from foot to foot.

"You look cold." James gestured toward her with his meat pie. "Want to get a bite to eat?"

In response, her stomach grumbled louder, like it was telling her to stop being an ass and say yes. Damn body, making her look supes uncool.

"I think that's a yes," James said.

Lucy swatted him on the arm, encountering a lean slab of muscle. Sweet sugary tingles trickled up her arm. *Be cool, Lucy.* "Fine."

****

He took her past many of the seedier-appearing bars to a black-and-gold painted pub with a carved lion's head beside the door.

"Don't worry. This place is all right," he said. "A lot of pubs don't serve food, but this one has a decent fish and chips."

Lucy's stomach rumbled again. "That sounds great." She followed him to the polished bar where they placed their orders. "Here, let me pay." She wasn't sure what impulse made her pull out the pound notes but could tell from James's expression that it had been the wrong one. His face tightened slightly as he slid her bottle of lemonade to her.

"I've got it."

She was making a muck of this.

Feeling chastened, which did not sit well with her, Lucy followed him to an empty table in the back corner. It smelled like lemon cleanser and the cracked leather bench squeaked when she sat on it.

"I'm sorry," she said, playing with the cap on her lemonade bottle. "It's a thing I do, where I automatically offer…I wasn't trying to—"

"I know." James sipped at his pint of beer, then finally met her gaze. A warm, sticky sweet sensation slid down her spine at the expression in his eyes. They weren't just hazel, but dancing shades of light and dark and ochre. "It's not you. It's my own problem. I showed you where I live, and my mum, and…" His cheeks flushed pink, making his freckles stand out. "I'm not used to showing people…so much of myself."

"I get that." It was an understatement, but about as much as she could manage at the moment. At a loss for words, she sipped her lemonade, which fizzed a pleasant sweet-tart taste in her mouth. "You have a lot of friends, though." She wondered if he had any particular friends, girl or boy, but wasn't entirely sure how to ask.

The corner of his mouth tilted upward. "Are you

trying to ask if I have a girlfriend?"

That sort of answered her question. "No. Just commenting on what it's like, living in the same place your whole life." She drank another gulp of her lemonade, the fizz making her cough this time.

"So you're a lifer, too?" He relaxed backward into the booth seat. "And no. Even though you didn't precisely ask. I don't have a girlfriend."

The rush of pleasure that coursed through her at this admission was definitely due to the arrival of the fish and chips. It glistened in the low glow of the pub lights and looked delectably crispy, like a food stylist's dream.

"That's cool." She watched as James poured malt vinegar into a cup and dipped his French fries in it. "I've never tried it that way. May I have some?"

"Of course. It's the only way, really." He poured some vinegar into a small cup for her and handed it across the table. For an instant, his fingers met hers and her skin lit into glittery sparkles.

She snatched her hand back. "Thanks. I appreciate it."

His gaze burned through her even as he continued to eat. "So, how did everyone take the news?" he asked.

"News? Which news?" Her mind drew a complete blank. She played with a French fry in the malt vinegar, dipping it then licking some of the salty sourness from the potato.

He laughed a little and broke a piece of fish apart before popping it in his mouth. "I suppose you've had a lot the past few days. I meant with everything that happened yesterday, at the peat bog."

"Oh!" Finally, a topic that seemed relatively safe

and had nothing to do with all the tingly, twirly emotions running through her. "I told Anita and Patrick. My parents had heard that the body was found, but I had no desire to tell them…um, exactly how."

His eyebrow arched, making his eyes twinkle even more in the low light of the pub. "So you keep secrets from your parents?"

Why did that feel like a loaded question? She snapped a piece of fried fish, watching the steam rise from the white flesh within. "Doesn't everyone? Why? Did you tell your mom?"

He sighed and reached for the ketchup bottle. "She already knew, of course. Word travels fast. Pete's mum called her, I think."

"Are you in trouble?" It seemed like a piece of her life hinged on his answer. Of all things, she didn't want to be responsible for James getting in trouble. He was too…well, nothing she really wanted to consider at that point. In lieu of thinking about it, she ate some of her fish, focusing on the salt and vinegar melting across her tongue.

He grinned. His lips were shiny from the fried food, but she was definitely not looking at them. Of course not.

"Are you worried about me, Lucy?"

"No." It came out too quickly, with far too much emphasis. She wanted nothing more than to get back to neutral territory. "I worry about your mom. She's really nice."

He relaxed further, his features settling into a pleased expression. "I'm not in trouble. Mum knows she can trust me. If I needed anything, I'd ask."

Oh. Lucky. Not that her parents didn't trust her, not

really. They probably wouldn't if she actually confessed to everything she held back.

They ate their meal in silence for a few minutes, the only sounds the snick and crackle of fried foods snapping in their fingers and teeth.

The easing of her hunger apparently loosened her tongue, too. Maybe it was watching his hands, too, the way his long fingers gently pared the food into manageable pieces. During the foxtrot, his hands had been so…perfect. "So, where did you learn to dance like that?"

"Like what? Like you?" he asked, the teasing evident in his tone. "All prim and proper?"

"I'm not prim and proper, thank you."

The expression in his eyes darkened, and his mouth tilted on one side. "No. No, you're not."

Heat flared through her. Damn blushing. "That's not what I meant," she said, over enunciating like she wasn't bright red at the moment. "If you dance that well, why aren't you competing?"

"Maybe it's because I don't have a partner."

Yes, the food definitely had improved her mood and sharpened her wit. "Aww, poor James. No girl will have you?"

"Maybe not the one I want." He accented this with a pointed look directly in her direction and a nonchalant pop of a French fry into his mouth.

Lucy had never had occasion to use the word "blackguard" before, but it seemed to suit him at that moment. She bit back the smile that threatened to ruin this whole cool-girl act she was playing. "Why don't you just answer the question?"

"Fine. For you." He emptied the rest of his pint of

beer, then rested his elbows on the table. "I started dancing when I was eight, because my mum wanted me to learn. She said all good men know how to dance."

"Like your uncle?" She thought of dour, sharp Mr. Butler and didn't fully see the resemblance.

"No, I don't think he dances." He said it in a thoughtful way, as though he'd never considered it before.

"But you work together," Lucy replied. "Do you know him pretty well?"

"Not really. He lived in South Africa for a long time. He only came back to England about eight months or so ago. I suppose for the job at Gryphon House."

"Wow. He really knows about the house, though. He must be a quick study."

"History and architecture are some of his passions, at least according to my mum." James picked up the last piece of fish on his plate and dipped it into the vinegar. "Anyway, I danced for a number of years, but money was tight and it never really…I don't know. It never really clicked for me."

The silence that followed seemed to fill with the words Lucy hadn't realized she wanted to hear. "*Until today*." That was what she needed, what she wanted, and knowing that filled her with an aching sort of sadness.

"That's too bad." Instead of looking at his sweet, handsome face, she peeled the label off her lemonade bottle. "You're a really great dancer."

"Thank you. So are you."

Silence again descended, thick like the misty rain outside the pub. Lucy glanced out the window but couldn't see much through the heavy haze.

James cleared his throat. "Would you like another drink? Something else to eat?"

"No, thank you." It felt inadequate, but she wasn't sure why.

"What are your plans for the afternoon? Hopefully not riding the death traps at the amusement park."

"They didn't look quite up to code."

"They're not."

"Let me guess, you have a friend who works there?" Her warmth returned with the comfort of the banter. James was simultaneously the easiest and most difficult person she'd ever conversed with.

"I do. He warns me off them. Especially the fun house. You wouldn't believe how little those mirrors get cleaned, or the things that happen in the shadows."

Lucy laughed and relaxed again. "I'm definitely counting that out. Sounds like a setup for the Blackstone ghost."

James's eyes twinkled. "Aye. A few years ago, a woman vanished from there. She was a pretty thing, too. A dancer."

Lucy rolled her eyes. "I don't scare that easily."

"I didn't think you did."

Something in his tone sent spicy tingles up her spine and another flush up her neck. "My parents wanted me to go back to the dance festival and watch the American smooth performance." She had the ticket on her phone and everything.

James played with his empty pint glass, sliding it a few inches across the table between his open palms. "It sounds like you're not too interested."

"I don't know. Maybe I don't feel like being alone. I mean, normally I'm fine with it. It's not a big deal.

Anita and Patrick are great, really, but they have their own stuff."

James caught her gaze again, and the warmth in his expression melted a bit of the loneliness that lingered inside her when she wasn't trying to drown it out. "Maybe you'd like to go with a friend?"

She glanced down at his open palms and the empty glass between them and wished, just for a second, that she could be there again. In his arms, flying. "Maybe I would."

****

It wasn't difficult to get James a ticket for the day's festivities, particularly as they were half over by the time they arrived.

Lucy hadn't fully appreciated the Crystal Gardens ballroom when she had first entered. She chalked her inattention up to nerves and was pretty sure anyone could forgive her for that. But now, with James, she had a chance to admire the building.

The Crystal Gardens lobby and ballroom were set up like an old theater, with a grand lobby lit by glimmering chandeliers dangling from the ceiling. On either side, large, curved staircases led to the mezzanine. There were a few vendors here and there, selling expensive dresses or dance shoes, but far fewer than she had seen at any competition in the United States. She was suddenly grateful for Anita's foresight in packing everything including the kitchen sink, because they likely wouldn't have been able to buy much here.

The ballroom was done in an old-fashioned style that reminded her of Victorian-era TV shows. Gilt and mirrors edged with the patina of time. On every side except the far one, where the DJ and judges stood, were rows and rows of faux-gilt theatrical seats. There was a mezzanine and balcony-level seating as well, with boxes closest to the stage where the judges and DJ stood.

"It's grand, isn't it?" James asked beside her, following her gaze to the epically large central chandelier hanging over the center of the ballroom. "You know, they used this building as a hospital during both of the world wars. My granddad was in the RAF, and they kept him here for recuperation after he got shot down."

"Wow." Lucy was still captivated by the light from the chandelier over the couples twirling on the floor. "My grandparents left Vietnam in the late sixties, but I don't think they ever fought."

"They didn't talk about it?"

"No." Not at all. Her mom had never mentioned what they'd gone through, and Lucy had only asked once, when she had a term paper on the Vietnam War at school. Once was enough to tell her that she'd better get her information from the History Channel. "Only my grandmother's still alive. My Ba died about ten years ago."

"I'm sorry." James's hand found hers and squeezed it. "Mine did, too. It wrecked my mum."

"Same." Her mother hadn't been the same for months afterward, and when she finally rallied, she had thrown even more attention onto Lucy.

"Come on," James said, his fingers still laced with hers. "Let's go find a place to watch."

****

They spent the afternoon in the nearly deserted

balcony of the ballroom, chatting about TV shows, books, and even occasionally the dancers. James produced packets of chocolate cookies and cheese- and onion-flavored chips to accompany the afternoon.

Not that it was a date, but it was still one of the most enjoyable afternoons Lucy could remember.

They applauded when the final heat in the semifinal twirled to their curtsies.

"I guess we have to go." She hadn't realized her voice would be so edged with disappointment.

"What do you mean?" James balled up the empty cookie and chip packets and stuffed them into one of the pockets of his coat.

"I don't have tickets for the evening show."

The balcony had filled in slightly as the number of couples in the quarter and semifinals narrowed. James leaned in close to her, his breath warm as summer rain on her ear. "Maybe we don't need tickets."

Lucy turned to him in mock shock. "What are you suggesting? I'm going to be an officer of the law one day. I'm not breaking and entering anything." In the loosest possible sense of "not."

"I would never suggest that. I'm just saying, there's always a back way."

The part of her that she never really let out, the rebellious little hellion who tired easily of following the rules, brightened. She would only be a teenager once, and in terms of rebellion, this seemed pretty minor. It could barely even be considered a gateway crime. "I'm in."

Chapter Twenty-Three

After the strained morning, the only thing Anita wanted to do after practice was go for a nice, long walk. Which the weather made impossible.

"Of course it's raining," Anita said, knowing exactly how grumpy she sounded. It wasn't her fault. At first it was her parents' constant texts and messages that had irked her, but now they had both been silent for a suspiciously long while. She stared out the window of the cafe, letting the steam in her green tea with honey evaporate.

"Look on the bright side." Patrick speared several pieces of vegetables from his roasted veg salad. "We found a partner for Lucy."

"Ugh." Anita grimaced, feeling gravity pull the lines of her face southward. "Carter Chatelaine? I refuse based solely on principle."

"Hard pass. Absolutely not. I meant James." Patrick shoved a mass of zucchini and eggplant into his mouth and sighed, contented.

She envied him that. "James?"

"Come on, you saw it, too. They were perfect together. No choreography, nothing planned, and the two of them clicked." He gave her a goofy, endearing, only-Patrick-can-make-this-look-sexy smile. "Like us."

Alarm bells rang in her head. "Like us? No. No, I can't deal with teenaged hormones on top of everything else this week."

"Relax. Lucy doesn't need hand-holding." He held up his phone, showing her the text message from Lucy on the lock screen. "She says she's fine and she doesn't need us."

"Please. She found a dead body yesterday." Anita stabbed her fork repeatedly into a poor, defenseless sprig of asparagus.

"And she seems fine with it. We don't know what she saw when she was working with John and the police department. She's strong enough to ask for help when she needs it."

The tiny appetite she had mustered fled.

"Look, Anita." Patrick reached across the table and took her hand, running his fingers over her knuckles. "Our routines are great. Nigel says we're smashing, and it takes a serious amount of weight to get that level of approval from him. We'll talk to Lucy and James about their potential. We don't need to see Lucian Chatelaine ever again if we don't want. Everything is going to be all right."

Then, like a delivery straight from Anita's personal hell, the cafe door opened and in walked her mother.

Her fork clattered on the plate between the vegetables she had shredded in anger. "Mom?"

"Anita!" Her mother shook the rain from her dark curls, ran across the cafe, and wrapped her in a big, enormous hug. One that she'd have to be made of stone not to like, and Anita was far more sand than granite. No one would blame her for leaning into it for a moment and inhaling her mom's signature scent. "I'm so happy Nigel told me where to find you. Didn't you get an international plan? You haven't answered any of my texts."

Anita was going to kill Nigel.

"Hello, Marina." Patrick, excellent buffer that he was, insinuated himself between them and kissed her mom's cheek. "It's so good to see you. I should probably go."

Like some misguided sitcom, Anita shouted "No!" at the exact time that her mother said, "Oh, yes, that would be lovely."

Patrick stood frozen between. "Um, okay. I'll just go get you a chair, Marina. Be right back."

There went her cheerful buffer.

Her mother touched her elbow, guiding her into her seat. "You look wonderful, darling." Her upper lip trembled slightly, and she put up a hand, the one still wearing her wedding ring, over her mouth to hide it.

Maybe it was that or maybe it was how her mom's Cypriot accent always got stronger when she was nervous, or possibly it was because she had flown all the way from Philadelphia to the northwestern coast of England. Whatever it was, Anita softened.

"It's good to see you, Mom." Her spine was still steeled, but the relief on her mom's face, laugh lines and all, warmed her more than her hot tea had. "What are you doing here?"

"You won't talk to me at home. I thought here, maybe you'd be a captive audience." Marina pushed her hands through her thick tousle of black curls, and the water droplets still clinging to them dripped to the floor of the cafe.

Anita's mouth felt sticky dry, but the thought of raising a glass seemed unbearable. Where the hell was Patrick? How long did it take to find an extra chair? He must be giving her extra space, the sweet, misguided man.

Marina cleared her throat. "How did Lucy's dance go?"

Anita's shoulders relaxed a bit. Work, she could talk about work. "It went well. They made it to the second round before they were eliminated, but everyone was pleased with that. It's so hard to find space in those first few rounds."

"That's good." Her mom's smile was warm, and so welcome it made Anita feel almost homesick. "It's because of your teaching."

"Patrick's a great teacher, too." And had been Lucy's first instructor, through the Lewis High ballroom dance club.

"He is. But you, my love, are something special."

Tears pricked at the backs of her eyes. Why did her mom always know what to say? Even if she couldn't take it in. All the anger she'd kept from writing in a text message flooded through her, making her blood race. Bitterness spilled across her tongue. "Why are you here? Are you going to tell me you and Dad are getting divorced? That's fine. Great. Live your best life, Mom. You deserve it after what he did to you." After he cheated. After he got addicted to drugs and ended up in rehab and had his medical license suspended. It was his own damn fault, and he had brought it on himself, and was she supposed to help pick up the pieces? No. Anita had her own stuff to deal with.

Her mother played with the teaspoon on the table, running her fingertips over the lines. "Your father and I are…talking. That's all. We are trying to find our way back to each other." She looked up, and her gaze was so full of hope and pain that it stabbed Anita in every vital organ. "We are trying to find our way back to you."

What was she supposed to say to that? Her cheeks itched, and when she wiped away tears, she barely felt surprise. "I don't know, Mom."

Marina reached across the table and took one of Anita's hands in hers, rubbing the knuckles. The way Patrick did. "I know you're angry and hurt and you've been through so much and been so strong. But we are still family. Yours is growing." She gestured toward the cafe counter, where Patrick stood, chatting with the owner. *Not* finding Marina a chair. Traitor. "We want to be a part of that. I don't want you to be scared to take this next step."

Anita snatched her hand back. "I'm not scared." Okay, she was terrified, but she wasn't about to admit that. After living her entire life thinking her parents were happy, contented, solid, and then have it all come crashing down?

Her mom's exacting eyes must have seen something Anita had not intended. "You know, Patrick is not like your father, Anita."

"Of course he's not." She glanced over, watching as Patrick now played with a toddler, entertaining him with goofy magic tricks while his mother ordered lunch. No, Patrick was nothing like her father. He wasn't exacting, or dismissive of her dreams, and he thought Anita was the center of the world.

As if he knew she was thinking about him, he glanced up and grinned at her. Patrick's smile could light the way during a solar eclipse.

"Anita?" Her mom asked. "Talk to me. It's been so long."

Hadn't she put her mother through enough? It wasn't her fault her father had torpedoed their lives so spectacularly. Besides, it was absolutely exhausting, holding on to her resentment. "I miss you, Mom," she said. Or at least thought she said it. Her voice was almost too quiet, drowned out by the patter of raindrops against the panes of the cafe windows.

But she must have said it, it must have been heard, because her mom was tearing up across the table.

"I found another chair," Patrick announced, brandishing his discovery. "And the finest coffee in all of town for you, Marina."

Anita wiped away the moisture beneath her eyes, but her mom's brimmed anew.

"So," her mother said, an enormous smile lighting her face, erasing the lines of jet lag and fatigue. "Have you two set a date for the wedding yet? I've brought all sorts of ideas with me."

Sighing, Anita simply sat and sipped her tea.

Chapter Twenty-Four

The rear entrance to the Crystal Gardens Ballroom was far less grand than the front.

"It's an alley," Lucy said, feeling a need to keep her voice down despite the fact that there was no one else around. Not just an alley, but a run-of-the-mill, super-creepy alley filled with cigarette butts and dumpsters that might as well have stink lines coming from them. "How are we going to get anywhere?"

James took her hand, pulling her out of the rain and into the snook of a doorway that offered minimal shelter from the weather. "Trust me."

A thrill shot through her, warming her more than even a fire could. *Why not?* her inner secret rebel whispered. The secret inner rebel who also found it necessary to appreciate how cute James looked, his hair shaggy with rain, his overcoat clinging to his frame.

James checked twice, likely to ensure no one else was coming, then pulled Lucy through the door and into a small vestibule. Surrounded by four walls, it didn't seem like much of a hiding space, particularly not if they wanted to watch the evening American Smooth finals.

"Where are we?" Lucy giggled, and didn't even have time to hate herself for it.

James grinned at her, his smile open and free. "Come on."

By that point in the day, a little high on rebellion and damn fine British cookies, Lucy might have agreed to anything. "Is this about the Blackstone ghost?" she asked. She waggled her fingers toward him like phantom octopus tendrils. "Woo-woo."

He playfully tapped her hand. "Hardly. But there is definitely a ghost. I've heard it before, moaning and crying in the walls. She's a woman, lost and alone."

That sounded eerie and far less date-like than she had been thinking. "Seriously? You're going to invoke the ghost thing? We're at a dead end." She gestured around them at the four blank walls of the vestibule. "Unless this is some sort of weird locked-room mystery, Sherlock."

James arched an eyebrow. It should have been a thoughtless gesture, not in the least bit appealing or sexy, but damn her if she didn't want to kiss him.

And Lucy never thought that way.

"Come on, Watson," he said. He pressed a flat palm against one of the empty walls, and with a loud and final-sounding click, the panel swung open.

Lucy's mouth dropped open, and she physically had to restrain herself from clapping her hands like a five-year-old at an amusement park.

The staircase was dark, musty, and spider-webbed, and Lucy had never seen anything cooler.

James laughed as he led her toward the stairs. "You are the first person I've ever met who appreciates this."

"That cannot be true. It's a freaking secret staircase in a wall!" It smelled like mouse droppings and rancid soup broth, but still. So cool.

"It's even better up top." He squeezed her hand then, like they were joined in this conspiracy, and her heart flip-flopped like the traitor it was.

"Okay." It wasn't the best repartee she could muster, but maybe she could be forgiven because *secret staircase*.

She followed him up two flights of stairs, picking her way up the termite-thinned steps. "I guess they don't do maintenance back here."

"It's an old servants' stair. Most people probably don't even know it still exists."

"Was it this decrepit the last time people used it?" She dodged the half-rotten railing, bracing against the slightly sturdier wall.

"Probably not. Otherwise there'd be bones below." He led her higher.

"How did you find it? Let me guess. You have a friend."

"I have a lot of friends. Maybe I'd like one more." He paused on a landing. Above them was another flight leading to a vestibule, and below was the staircase they'd just climbed. Anticipation tingled through Lucy's body. She was close to him now, only a few inches away.

Why not? Her inner rebel repeated.

She stepped forward, closer to him, gazing up at him through her lashes like she'd always secretly wanted to try. "But not a girlfriend?"

A hint of a smile flickered across his features. "No. What about you?"

"Do I have a girlfriend?" Who was she and what had she done with Lucy? She didn't care. "No. No boyfriend, either."

"Really." It was half-statement, half-question, accented by his moving a step closer to her.

Her heart pounded in her chest. She had never felt this way with her ex-boyfriend. All tingly and alight, like if she raised up on her tiptoes, she might burst into flames. She liked it. “Really.”

Just for the joy of it, she raised up on her tiptoes, and James responded by sliding his palm along the line of her jaw. Who knew that was an erogenous zone, but it sent electric thrills through her. He tilted his head toward hers, his mouth mere centimeters away…

And that was when they heard the scream.

****

James’s grip on her tensed, but she stepped away. “What the hell was that?” she said.

He shook his head, his face lined with concern. “I’m not sure.”

“You’re not going to tell me it was the Blackstone ghost?” She’d meant it as a joke, but her voice came out too soft for it to fly.

The direction of his gaze was everywhere but at her. “I don’t know.”

There was a sound of crying, and another muffled scream. Lucy’s inner resolve stepped up. “Then let’s find out.” She reached out, mimicking his earlier actions, pressing her palm against the panels of the landing. No movement. “Rude,” she hissed.

“It sounds like it’s coming from below.”

She followed James back down the stairs to the first vestibule where they had entered. “Is there another hallway?” she asked.

“I don’t know. I only know this passage, and it opens down in the alley and up on the third floor balcony, by the bathrooms. I don’t hear anything anymore, either.” James shook his head. If he was anywhere near as frustrated by this as she was, she couldn't really tell.

It wasn't her preference to sit around and wait. She walked around, pushing every single wall panel, encountering nothing but resistance. A little moisture, too, which, ew. The lack of benefit only irritated her further, and she slammed her open palm against the bottom of another wall, the one closer to the ballroom entrance, and met a sharp click.

"Holy shit, that worked?" she said, eyes round. Behind the secret panel was a dark passageway with no light to show the end.

James eyed the opening with a critical eye. "It's not very large. I don't know if I'll fit."

Lucy appraised the breadth of his shoulders, for research purposes only, obviously. It didn't hurt that, beneath his shirt, she could appreciate the ridge of muscles. No, he wouldn't fit through the opening. "It's fine. I'll do it."

He arched an eyebrow. "You want to get in there?"

She re-examined the opening. It wasn't large, a few feet by a few feet. Probably lined with cobwebs and rodent droppings and other things she'd better not think about. Still, someone had screamed, and she didn't fully believe in ghosts. What would John Flaherty do? He'd suck it up and find out what was happening. "I'll be okay." She pulled her phone from her pocket and activated the flashlight function, her finger slipping only slightly over the screen. But she wasn't nervous.

"Lucy—" No, she couldn't let him stop her.

"I'll be right back." With that, she ducked her head, took in a deep lungful of clean air, and pressed herself head first into the crawlspace.

Because, now that she was there, wedged and almost literally locked in, that was what this was. A crawlspace. Just as fusty and grody as she had expected. Wonderful. At least there was a shower awaiting her back at Gryphon House, and the layers of dust and grime would be a good prophylactic against any other kissing-type notions James might have.

Not that she was interested in doing any of that.

She crawled along the path on her stomach, using her elbows to drag her body forward. The light from her phone wasn't the brightest, but it gave her some comfort.

"Are you okay?" James called, his voice so full of concern it sent warm tingles up her spine.

"Fine. I don't see anything yet." It occurred to her that if she was looking for some signs of the ghost or whoever it was who had screamed, she might want to keep her voice down. Though if she thought more about that, she was likely to lose her nerve. And Lucy, if her ex-boyfriend were to be believed—which he hardly ever was—had a lot of nerve.

She crawled along, wincing as her face broke through decades-old cobwebs. That couldn't be an insect scurrying over her wrist. If she gritted her teeth, she couldn't smell the ferric, mineral scent of aged cellar. It only called to mind every horror and thriller story she'd ever read or seen.

"Lucy?" James's voice sounded even farther away now, like he was at the bottom of a long, deep well.

If she looked back to see how far she'd gone, or what she'd crawled through, she wouldn't keep going. The instinct at the back of her neck tickled, telling her she was getting close.

"Lucy?" she thought she heard, but the voice was now so distant, she wasn't sure she was even in the walls of the Crystal Gardens ballroom anymore. How long had she been doing this? What if she had crawled back in time?

That would *so cool.*

Then the light from her phone flared slightly, as the crawlspace opened up into a little cavern. It was barely large enough to sit up in, but she wasn't huge, and by that point, she was a little ready to head back. The time stamp on her screen told her she'd been crawling for only five minutes, but it felt like hours.

Using the light, she examined the cavern. There wasn't much in terms of variety in the crawlspace, but there was a window vent along one wall. When she saw that, she dropped the flashlight so it didn't shine through the slats. Excitement and anticipation rippled through her tired arm muscles. She'd thought she was in shape, but dancing didn't necessarily prepare her for a full-on army crawl.

She bent as close to the vent as she could, trying not to breathe in through her nose, but she couldn't hold back the gasp that escaped her.

She looked out into a room, lit by a single, dim overhead bulb. Would it kill people to switch to LEDs? Besides the energy efficiency, it would make it far easier to tell what was happening.

It looked like someone had been there fairly recently. There was a plain mattress along one wall, a few buckets, and some empty cans and packets scattered across the stone floor. If only there were papers, or something more identifiable. She leaned in closer to the vent and switched from the flashlight function to the camera on her phone. All she needed was one picture.

But at that moment, just as she pressed the red circle and the flash she'd forgotten to turn off lit up the crawlspace, there was an angry skittering sound and some animal she didn't want to contemplate scurried across her ankles.

She shrieked and threw her body backward. Nope. Hard nope.

If she had to get a rabies shot, there was absolutely no way she was ever doing anything like this again. The crawl back was faster, but she felt every greasy, ashen line of broken insect carcasses and grime against her skin. The ick factor was so strong she almost threw up.

Would John Flaherty throw up? Hell to the no.

So she closed her eyes, bent her elbows, and crawled like she was at boot camp.

"Lucy? Lucy?" The voice got louder the farther she went, and was so welcome she almost wanted to cry.

Even though she kept her eyes closed, she felt James's warm hands around her, pulling her from the crawlspace, wrapping her against his body. This boy was heaven.

His breath brushed her hair, and he talked almost too quickly to make out what he was saying. "Are you okay? I couldn't see you. I tried calling. Could you not hear me? You're okay, you're okay." He tugged her closer, and though it crossed her mind to wonder if he was bothered by her current gross-out state, he didn't seem to care about it.

In fact, he seemed to care about her. What exactly was her stance on dating again? It all felt fuzzy in her brain.

Tentatively, she wrapped her arms around him and returned the hug. “I’m okay, James.”

He kissed the top of her head. “I was so worried.”

“I mean, I almost got eaten by a rat, but I’m cool.” She pulled away from him. Moments like this were always a lot for her. Too much emotion. It was better to make jokes, to laugh. “And, I got pictures.”

James’s face was streaked with grime, which only indicated that she must look a thousand times worse. Despite that, he cupped her chin between his palms and swiped his thumbs across her cheeks. “You are the coolest person I’ve ever met, Lucy Knight.”

That was when he kissed her.

Chapter Twenty-Five

"I hope Lucy's afternoon was less eventful." Patrick unlocked the front door to Gryphon House. After watching Anita feign interest in her mom's massive wedding planning scrapbook and dodging every mention of "they just need a date," Patrick had a desperate yen for alone time.

"What do you say to yoga, a light dinner, and early bed?" he asked. Definitely not bringing up any wedding or father-related issues.

"Yes, please." She snuggled against him, warming him despite the early evening chill.

"Good." He kissed the top of her head and pushed the door open.

The foyer lights were off, but Patrick could hear sounds coming from the sitting room ahead of them, and two side table lamps emitted a soft glow. "Lucy?" he called. "Is that you?"

Lucy's head popped up over the side of the couch. Her normally straight hair was ruffled, and her cheeks were flushed. "Wow, hi. I didn't think you would be back so soon."

"Yeah, we got a ride share." Patrick removed his coat, but Anita was tugging on his arm. "What?"

Anita nodded toward the sitting room, her eyes twinkling with mirth. "Turn around."

"Why?"

Anita put her hands on his shoulders and forcibly rotated him away from the sitting room. "Trust me. Give them a minute."

"Why do I need to—oh." His stomach simultaneously leapt and froze. Honestly, the foyer closet was fascinating, far better than seeing whatever was going on in the living room. No ghosts or weird lights there now. There were even fur coats far in the back, like something out of a C.S. Lewis novel. Maybe he could hide in there among the furs and emerge only for food and dance competitions.

No, he was pretty done with closets.

"Patrick." Anita's tone implied what he already knew. "You're being a little ridiculous."

"Seriously, what are you two doing?" Lucy asked.

Patrick relaxed when he saw she and James were standing beside each other, a respectable distance apart.

"I am not prepared for this," Patrick grumbled, and Anita smacked him in the arm.

"Way to make this awkward, Patrick," Lucy said. She crossed her arms over her chest.

She was right. Anita was right. He was the one being an idiot. Lucy was seventeen and his student, not his kid. So what if she was making out on the couch with James Barrow?

Absolutely. Positively. None of his business.

"Right, I'm cool." He nodded to James. "How was your afternoon?"

Lucy paled and James shifted from foot to foot.

"So, you two didn't spend the whole afternoon making out?" Anita asked. "Let me guess. You went looking into the Tom Havens thing."

Uncharacteristically reticent, Lucy traced her toe

along the floor. "Of course not. I don't really know much about British procedures."

"Like that's ever stopped you before?" Patrick asked.

James cleared his throat, and despite Patrick's overall sense of extreme embarrassment, he appreciated James's tact. "I'm so sorry, but I've got to get home to my mum." He flushed slightly, kissed Lucy's cheek, and plucked his coat from inside the foyer closet. "Bye."

With that, James escaped. If only Patrick could.

Lucy sighed. "This is only weird if you make it weird."

"It's not weird," Anita said. Thank heavens she was taking charge of this situation. "Come on. We brought curry back for dinner. Let's eat and talk."

****

After a decent portion of the vegetable curry and brown rice, Patrick finally relaxed. "So seriously, what did you do this afternoon?"

Lucy shrugged and speared a large piece of green bean. "Not much. James and I watched the American Smooth competition."

Relief flooded through him. "That's awesome. Anything you really liked?"

Without looking up from her plate, Lucy said, "Well, we were going to sneak back in to watch the evening performance, but we heard someone scream, so we went to investigate."

Ah, there it was, back again, the terror that he was somehow responsible for this person who took extreme liberties with her own safety.

His fork clattered beside his plate. "Lucy—"

"You did what?" The voice was unexpected. Patrick whirled to see Mr. Butler standing behind them, wearing an apron over his suit and holding, for some reason, an iridescent-colored wine key.

Where had he come from and how was he the only person who knew how to open that massive front door without setting off its gong-like creak?

"Hello, Mr. Butler," Anita said. Naturally she would be the peacekeeper here. "Would you join us for dinner? We have plenty."

"No, thank you." His voice was stiff and his jaw barely moved. "Where were you and James this afternoon, Ms. Knight?"

Patrick glanced at Lucy, whose expression was drawn, but she looked back at Mr. Butler with fierce determination. "At the Crystal Gardens ballroom. We were watching the competition, and then James drove me back here."

"Is that all?" Mr. Butler said it in the manner of someone who knew there was far, far more to the story.

Patrick's curiosity was now a bright forest fire inside of him, but Lucy didn't deserve this second degree. Apart from trying to sneak into a theater, which on the list of teenaged bad decisions ranked somewhere around drinking milk straight from the bottle, she hadn't done anything wrong. And even if she had, it was none of this stranger's business. "If she says that's all, Mr. Butler, that's all."

As if seeing him for the first time, Mr. Butler slowly rotated toward him. When he spoke, his tone would frost an ice castle. "It's best, Mr. O'Leary, for all of you to go to your little competition and mind your own business." With that, he took the wine key and vanished down the hallway.

The three of them were silent for a long moment.

"Do you really think we should have let him walk out of here with that corkscrew?" Lucy asked.

"Technically, it's a wine key." Anita shook her head. "It doesn't matter."

Patrick exhaled. "That was weird, right?"

Lucy nodded in vigorous agreement. "Absolutely."

They ate in silence, though at least on Patrick's side, his appetite had completely vanished.

"So you went to investigate a woman who screamed?" Anita's tone was conversational, but she stared a little too intently at her sweet potatoes.

Patrick thought briefly about making a joke about the Blackstone ghost, but Anita silenced him with a quick arch of her eyebrow.

Lucy pushed her food around her plate. "I shouldn't have said anything."

"But now you have, and we want to help." Anita set her fork down beside her plate. Patrick did love the authoritative side of her. "You're not alone in this."

Lucy exhaled through her teeth. "Okay. So, there's this secret boarded up staircase at Crystal Gardens that we entered through the alley."

This was news to Patrick. He had been to many ballrooms and many hotels in many different countries, but he had never been so fortunate as to find a hidden staircase. It wasn't his fault he couldn't keep the jealousy from his tone. "You found a secret staircase?"

Anita laughed, rolling her eyes. "You're living Patrick's dream vacation. So then what happened?"

Lucy didn't fidget. "We heard a scream. So we followed the sound to the landing, and when we looked around, we found a door to a crawlspace." Patrick's skin itched and he retched in sympathy, but Lucy just shrugged it off. "So I went in. I found this vent over a room, where it looked like someone had been staying. I, um, couldn't stay, though, so I took a picture and left."

"Ah, the invulnerability of teenagers," Anita said.

"Can we see the picture?" Out of pure idle curiosity, of course, and not because he was positively dying to see the secret room.

Lucy took out her phone from her pocket, tapped the screen a few times, and tilted it toward them. "It didn't come out super well. Probably the lighting or the flash or something."

"Is that a rat?" Anita visibly recoiled as she gestured at a shadow across the screen, long and thin and whip-like. "Yeesh."

Lucy swallowed. "It was not an experience I think I will repeat."

Understatement. Even though the picture lacked a bit of quality, it was clearly taken in a cramped, not-entirely-pleasant space. Patrick couldn't see much, but he could discern what looked like a mattress and some buckets.

"Who would want to live there?" Anita asked.

"Mole people," Patrick and Lucy said simultaneously.

Anita shook her head. "You two are way too much and I'm exhausted." She scooped up dishes, and Patrick followed suit in clearing the table. "I'm washing these and I'm off to bed."

Chapter Twenty-Six

What was sleep compared to hours and hours of internet research, trying to break into the local police department's system to read the report on Tom Havens's death?

Not worth it, in Lucy's opinion.

When she finally succumbed around three in the morning, after countless minutes of frustration and repetitive reading, because why couldn't wire services take the time to get more original information, it was only for a few hours.

Though this time, instead of a dead body, it was the thought of James that woke her.

She braided her hair over one shoulder. So what if she and James had made out for a while on the couch last night? They had made it clear neither of them was in a relationship. After they'd returned from Crystal Gardens and she had showered twice to rid herself of ventilation duct goo, it had been the most natural thing in the world. Comforting, even, to fall into his arms. He was a fantastic kisser, for one thing. Lips that were soft and hands that teased just enough to comfort but not enough to push her past her limits.

So then why did she feel like something was amiss?

She agreed to the run with Anita and Patrick only to clear her head and avoid the buzzing of her phone, reminding her of the school assignments she was neglecting.

When they arrived back at the house, Patrick disappeared to shower and touch up his spray tan, leaving Anita and Lucy in the kitchen with two enormous glasses of water.

"Anita?" This was probably a bad idea, but she had very little experience to go on here. She and her ex, Daniel Riley, had been set up by their parents, dated for a while because it was easier than to argue, then split up when she couldn't handle his irritating personality quirks any longer. Besides, Anita was now in a healthy relationship. Why not avail herself of an older woman's wisdom? "Can I talk to you?"

"Sure." Anita set down her empty water glass and refilled it. No wonder her skin glowed, with her dedication to hydration. "What do you want to talk about?"

This was the main reason Lucy liked her coaches so much. When they asked her a question, it truly was open-ended. There was no hidden judgment or derision.

"About James."

"Oh." Anita nodded. To her credit, there was no blush on her cheeks apart from the post-run flush. "I take it this is something you don't want discussed with your parents."

"Yes." Lucy wasn't worried. Anita was one who would take any secrets to the grave.

"Okay." Anita folded herself into a chair at the kitchen table. "Take a seat. Let's talk."

A flash of nervous energy rushed through her, but Lucy tamped it down. She didn't need to worry with Anita, but the words felt glued to the roof of her mouth.

"So…James."

"James." Anita raised her eyebrows, her expression playful.

Lucy opened her mouth, but nothing came out. She felt overwhelmed by the number of things she wanted to ask. To her utter horror, tears beckoned at the backs of her eyes, and she shut them to keep herself together.

"Why don't I start?" Anita said softly.

Lucy's shoulders relaxed with relief, and she opened her eyes. "Okay."

"You and James have a natural chemistry. You dance really well together. I know we haven't talked about the auditions yesterday, but I haven't seen you that free in a long time. I think he's good for you. Obviously, there are a lot of discussions to be had, but if you and he are willing, maybe he can be your partner."

Sunlight broke through the slats of the kitchen window, illuminating the room. Or maybe it had already been there, and Lucy only just noticed.

"Wait, is that, like, possible?"

Anita shrugged. "There are a lot of logistics involved, but it's certainly possible. If that's what you want."

Lucy wanted to say yes, really she did, because this was a solution that had nothing to do with creepy Chatelaine progeny and would somewhat satisfy her parents, but every time she tried, the word stuck in her throat. "Wow," she finally managed.

Anita stood and moved over to the kettle. "Is that what you want?"

Lucy was grateful for the tea-making process, as it occupied her teacher for a while, filling the kettle with water, setting it in its electric base, taking out mugs and tea bags.

What did Lucy want?

"I don't know." It sounded small, insignificant.

The kettle boiled, and Anita poured water into the mugs before carrying them over to Lucy. "Maybe just start talking. Sometimes we deny ourselves the things we want because we feel like we don't deserve them, or they might disappoint someone. There is a lot of power in naming what you wish for. Giving it air helps breathe life into our dreams."

There was an aura of world-weariness in her words, but also hope.

"So I just start talking?" Lucy warmed her hands around the mug, pleased to smell the pleasant scent of chrysanthemums steeping. "Like when? Right now?"

Anita opened her arms wide. "Whatever. No judgment."

So Lucy did. She turned off her inner critic's microphone and let the words flow. "I want to solve Tom Havens's murder. I want to be a detective, or a federal agent, someone who solves cold cases and brings people to justice. I want my parents to look at me like they understand me. I want school to be easier, not schoolwork-wise, but interpersonal relationship-wise. Friendships are so freaking complicated." The steam from her tea invigorated her, and as she talked, the words spun faster from her. "I like dancing, but I want it to be fun, not something with an end date or a world championship goal. I don't want to give up the other parts of my life for it. If I have to dance, I want to dance with James, or someone like him." Wait, had she said something that might be harmful to Anita? The older woman gave no indication that she'd messed up, so she kept going. "I want to go away to college, as far as I can. Not to get away from my family, but to experience new things." The flood of wants trickled to a rivulet. "I want to choose my own future."

She stopped, breath coming faster than she would like it to, and sipped her tea.

Anita waited for a few moments, a soft smile on her face. "How do you feel?"

Free. "Better. Lighter, really."

"Good." Anita sipped her tea. "Do you want to work on any of those wants?"

She wished she had written them all down. Maybe later, on her laptop, during a hacking break. One thing kept spinning in her brain. "James."

"Great. What do you think?"

"I think you're pressuring me to come up with my own ideas. Are you a therapist or something?"

Anita shrugged. "Therapy is good for people."

"True. Okay." Lucy sighed and sipped her tea again for strength. "Is it wrong to want to, like, date James?"

Anita's brows knit together. "What do you mean? Is he in a relationship?"

"No." Lucy felt color rise to her cheeks. "Because he lives here and I live in Lewis. Because he's older than me."

"He's, what, a year older than you? That's not terrible. He's going to college, you probably will, too. Blackstone isn't the moon. It's not even a huge time difference." Anita shrugged and sipped at her green tea. "I'd say doable. Particularly since you're young, and it's your responsibility to try lots of different things. If it doesn't work out, it doesn't work out. We live and learn."

Lucy couldn't resist. She'd overheard so many bits and pieces, but never full stories. "Like you?"

Anita paled slightly but she laughed. "Yeah, sure. Like me."

"Thank you." Not for the first time, Lucy was immensely grateful Patrick had started the ballroom dance club at her high school. "I know you're really busy today."

"I don't mind." Anita hesitated before continuing. "I know what it's like to feel like your parents don't understand you. But you could never disappoint anyone, Lucy."

An unfamiliar, undesired crushing sensation weighed on her. She took her mug to the sink and rinsed it out. "Thanks, Anita. I'll see you tonight at the Team Match."

Lucy bolted upstairs to her room, where no one could see her cry.

Chapter Twenty-Seven

The best part of only having to dance for the evening competition was that there was more space available in the preparation area.

The other best part was that since this was an event for professionals, Anita and Patrick recognized almost everyone. Even the few they now avoided since they used to date.

"Talk about awkward turtles," Patrick whispered to her when they spied two of their exes. "The last time we saw Giorgio and Eva, they were doing the horizontal mambo."

Anita blanched. "Why would you remind me of that?" Stuttgart, ugh. "So I made some mistakes in the past. Are you ever going to forgive me?"

Patrick wrapped his arms around her and pulled her close, pressing his lips to her temple. "Always. It's us now, right?"

Eva waggled her long, poison-green nails in their direction. Anita wouldn't mind kicking her ass in the Team Match, the way she looked at Patrick.

Laurie Donovan wove through the departing pro/am competitors and wrapped them both in an enormous hug. She smelled of coconut self-tanner and acidic hairspray. "Thank God you two are here. Mikhail keeps name-dropping. I think he's in total awe of our competition." She rolled her eyes. "We're going to kick ass." She followed the direction of Anita's gaze and grimaced. "Ugh, Eva? That bitch told me once marriage was between a man and a woman. Puh-leez. Is she on the Euro team? Standard or Latin?"

"Latin," Anita replied. At least it meant Evelyn Zhao wouldn't need to deal with her. "I'm shocked she and Giorgio are still together, but maybe their personality disorders match."

Laurie nodded and unpacked her dance bag onto a table beside theirs. "Total *folie a deux* situation. Danger, danger, right?"

Too true. Anita stuffed down her anxieties and focused on preparation. The Americas team was going for uniformity with their look, all blue and silver, hair simple with a line of crystals down the part, smoky eyes. She could make this all work.

"Standard dances first?" Patrick bounced up and down on the tips of his toes, warming up.

"Yes." Anita glanced across the room at their counterparts dancing the five Standard dances. The teams were already dressed and joking freely together, to the point where Alexei squirted water from his nose. "They look like they're having more fun than we are."

On their side, the teams competing in Latin had all retreated to their own corners to get ready.

"Talk about collegiality," Laurie said. "I'm not going to worry about it. We're here to have fun and do the best we can, right?"

"Exactly." Anita set up her travel mirror and makeup case.

"I'm going to the bathroom. Be right back." Patrick kissed her cheek and headed off.

She and Laurie plucked and dabbed and gelled and

painted side by side for a few moments. The movements restored her, and she'd forgotten how pleasant it was to sit beside someone as they beautified themselves.

"So…Patrick." Laurie arched one eyebrow to highlight it with shimmery cream.

Anita blended in her contouring with percussive dabs. "What about Patrick?"

"I mean, he's gorgeous, funny, and completely devoted to you." Laurie gestured to the rose gold band and diamond on Anita's left third finger. "Are you two going to run off to Gretna Green like in some Austen novel? When's the happy day?"

Like that, all the air in the room dissipated, and the hand blending in light and dark contour powder faltered. Anita clenched her hands into fists and forced a smile before returning to aggressive blending techniques. "We haven't set one yet."

"What's stopping you?" Laurie turned her face in multiple directions, checking the symmetry of her eye makeup.

Significant doubts, for one. "It's—I don't know."

"Complicated?"

Anita nodded. "With a capital C."

At that moment, Jackson Alder entered the ballroom, avoided the Latin side, and made a beeline for Evelyn and Alexei.

Grateful for the distraction, Anita laughed lightly. "What's that about?"

Laurie swiped her undereye area with the brush, eliminating the specks of eye makeup that had fallen there. "I heard they asked him to judge tonight, and when he said it wouldn't be fair, since he and Evelyn are dating, they insisted he judge the Latin instead."

"I wouldn't have guessed Tom Havens was this important," Anita said. "How do they not have enough judges?"

"Beats me. There have been so many weird things this competition. Did I tell you I shocked Mikhail this morning?"

"No. What happened?" Finally she didn't have any gaping spots in her contouring. She set down the large blending blush and picked up her blush and kabuki.

"So, we came early since Mikhail had a couple students in the pro/am." She rolled her eyes. "None of them made it past the second round. I keep telling him he needs to stick to the syllabus, and his students need to master the basics before they move up. Not that he listens to me."

Anita waited, swiping blush over her cheeks.

"Anyway," Laurie said. "So while he was competing, I wandered around, chatting with some people. I ended up in this balcony hallway, above the mezzanine?"

Anita nodded, like she had any idea where this story was headed.

"So, I went to the bathroom up there. Those bathrooms are much less crowded, FYI. Super nice, too. All ornate, a little vintage. So cute. My girlfriend would die. She's been wanting fixtures like that."

Making some sound of assent, Anita moved on from blush to curling her lashes and prepping her two sets of falsies.

"Okay, so here's the thing." Laurie placed a hand on her arm and leaned toward her in a conspiratorial manner. "I was coming out of the bathroom, and I heard the Blackstone ghost! There was all this grunting and crying and it was so real! I walked up to the wall, but, like I wasn't going to press my ear against it or anything, because ew. Isn't that crazy? I told Mikhail and he flipped out."

Anita paused, one hand gripping the false set of eye lashes so tightly she wasn't entirely sure they weren't going to rip and drop little false lashes all over her carefully constructed face.

"Wow," she finally said, as Laurie seemed to be waiting for a response. There was so much to unpack in that story, so many idle aspects that pinged around in her brain like a super-bouncy rubber ball filled with battery acid.

"I have to be honest," Laurie said. She fluffed her hair before pulling it into sections. "I did not believe in all that rubbish about a Blackstone ghost. But maybe it's real, right?"

Snake-like anxiety coiled in Anita's belly. "Maybe."

Patrick arrived, his cheeks slightly flushed. "What did I miss?"

****

It wasn't long before pretty much everybody realized the European Standard team was going to crush it. In Anita's opinion, this was entirely due to Evelyn and Alexei. Even though they were only one couple, they commanded the attention of everyone in the ballroom.

Almost everyone.

"Where is Mikhail?" Patrick asked. They stood with their team counterparts along the edge of the ballroom, cheering them on.

Anita shrugged. The live band added a lot to the evening performances. She was content to let the music and general atmosphere of excited anticipation get her through this next hour of her life.

"I'll text him." Laurie picked up her phone from the dance bag at her feet and stepped away. "He's been so scattered this whole trip."

"Are you okay?" Patrick slipped his arm around Anita's waist. "What's going on?"

"Nothing." Anita bit her lip. "I'm just focused, that's all." No need to worry him with her vague, needling anxieties. The balcony hallway…

"Okay." He frowned slightly. "My therapist does say it's better to talk, to get things out into the open."

She covered his hand with her own and squeezed. "I know. We can talk later tonight."

At that moment, Lucian Chatelaine approached them, not even pretending to watch the Standard couples. Miranda walked beside him, her pretty features strained, in a stunning silver gown that draped around her curves like a glittering second skin. "Ms. Goodman. I haven't heard from you about my son and your student."

Her spine stiffened, and she used the warmth of Patrick's arm around her to keep herself from launching into a tirade. "I don't think this is the time, Mr. Chatelaine."

His eyes narrowed, and Miranda did not make eye contact with her. "I made allowances for you to be here, Ms. Goodman. Do not forget that."

Don't forget that he was basically trying to ruin the reputation of the world's oldest and most well-respected ballroom dance competition? Don't forget that he had stacked the juniors competition in favor of his son?

Fury rose within her, stoked by this asshole's presence, her overall unease with all the talk about a ghost, and her general dissatisfaction with her own ridiculous reluctance to marry Patrick.

As if sensing it, Patrick squeezed the side of her waist gently, the peacock-blue sequins scraping against her skin. "Thank you," he said, far more evenly than she would have. "We have to get ready. We're almost on."

Chatelaine opened his mouth, about to retort, but the audience broke into a fever pitch of applause at the close of the tango. Anita didn't miss his sharp glare or the way he tugged on Miranda's arm as they moved away.

"You're not going to expose Lucy to that dickhead, are you?" Patrick asked.

"Not a snowball's chance in hell."

Laurie reappeared beside them, her expression drawn despite the feathers she had painted at the corners of her eyes. "I didn't hear from Mikhail. He knows what's at stake. I'm sure he wouldn't miss this for anything."

Privately, Anita agreed. An opportunity for Mikhail to show off that he had been chosen among all other competitors? Especially since "winning" meant all of their scores were totaled, so it wasn't totally riding on his performance. Anita knew Mikhail wouldn't be satisfied with anything less than a trophy.

As if anything could possibly get worse, Anita saw her mother weaving through the crowd, waving at her.

"I just wanted to wish you luck!" Her mother

embraced her, careful not to muss her costume or hairstyle. "Not that you need it. You look gorgeous."

At least on that Anita agreed with her mother. The costume suited her particularly well. The bodice was a net of thick silver braids woven around her curves, and the skirt flared into an asymmetric twirl of peacock feathers.

If Anita could have chosen another, she liked Laurie's second best. The leotard was long-sleeved silver mesh, the bodice peacock blue and green shot through with sparkles, with silver fringe covering her bottom. She looked completely stunning.

"Good luck to you, too, Laurie." Marina pushed her curls out of her eyes. "I've seen you on *Dance with Me*. You are such a beautiful dancer."

"Aw, thank you, Mrs. Goodman."

Anita bristled at the moniker but it didn't seem to faze her mother at all. "Anita, your father would just love to see this," Marina said.

Unable to hold back the scoff, Anita crossed her arms over her chest. Sure, she was exposed from a clothing standpoint, but this was entirely different. "Seriously? The man who hasn't come to a single one of my performances since I graduated from high school?" She felt Patrick step closer as Laurie distanced herself from them. Anita could care less. "Why do you care what he thinks? He cheated on you, Mom. He treated you terribly."

In the light reflected from the dance floor, Marina's dark eyes glistened with tears. "I know what he did. I know what I did, by not standing up for myself. I don't make those mistakes anymore, Anita. And your father deserves another chance. He's not a bad person, just an ordinary one who made wrong choices. He wants to make things right with you."

"He could start by showing up once in a while." On the floor, the couples ran through their Viennese waltz routines, like a bevy of colorful tops swirling.

"Anita." Her mom placed a warm hand on her arm. "You know, your father would be there for your wedding."

"I'm sure he would, Mom. But he'd be there for appearances, not for me." Anita bit her lip, holding back the tears because she had to compete in a very short time, goddammit, and she wasn't going to cry now. "I think cake rates higher than my career and happiness at times." Eloping sounded vastly preferable to that kind of performance.

"Anita—"

In one of the three lifetime instances where his arrival was welcomed, Mikhail appeared at that moment, stepping between the two women. Anita had never been so grateful for his obliviousness.

"Where the fuck have you been?" Laurie hissed at him, swatting his chest. Mikhail returned it with a nonchalant shrug.

Her mother stepped away. "I'll find my seat. But I'll see you later?"

Anita stretched up on her toes, feeling the muscles of her legs lengthen and warm. "Great."

"I can't believe you," Laurie said to Mikhail behind them. "The biggest competition of our career—"

"I had a thing," Mikhail replied.

Anita knew him well enough that whatever the thing was, it had not been good, or possibly even legal.

Patrick leaned down beside her and kissed the shell

of her ear. "Are you eavesdropping so we don't have to talk about your mom?"

"No." So what if she was?

On the dance floor, the couples had ended their Viennese waltz routines and moved into foxtrot.

Anita caught sight of Jackson Alder, standing at a respectful distance from the dance floor. He watched Evelyn sway and move, and it was like his body moved with hers. Then Lucian Chatelaine sidled up beside him and whispered something in his ear, making Jackson go stiff as an icicle.

"I really don't like that guy," Patrick said, following the direction of her gaze.

"Me neither." Anita closed her eyes and tuned out everything but the feelings in her body. The quickstep, the final Standard dance, was almost complete. Her heart pounded in her neck and wrists, and her skin tingled everywhere. She was alive, and she could do this. She would throw herself into the music and rhythms and forget everything else.

"How are you feeling?" Patrick applauded for the Standard couples, who took their bows.

Anita's eyes snapped open. "Fucking fantastic."

Chapter Twenty-Eight

Since he was not an oblivious dickhead like Mikhail, Patrick knew something was wrong with Anita. It wasn't just fighting with her mom in public, which was a completely unexpected turn of events. It wasn't even that she seemed angry about Lucian Chatelaine's assholery. It was that she thrummed with energy, like a live wire struck by lightning.

Patrick straightened his posture and readjusted the lapels of his dance shirt, which exposed a decent but not obscene amount of his chest. Waxing chest hair was not something he had missed when he had quit performing a few years ago.

The Standard teams filed off the floor, with congratulations and best wishes reverberating in their wake in several languages.

Then the announcer called the start of the Latin Team Match, and the crowd roared to its feet. Patrick understood. There were some superstar dancers competing tonight.

As he watched the European team, then the Asian team called forward, Patrick found his gaze drawn to Anita's mother. She sat beside Miranda, the woman from the Pleasure Palace Dance Hall, and the pair of them appeared in deep conversation.

Worry tingled at the back of his neck. What on earth could they have to talk about? Of course, Anita's mother was the consummate host, always making everyone feel welcome and sussing out dark secrets. She had done the same for Patrick many times.

They called Team Americas, and Patrick and Anita strode onto the dance floor behind Hanna and Markus. He led Anita around in a tight circle before they found an unoccupied corner of the floor, perfect for starting their cha-cha. The other competitors had their hands raised, clapping along with the calls and rousing the crowd, so Patrick joined in, giddy with the party-like atmosphere. Who could blame him for being thrilled to be here, on this floor with these competitors? Maybe there really was something magical about Blackstone, and it had nothing to do with a ghost.

"Ladies and gentlemen!" the announcer called. "Welcome everyone to our Latin Team Match. We have some amazing dancers here today, some you may recognize from television or internet fame, but they are here live for you this evening. And it's time…for cha-cha."

From the opening strains of the live band's version of Earth, Wind, and Fire's "September," Patrick could tell that this performance would be different. Patrick let his hips roll, but in front of him, Anita moved with exquisite precision.

He was completely biased, and she was always a gorgeous dancer, but this was new. Her flair was brighter, her smile broader, her steps effortlessly sliding from percussive to sinuous. It was all Patrick could do to keep up. And not kiss her senseless every time he wrapped her close to him.

Halfway through their rumba, he let his lips touch her hair while they moved together, her body pressed against his. She wasn't so much getting lost in the music as conquering it, and he was her beloved golden retriever, following wherever she led.

The audience responded, too. Beyond the dim haze of their dance bubble, Patrick could hear the three-beat chant of Anita's name. Of course, everyone had their favorites, but Anita's assertive, flirtatious performance was doing a lot for a lot of people.

Including him.

"You need to slow it down," he whispered to her during a samba roll. "Seriously, we might have to avoid the jive and find a dark corner somewhere."

Anita snaked her hand through his hair, then spun away from him. "Just keep up."

So he did. He matched her energy, jive kicking in sync with her. When the music finally ended, they both stepped out to bow, then he pulled her into him and hugged her tightly. "You okay?" she asked.

"Perfect."

It was clear from the crowd's reaction that they had loved the performances as well. Everyone in the ballroom was on their feet, clapping and cheering. Patrick scanned the crowd for Anita's mom and saw her bouncing on her feet, crying and laughing and applauding. A thought tried to force its way through his energized brain. Where had Miranda gone?

It didn't matter, though, not when they could barely leave the dance floor for the acclaim that was still happening. A twinge of guilt ran through him. The Standard dancers had also received enormous affirmation from the crowd, but it hadn't gone on quite like this.

The band on the far end of the ballroom started to

play, but the emcee—Horace Brixley again—was nowhere in sight.

It was as though he was in a movie, and at the part where everything else faded until he became aware of a single sound.

A scream, piercing through the applause and chatter and music.

Patrick stiffened. "Did you hear that?"

It came again, plaintive, louder, echoing around the grand ballroom.

Now it seemed other people had noticed, as well. "It's the Blackstone ghost!" Eva cried across the floor.

It wasn't. The crowd parted like the Red Sea, as though everyone was afraid to touch her in case she might, indeed, be spectral.

But Patrick could tell she wasn't. She was gaunt and frightened and half-naked, but she was as real as Anita.

Anita pushed past the inertia first, running in heels and full costume to the woman as she collapsed at the edge of the dance floor. Patrick was there only a second behind his fiancée, and for once, his timing was excellent, because he could catch the woman before she hit her head.

"Help," she said in a voice cut through with dehydration, grief, and fatigue. She was beautiful beneath the layer of streaked makeup.

Then she promptly passed out.

Chapter Twenty-Nine

Lucy had every intention of keeping the promises she had made to her mother and Anita. She would finish up the assignments that she had taken on vacation with her. She would shower and exercise and eat vegetables.

It wasn't her fault that James showed up a few minutes after Anita and Patrick had left for the ballroom. It was definitely not her fault that he looked all rumpled and sheepish and completely delectable. "Hello," he said softly, eyes turned to the floor. Why was that so stinking cute?

She'd ask for forgiveness later. Wrapping her arms around his neck, she pressed her lips to his and indulged in the kinds of kisses she'd avoided thinking about the night before.

When they came up for air, he brushed tendrils of hair from her face and smiled. "I've been thinking about that all day."

"Um, ditto. Why do you think I threw myself into online sleuth mode? It was the only thing that could distract me." She linked her hand with his and pulled him into the house. The door shut behind him with a satisfying creak and groan.

"Did you find anything?" James leaned down—she loved that he was just taller than her, enough to lean down for kisses, though if she thought about it too long she might wonder about the longevity of his back and neck muscles. But that was a rabbit hole for another day.

Lucy shrugged. "My hacking skills are no match for your police department's records. I knew I should have taken that dark web class sophomore year."

He laughed, pulling her toward the kitchen. "I'm starving. Come on, let's get some food."

He didn't seem to mind that she was terrible at flirting. Score one for Lucy.

"How's your mom?" She pulled a loaf of bread from the fridge along with butter.

Screwing up his nose in a gesture of frank disgust, James pointed at the bread. "You put all that in the refrigerator? My uncle would have left it out. How in the world does the butter spread?"

"Without salmonella, of course." What would Madison Templar, resident queen Resting Bitch Face, do in this situation? Probably toss her hair and pull the neckline of her shirt down. Lucy glanced at her Arcade Fire tee and promptly ruled out both ideas.

"Does butter get salmonella or just go rancid?" James filled the kettle with water and set it back on its electric base.

"I'm pretty sure both will ruin your day." The toaster dinged and she buttered and marmaladed the two slices. "Here. I'm trying to impress you with my mad toast-making skills."

A half-smile on his face, James stood before her, arms along her sides, hands resting on the countertop. "Toast aside, I'm already impressed."

Then followed another session of intense, soft kissing, wherein Lucy lost time. Normally she would hate this but James tasted so good, and his body felt so nice pressed against hers.

At last, though, the crispy toasty smell of their snack and the whistle of the kettle broke them apart.

"Here's the bad news." Lucy took her mug and plate over to the kitchen table. "I learned absolutely nothing new about Tom Havens's death because wire reporters are lazy and basically repeat the same story over and over."

"That is true. None of them said anything about how he ended up in the peat bog?" Crumbs showered down James's soft gray T-shirt, and he brushed them off the side of his hand. "Is it possible it's an accident?"

"Nope. Besides not knowing anything about how the body got there, it's a complete mystery where he was murdered. The one consensus is that he was, in fact, murdered, but not how. One story said stabbing, one said gunshot."

"How helpful." James sipped his tea.

"Tell me about it." Lucy mimicked his earlier movements, adding a little cream to her own tea and sipping it. Nope, she still preferred it plain. "What did you do last night?"

"Me?" James leaned back, a smirk on his face and his eyes lit with glee. "I made you a mixtape and wrote some shitty poetry."

Why was this boy so perfect? "Now you have to read it."

James shook his head violently. "On your deathbed. Nah, my mum and I watched telly and went to bed. Certainly no late night sleuthing."

"Does your uncle live near you?" She picked off the crusts from her toast, leaving only the satisfying middle.

"My uncle? Hardly." James finished his tea. "He's only been back from South Africa for a minute. And he and my mum had some sort of falling out before he left a few years ago. He lives just north of Blackstone, but before he gave me this job, I hardly ever saw him."

"That's too bad. I'm an only child, and I've always wanted a sibling." A confidant. Someone who understood what she went through in the Knight household. Not that she was complaining, but still. It would have been nice.

"Same."

They sat for a few moments in silence as Lucy forced down the rest of the tea she'd prepared. It was rare to find someone like him, someone to sit beside without speaking. Normally Lucy felt like she had to carry the conversation, but not now. It was…nice. More than nice.

"What do you want to do now?" James asked. There was no pressure or hidden meaning in his tone, and that made her fall a little bit more for him, too.

"Hmm." She sat back in the chair, letting the wood frame hold up her posture. "This is an old church, right?"

If she looked up "taken aback" in the dictionary, that would be James's expression. "Um, yes."

"Cool. So there's hidden rooms here, too?"

James found her gaze, a smile sparking across his lips, as he nodded. "Wicked."

Chapter Thirty

James didn't need a map or blueprints of the house. He showed her the panels that covered hidden stairwells to servants' quarters, like the one in the far back of the pantry, behind the cans of baked beans and packets of crisps. They had moved everything aside before opening the door.

"A lot of these entrances got boarded up when the house was renovated. No one had need for servant quarters or things like that."

Lucy shone her flashlight into the dark, cobwebbed stairwell. After her last experience, no way was she climbing in there. "So what happened to them?"

James shrugged, his T-shirt riding up enough to expose a single inch of toned abdomen. Though she wasn't usually one to ogle, this time could be forgiven. "I imagine they're still there. Full of animals or whatnot." He examined her face carefully. "Lucy, you can't be thinking about going up there."

"Who, me?" She flattened her palm against her chest. "If it isn't crawling through guano, and merely climbing stairs, I'm kind of into it. Hello. Secret staircase."

"This is what always happens in horror movies. The young couple sneaks off to make out, like dust and cobwebs are sexy in any way, and they end up with their heads chopped off."

"That seems a bit extreme." Lucy rolled her eyes. "We wouldn't be sneaking off to make out. We can make out here, where there's hot tea and a fireplace and a relatively clean couch."

Laughing, James slid his arm around her waist. It was surprisingly cozy in the back of that pantry. "I have to be honest, I'd much rather make out than go looking for creepy abandoned rooms. What if there are dolls in them?" He shuddered. "With those glass eyes looking onto nothing? Ugh."

"Thinking about empty-eyed ancient dolls is not making your case." Still, she kissed his cheek anyway, because he really was kind of perfect and she wanted to take every opportunity while she could. "Come on. Five minutes. It will distract me from the fact that I can't find out anything about the Tom Havens case." Summoning whatever inner female part of her might know how to flirt, Lucy attempted to bat her eyes. It felt awkward and bizarre. "Oh, that was weird. I'm never doing that again."

James traced the line of her cheek with his finger, his touch warm and welcome. "You really are one of a kind."

Heat built and coiled in her stomach. "So are you." She didn't want heat, not now. Something about her parents being out of town and knowing that this could end. She wasn't ready. Deflection was better. "Now, come on. Show me the secret servant quarters where all sorts of chicanery went down."

James laughed. "I don't know if you're using chicanery properly."

"Who cares? We'll look it up later. Lead on."

****

With both of their phone flashlights illuminating the space, it looked vastly less murder-y and haunted house-ish. Far more rundown and sad.

"Do you think they used stairwells like this to hide people?" Lucy asked. "Like during World War Two?"

"On the mainland, for sure." James squeezed her hand like he wanted to remember she was there. Aww, he was so cute. "Not as much here. Though I'm certain over the centuries many people needed sanctuary."

"Ooh, like *Hunchback of Notre Dame*?"

"I knew you'd read Hugo. Of course you have."

She had, but the teasing was too fun to stop. "They should do a reboot of it, but with robots and space puppies."

James's laughter reverberated off the cold stone walls of the stairwell.

"It's freezing in here," Lucy said. However little she knew of romance and attraction, chattering teeth were probably not considered sexy. "Poor servants."

"Seriously. They worked their arses off and get cold, wet stone. Bloody tuberculosis."

"Like factory life was better? Score zero for the Industrial Revolution."

They reached the landing at the top of the stairs, revealing a long, wide corridor with rooms set on either side. Plain, cracked wooden doors hung askew on rusty hinges. Cobwebs covered substantial surface area, and she didn't want to think about what was in the dust she disturbed with her feet. "Yeah, you were right. Why do people in horror movies think any of this could be sexy?"

James tickled her side, and she leapt away, laughing. "Maybe they hope if they scare you, you'll jump into their arms, looking for shelter."

"So, basically you're saying the jump-horror genre is one thousand percent supportive of the patriarchy?" She was not proving her point by settling into his hold, into his touch, but whatever. She would only be young once, and he seemed to like her smartass remarks. "We need male protectors, right?"

Laughing, he touched her forehead with his, his soft hair brushing against her skin. "Of course. That's exactly what I meant."

His lips touched hers, soft and warm and tasting like milky tea and sharp, sweet tangerine jam. If she had known kissing could be like this, would she have pursued it more?

Probably not. James seemed like a once-in-a-lifetime opportunity.

She wound her arms around his neck, pulling him closer, falling further into the kiss.

The first time she heard the moan, she thought it had been hers. It certainly hadn't been James's, as she could feel the wave of his breathing against her chest.

When she heard it a second time, softer but still echoing in the otherwise empty hallway, she broke away from James. "Did you hear that?"

"What?" He looked dazed and a little lost, his eyes darker than usual and lips swollen. It would be so tempting to forget what she'd heard and slide back into…

But no. There it was again.

Lucy snapped every neuron in her body to attention. Without waiting for James, she turned down the servants' hallway, using her lightest tread, listening every few steps.

"What are you doing?" James hissed. He had caught up to her but followed a few paces behind.

"Shh. I need to hear." She closed her eyes, leaning into her other senses.

There, behind the third door on the right, the one with the only door that looked like it actually closed. A whimper, some rapid breathing.

Without fully processing what she was about to do, Lucy pushed open the door and gasped.

There, on an incongruously clean mattress with brightly-patterned floral sheets, was a thin slip of a woman with pale skin and long, thick dark hair haloed around her. She looked older than Lucy, but she was stunningly beautiful, and shivered despite the layers of blankets on the bed.

"Oh shit," Lucy breathed. "James, call the police."

Chapter Thirty-One

The entire ballroom was chaos after that, but Anita barely noticed.

"She needs water," she said to no one and everyone at the same time.

"Here." Jackson Alder pressed a plastic bottle of water into Anita's hands. She wasn't sure when he and Evelyn had appeared beside them, but she was grateful.

Anita unscrewed the bottle top and dripped a little water into the woman's mouth. She groaned.

Patrick brushed the woman's hair off her face with gentle strokes, and Anita was so intensely grateful to him, she almost would have married him on the spot.

"I called the police," her mother said. She stood behind Patrick, hands clenched together.

"Good. Poor woman needs an ambulance." Beside her, Evelyn was a pile of skirts and tulle, but she picked up the woman's hand and held it.

Something about all of these demonstrations of tenderness toward a complete stranger hit Anita like a bout of nerve pain, lancinating through her, quickly followed by guilt. People had larger problems than she did. Why couldn't she just get over herself?

The woman's eyes opened, revealing bright green contact lenses, and her gaze found Anita's, holding her rapt. "Help," she said, her voice soft and barely audible amidst the din in the ballroom.

Anita squeezed the woman's hand. "The police and the ambulance are on their way. What happened?"

The woman shuddered and seized, but Patrick, to his credit, continued to cradle her.

"Are you in pain?" Evelyn asked.

The woman shuddered again and opened her mouth, as though about to say something. But they never found out what it was, because her electric-green gaze caught on something over Jackson's shoulder, and she loosed a primal shriek.

****

The ambulance preceded the police only by a few moments, and Anita and Patrick moved to the side of the excitement as they strapped the woman to a backboard and carried her out. "What will happen to her?" Anita asked one of the paramedics.

"Sorry, ma'am, but I'm not at liberty to say. We're taking her to hospital." He tipped his hat toward her and left, heaving an enormous kit bag over his shoulder.

Horace Brixley, his bow tie crooked and his neck glistening with sweat, stepped up to the podium, a police officer beside him. "Um, ladies and gentlemen." At least he was appropriately subdued. "Unfortunately, the police have asked everyone to stay until they've finished questioning people. We'll set up water stations in the back."

Mikhail materialized beside Anita, his presence as unwelcome and sudden as a mosquito bite. "Aren't they going to announce the winners?"

"Seriously?" Patrick said. "There are more important things right now."

Mikhail grunted. "I've been taking boxing lessons, Patrick. Don't tempt me."

Fury rolling through her in waves, Anita turned on him. “Don’t tempt *you?* Don’t tempt me.”

Mikhail cowed, which was an immensely satisfying sight, cooling the rage inside her. “I’m going to get some water.”

“What a dick. I’m going to get my phone from my dance bag. Be right back.” Patrick kissed her cheek and disappeared, but for once, she wasn’t attuned to him.

That dubious honor belonged to Mikhail, whose progression across the room had been halted by Lucian Chatelaine and Horace Brixley. They appeared to be having one of those almost-arguments, where no one wanted to raise their voice because they were in a massive crowd, but their body language conveyed all of the latent anger.

What in Dante’s hellfire was going on around here?

Laurie approached her, wrapping a long, thick robe around her costume. “Are you all right?”

“I’m fine. You danced beautifully.” It seemed like the entire wrong thing to say at the moment, but Laurie seemed to appreciate it.

“You too. What a fucking mess, huh?” Laurie sighed and brought a Thermos to her lips. “I wish this tea had booze in it.”

“Tell me about it.” Anita’s attention wandered again to Mikhail. “Do you know what’s going on over there?”

Laurie shook her head. “I’m not sure. I know Mikhail’s been angling for a spot on *Dance with Me*. He keeps asking me to put in a good word, but I can’t do that to my colleagues or the other contestants.” She shivered, cupping her hands around the Thermos. “I really don't want to dance in the open Latin with him. He's ruining my cred for future partners."

"That's not true," Anita replied. "You're amazing and anyone would be lucky to dance with you."

As if this night was not bizarre enough, Patrick streaked through the crowd, holding his phone aloft. "Anita! You have to see this message from Lucy."

This night was never going to end, and of course she would meet it in peacock feathers.

Chapter Thirty-Two

She didn't wait to ensure James would take out his phone and call.

Lucy ran to the mattress and the woman. "Are you okay? Are you hurt?"

The woman opened her eyes but didn't seem to see Lucy. Maybe it was the violet-colored contacts. Underneath, her eyes were a lovely dark brown color.

"I'm Lucy, and this is James. We're here to help. I'm going to touch you, but only to check your heart rate. Is that all right?"

The woman's mouth opened, but she didn't say anything, and the effort seemed to exhaust her. She looked surprisingly hydrated for being locked in a secret attic.

Which brought up the question of how she came to be here. Dread pooled along Lucy's spine. The only other person she could think of who would know about this would be James's uncle. It wouldn't be James. Would it?

Hiding her thoughts, Lucy took the woman's thin wrist and checked her heart rate. Steady, metronomic.

"Thank you," James said into the phone behind her. "Lucy, the police are on their way."

Lucy didn't want to look at him. She stared instead at the woman who had fallen asleep on the mattress. Now, she picked out little details she hadn't noticed before. The large reusable water bottle, the insulated Thermos for tea, the wrappers from packets of snacks and biscuits. A plate with crumbs and a half-eaten stalk of celery.

She recognized that plate. It was the same as in the kitchen downstairs at Gryphon House.

"Lucy." James breathed her name into her ear, and it was too intimate, too much. "I called the police. They're on their way."

"How did she get here?" Damn it, she hadn't realized she was crying, but it made it easier, somehow, not to look at him. "Did you know?"

"No." He took her hands, pulling her toward him, but she couldn't look him in the eye. "I'm as surprised as you."

She wanted to soften, wanted to fall into his arms and trust and believe that yes, sure, this time it wasn't what it seemed. It wasn't that someone had trafficked this lovely woman and locked her into a dusty, likely vermin-infested attic. There were no Blackstone ghosts and no bad people, and there was only James. James and the way she was falling in love with him.

"What are you two doing here?"

With a wrench, strong arms lifted her up, away from the woman and onto her feet. Why wasn't she struggling? Because Mr. Butler now had James. His hands were on James, and he was dragging his nephew out of this little room.

"What are you doing here?" Mr. Butler repeated. His expression was fury and, maybe, fear? It was difficult to tell through the veil of tears. "You can't be up here."

"What's going on?" To his credit, James didn't

back down from his uncle. “We’ve called the police. They’re on their way.” James took Lucy’s hand and pulled her behind him, shielding her.

“Aw, fuck.” Mr. Butler ran his hands through his hair and then tossed them in the air. “You don’t understand what you’ve done. What the hell am I going to do? You two, go downstairs immediately. You never saw any of this.”

“Are you joking?” Lucy found her voice again, grateful it was as steady as she had hoped. “You’re hiding a woman in an attic.”

Mr. Butler shook his head. “You don’t understand, and this is not the place for you. Go downstairs.”

But at that moment, footsteps pounded on the stairs, accompanied by shouts of “Police!”

Lucy steeled her jaw as she watched the armed police officers handcuff Mr. Butler, who was still protesting the entire thing.

In fact, she barely moved as the police swarmed the attic, followed by paramedics, who assessed the woman and carried her down the stairs. Likely to a waiting ambulance. Lucy barely moved as she answered the questions she could and listened to James’s responses. Analyzed them.

At last, it was just the two of them.

“Lucy.” James hugged her, but she didn’t return it.

Maybe she was better off alone.

“I have to go call Anita and Patrick.” And her parents, but that was a thing to be dreaded another time.

“I’ll go with you.” He reached for her hand, but she slipped from his grasp. She closed her eyes, not wanting to see the hurt etched on his face.

“I have to do this myself.” She turned and headed

down the hallway toward the staircase. “Goodbye, James.” She only wished it didn’t sound so final.

Chapter Thirty-Three

"Seriously, how long do we have to stay here?" Patrick shifted from foot to foot. He hadn't succumbed yet to sitting on the floor, like many of the other people awaiting police clearance, but at least they'd let him and Anita change out of their costumes. After their performance, his sweat-drenched dance pants had clung to him like a pair of jeans that had seen the polar plunge. He shivered just thinking about it.

"Why isn't Lucy answering her phone?" Anita growled at the apparently useless communication device in her hand. "She sends us an SOS, and then doesn't pick up?"

"Maybe we should call her parents. Ooh, or threaten to call her parents." Patrick bounced on his feet, willing circulation into them. It had fled approximately seven hundred hours before, but he was nothing but optimistic.

Anita rolled her eyes and dialed again. "I don't understand how she got into the ballroom."

Patrick did a few jumping jacks. "Maybe from that secret mole person room? I don't know. Maybe someone left a secret door unlocked."

"That seems unlikely." Anita cursed at her phone and tugged at her ponytail.

"At least there's only a few of us left." The remark didn't seem to improve her mood.

Lucian Chatelaine and Horace Brixley had been some of the first interviewed. One of those “rich men leave first” scenarios, Patrick guessed. Mikhail had disappeared before anything had ever gone down, which did absolutely nothing to endear him to Patrick. Seriously, in his mind, Mikhail was worth less than plant lint from a dying tulip.

Now, though, there were less than ten of them, and three police officers, so he put the odds on them getting back to Gryphon House by midnight were…fuck if he knew. Not only was he so tired that jumping jacks were the only things keeping his eyes open, but he never gambled. He’d put too much work into earning his own money to be comfortable playing odds.

****

To his immense relief, they did leave a shade shy of midnight, and he only almost fell asleep twice on the drive back to Gryphon House. Anita seemed to be powered entirely by rage, and couldn’t stop twitching, not even long enough for him to pass out on her shoulder. How rude.

He briefly rocked awake when the car stopped in the drive, and then again when Anita grabbed his arm and dragged him from the car.

“How are you sleeping?” she hissed. “After everything?”

“Sorry.” He dragged a hand down his face, working his fingertips into his muscles. Maybe pain would wake him up. Nope, no luck. Still totally beat. “I feel like I drank two pitchers of margaritas.”

Anita’s rage subsided and she rubbed his back. “Poor Patrick. Honestly, I could use a margarita right now.” She unlocked the door and pushed it open.

Every light in the house was ablaze. Again, how rude. Patrick longed for their bed upstairs, where he could fall asleep fully clothed, or even the couch in the living room. Both of these dreams were highly unlikely with the lights on.

"Lucy?" Anita pulled off her coat as she walked through the foyer. "Are you here?"

Patrick picked it up, intending to hang it in the foyer closet, but this seemed an oddly impossible task. The door to the foyer closet hung open, and everything inside had been either dumped out or pushed to the sides. Most fascinating of all, at the end of the closet was a panel that was shifting slightly back and forth, like from a breeze.

Now awake, Patrick stopped so abruptly his shoes made an unpleasant squeaking sound against the parquet floor. "Holy shit, is there a secret room inside that closet?"

From the living room, the sound of sobs echoed around the arched ceilings. Lucy sat upright on the couch, staring at them behind red-rimmed eyes and puffy cheeks.

Anita rushed toward her. Patrick intended to as well, but the discovery of the whole secret room thing had him trapped.

"Lucy, are you okay?" Anita dashed into the living room and wrapped her arms around Lucy, who broke into a series of heaving sobs.

Fighting his own inertia and promising his inner child to explore later, Patrick followed Anita, perching on the very uncomfortable wooden arm of the couch.

"What happened?" Anita asked, stroking the girl's hair. "We kept trying to call you back."

Lucy sobbed louder, doubtless unable to speak through her tears.

"Do you want me to call your parents?" Patrick wasn't sure that would help, but it seemed at least an option. "Where's James?"

That was the exact opposite of the right thing to say. As though he'd set off a bomb in the living room, Lucy bolted away from Anita and stood, her entire body shaking with grief and what seemed like rage.

"James is involved in a sex-trafficking ring!" She spat the words, expectorating with each syllable, before running for the stairs.

This was what shock felt like. Cold, frozen, numb indecision. "What the fuck?" It wasn't the best thing to say, he knew that, but it encompassed a lot of his current emotions. Apparently everyone had had a rough night.

Above them, he could hear footsteps pounding along the corridor, a door opening and shutting with finality.

Anita seemed as stunned as he was.

"Um, we should go after her, right?" Patrick asked.

Anita glanced over at the staircase. "Probably. What is going on?"

He shrugged and stood. If he projected confidence, maybe he would feel it. "Come on. Let's go find out."

They climbed the steps with iron in their feet. "Lucy?" Anita called. "We're coming up."

He appreciated that she warned her. It certainly hadn't occurred to him, but then he'd never been a heartbroken teenaged girl before.

"Did she really say 'sex-trafficking ring'?" he asked, keeping his voice soft as it carried in the old house.

“Yup.” Anita kept her gaze straight ahead. He’d be wise to do the same.

They arrived simultaneously at Lucy’s bedroom door, and Patrick knocked on the wood softly. Inside, he couldn’t hear any more sobbing. Maybe she’d fallen asleep. That had always worked for him before. Extreme grief, then a good passing out.

“Lucy?” Anita tested the doorknob, which wasn’t locked. “We’re coming in, okay?”

There wasn’t a response. Was that tacit approval? He would let Anita lead this one.

Anita opened the door with a gentle slowness. Lucy was not one for keeping her space tidy. Clothes spooled from the great dresser in the corner, and the desk was a collage of spiral-bound notebooks, a splay of brightly colored pencils, and nail polish bottles.

Lucy straightened as they entered, wiping underneath her eyes with the heels of her hands. “I had the worst day.”

Anita pulled over the desk chair, gesturing for Patrick to sit, then sat beside Lucy on the bed, wrapping her arm around her shoulder. “Tell us what happened.”

“I don’t know. It was all fine, at first. We were joking and laughing and eating toast. James said there are boarded up servant hallways in this house, and more, because it used to be a church.” Her eyes scrunched up into her face again, but she sniffed rapidly several times and exhaled, which seemed to calm her. “I know you’re going to say I’m crazy, but I know what I saw.”

“What did you see?” Patrick leaned forward in his chair, resting his forearms against his legs.

Lucy sniffed again and snuggled closer to Anita. "The woman, she was sitting there, on the bed. She looked so frail and pretty. And then *he* was there, and I just knew—"

"Wait, which he?" Anita gave him a sharp look for interrupting, but there were several potential players in the scene.

Lucy exhaled, pursing her lips and blowing out the air like she was blowing a balloon. "Mr. Butler. He showed up after we did, and he looked so surprised. I'd show you, but the police took everything."

"The police were here?" Anita got a pass for interrupting.

"Of course. We called them straight away when we found the woman. I mean, I just don't think there's any other explanation." Lucy pulled away from Anita and paced in front of her bed. "You take a woman hidden in a boarded-up room behind a secret staircase, and a man who clearly knows she's there, and knows this house. I don't know. Doesn't trafficking make the most sense?"

Especially after what they'd seen in the Crystal Gardens ballroom, Patrick couldn't disagree. "I think it makes some sense," he said, hesitating. "But why do you think James is involved?"

"Because it's his uncle!" She threw her hands into the air like it was completely obvious and he must be in a coma not to realize it.

"I don't know, Lucy." Anita tightened her ponytail, even though there was not a hair askew on her head. "He's a really good guy, and he clearly likes you. Why would he have even shown you the room if he knew what his uncle was doing?"

Lucy collapsed on her bed face first, her body

bouncing like she had landed on a trampoline. "Aargh. I wish that were true."

Anita reached over and patted her back. "It is true. Look, it's late. Get some rest. Call him tomorrow morning. We can figure all this out."

Lucy paused, then sat upright in a cobra pose. "I'm such an asshole. I didn't even ask how your performance went. I'm so sorry I missed it."

"Oh." Anita blanched, and from the numb feeling in his own face, Patrick had a feeling he looked the same. "It was, uh, eventful. We'll talk about it tomorrow."

"Okay." A wave of fatigue seemed to crash over Lucy, and she barely seemed capable of keeping her eyes open. "Tomorrow."

"Go to sleep." Anita stood and took Patrick's hand. "Everything will be okay."

Lucy was already under the covers and half-snoring as they let themselves out of the room and closed the door.

Anita wheeled on him, and he recoiled. Had he done something wrong? Probably not, as it looked like she was holding back tears.

"Everything is not going to be okay, Patrick." She burst into sobs, and he did the only thing he could think of. He pulled her close, stroked her back, kissed her cheek, and whispered sweet, soothing lies into her ear.

Chapter Thirty-Four

Anita would have preferred to be woken by a thunderstorm, not bright spring sun painting the inside of the room with incongruous glee. Especially today, when it seemed designed to mock her with its cheery promises and only drew attention to the puffiness of her face and general lack of ambition.

She rolled over in bed and groaned. Her playlist for today would have to include Springsteen, Journey, and definitely Roxanne. Some classic, some comfort, and some righteous female grit.

"Do we have to get up today?" Patrick mumbled into the pillow beside her. It took ages for her to roll over to face him, and when she did, she was greeted with a loud snore.

"Fuck it, I'm going back to sleep, too." She pulled the covers up over her shoulder and snuggled into the comfortable mattress. To hell with competition prep. So what if tomorrow was the Latin professional division? She was spent, done, an out-of-order vending machine at an abandoned gas station in the middle of nowhere, Pennsylvania.

Just as she drifted back toward beautiful, blissful sleep, her cell phone blared "Maghalenha" multiple times in a row.

She growled. Today, she hated everyone.

Her phone would not be silenced. Did the "do not

disturb" feature not work across the pond? Damn international plan.

Immediately after the song ceased, meaning that whoever it had been calling her had—thankfully—hung up, her text message alert chimed.

She lay in bed with her eyes clenched. Exactly how important was this text message? Was it likely to improve her day? Doubtful, as she'd only been awake for six minutes and already rued every moment.

When the alert chimed again, then flurried like a chorus of hostile doves, she finally sat up and slid the button on the screen to unlock the phone.

The first message was from the Blackstone Dance Festival. The eight that followed were all from the Team Americas chat group.

Of all the people who should have been allowed to sleep in, of course all of her teammates were bright-eyed and bushy-tailed. Bastards.

The words swam a bit, as her vision was still hazy from blinking sleep from her eyes. She read the one from the Blackstone Dance Festival first.

Due to the unforeseen events of last evening, we were unable to congratulate and award our winning Standard and Latin teams properly. All team members, please present to the Crystal Gardens ballroom at noon sharp today for the long-awaited awards ceremony.

"Long awaited?" Patrick said, and Anita jumped, nearly knocking him in the chin with her shoulder. "It was barely eight hours ago."

"I didn't realize you were up." She was grateful, really, that she hadn't wounded him. Patrick had such a cute chin, firm and strong. It would be a shame to harm it.

He yawned. "I'd rather be asleep, but your phone is loud."

"I thought I put it on vibrate or do not disturb or something." She cursed her own lack of technological skills.

"Don't worry." Patrick leaned over and kissed her softly, which was the only pleasant thing that had so far happened this morning. "We're both awake now, for better or worse. Let's caffeinate."

Okay, two good things. "Deal."

****

Thirty minutes of yoga and one cup of green tea later, Anita felt slightly less like a cantankerous fusty nuts and more like herself.

Patrick carried a bowl of fruit salad to the kitchen table and set it between the two of them, handing her a fork as well. "Lucy's still asleep."

"She needs it." Anita speared a slice of honeydew with laser precision.

Patrick twirled a halved strawberry on his own fork. "So, what do you think?"

"You're going to have to be more specific." Fatigue pressed at the back of her head, but she pushed it away. "About last night? About the state of the world? Superhero movies?"

"Last night. Mostly about the secret room thing." His voice twinged with excitement.

She should have known. Patrick loved a good locked-room mystery. "I'm not sure." She warmed her hands on her mug, but the tea was already cooling. Blergh. "Something doesn't feel right about it. It all seems a weird coincidence, the woman in the ballroom and then Mr. Butler here. Doesn't it strike you as odd?"

As she spoke, the tension in her brain eased, as if she was relieving herself of a weight she hadn't known she carried.

Patrick exhaled and set down the strawberry. "Exactly. I've been thinking the same thing."

"Oh." Validation was always nice. "I don't think there's anything we can do about it."

Patrick waggled his eyebrows and pasted on his Sam Spade impersonation face. "We can investigate, sweetheart."

Anita speared another slice of honeydew. "Patrick, I love you, but you really need to work on your Bogart."

Patrick shrugged it off. "Come on. Haven't you always wanted to climb a hidden, musty staircase to a chamber filled with secrets?"

Anita thought for a second, tilting her head and pressing a fist to her chin. "Mmmm, no, no, and no."

In an instant, Patrick's face morphed into that of a pleading puppy. "You're killing me."

"Hardly." She threw him a bone by plucking all the bits of his least favorite fruits out of his sight line.

Footsteps brushed along the floor, and Lucy entered the kitchen, looking marginally improved from the night before. "Good, you're both awake."

"Want some fruit?" Patrick popped a square of pineapple into his mouth.

"No, I'm okay." Lucy slid into the seat beside Anita and set her palms on the table. "I've been thinking a lot about what you said last night."

"You didn't sleep at all?" Anita nudged the bowl of fruit salad toward Lucy.

"No, I slept for a bit. Or I passed out. Whatever.

The point is, I need to talk to James and find out what's going on." Lucy nodded her head, as though this was the absolute and final word in the entire matter.

Unsure what she was supposed to say, and clearly Patrick felt the same, they both sat and waited.

"So what do you think?" Lucy prompted, glancing between the two of them.

Anita thought this entire week had not gone according to plan, but that was apparently becoming her norm. "That's great. You owe him the chance to explain."

"Besides, maybe there's something else going on," Patrick said.

Honestly. Of all the things to say to the world's most intrepid teenage detective.

On cue, her eyes brightened, and her speech ramped up to lightning. "Do you think so, too? I woke up at four, and couldn't get back to sleep, so I opened up my laptop. Do you know how many disappearances of young women there are in Blackstone each year? It's astronomical. A lot of it has been attributed to rumor and the Blackstone ghost, but I think it's worse than that."

"Worse than a ballroom-dwelling ghost who disappears young athletes?" Anita hadn't intended for it to come out in a sarcastic tone, but oh well. Her earlier bad mood had recurred in spades and had brought a massive migraine with it.

To her credit, Lucy processed the information and shrugged. "True."

An alarm pinged on Anita's phone. Her stomach dropped as she read the alert. "Patrick, we have to get ready. We have to be back at the ballroom in ninety minutes."

"You need ninety minutes to get ready?" Lucy was definitely feeling better than the previous night.

Patrick slid the fruit bowl to Lucy and stood. "Beauty takes time."

****

While primping and plucking and tugging, Anita's phone chimed again and again. The second she didn't have a hot curling iron in her hand, she was going to demand Patrick show her how to put it back on vibrate.

Stepping out of the shower, Patrick wrapped a towel around his waist, and for a moment, Anita forgot to breathe. As wonderful as Patrick was, sometimes it was easy to neglect his athletic build, the sharp contours of his muscles, especially with water from the shower pearling along the lines.

She really ought to marry the man. He was walking catnip.

Patrick leaned over, kissed her hair, and flipped a small switch on the side of her phone so it started buzzing. "Put your tongue back in your mouth."

Returning to her senses, she scoffed, "Don't antagonize people holding burning hot irons, then."

"It's cool. I'll shake my butt a little as I leave, to give you a show."

What else was there to do but laugh as he shimmied away, swaying his hips, the soft Turkish cotton towel flicking around his toned thighs.

Yup. Walking catnip.

She turned back to the mirror, running the iron through her long blonde hair to accentuate its natural curl.

Her phone buzzed again on the counter,

dangerously close to upsetting her jar of expensive makeup primer. Right. She couldn't ignore the group chat forever.

But when she swiped open the text message screen, the messages were not, in fact, from the Team Match group chat. They were from Lucian Chatelaine.

Chatelaine: —Need you to stay after the ceremony. Want to meet with you and Patrick re: opportunity.—

That was weird. She barely had crafted a mental reply before the next one came through.

Chatelaine: —Meet at my office. My asst will send details.—

Yet another wrinkle in her day. The migraine that had receded with the soothing getting-ready routine now teased at her temple again. It almost felt like the world didn't want them to compete tomorrow. "Patrick?" Even her voice sounded gritty and soul-crushed.

"Everything okay?" He called from the bedroom.

"We've been summoned." She checked her hair, the long, loose soft-yellow curls. Maybe she should cut it all off. That would be ridiculous, a foolish rebellion. Gathering it at the base of her skull, she fully intended to pull it all up into her ponytail, tight and floppy.

Yet somehow she couldn't do it. Releasing the knot, she let the waves float down to kiss her shoulders and back.

"Summoning sounds kinky." Patrick appeared in the doorway and leaned against the jamb. He had dressed in dark-gray slacks and a crisp white shirt. "Hair down? I like it."

"Thanks." It felt good, changing it up a little. Like she was a new Anita. Not totally new, but a little shinier, a little more polished. "And there's nothing kinky. It's Lucian Chatelaine."

"Chatelaine? What in the world could he want?"

Anita shrugged and applied a layer of primer to her face. "He says he has an opportunity."

"An opportunity?" Patrick scratched at his chin. She knew he had to shave for the competition, but she liked it best when he had a thin line of shadow along his jaw. "Maybe it's about the show."

"The show?"

"Yeah. *Dance with Me*. Ooh, maybe he wants us to be judges."

That seemed simultaneously unlikely and also a weird enough possibility to be true. "If it means working with him, hard pass."

"True. He is an enormous knobhead."

Anita applied the makeup, dabbing on foundation, blending with the brush. It didn't soothe the niggling ache in her temple. That Chatelaine was an enormous knobhead didn't shock her. She set down the brush in her hand and turned to Patrick. "Do you have the sense more is going on here?"

He nodded vigorously. "Too many weird coincidences. You almost ready?"

Chapter Thirty-Five

Lucy dressed in record time. Not that she usually dwelt for ages on her toilette like some Regency heroine, but she cut a lot of corners in her anticipation of seeing James.

It was that gut feeling, the one John Flaherty told her never to ignore. If everything seemed wrapped up and final, but he felt like something was missing, he would dig deeper.

Of course, John wasn't here and she was in a foreign country, so she needed help. Help with a lot of friends. And if that help happened to be positively delectable and the kind of kisser that launched a thousand heartthrob memes, who was she to argue?

"Lucy!" Anita called down the hallway. "Patrick and I have to go. Do you need anything?"

"Nope. Good luck!" She doubted they needed it. When Anita and Patrick were on their A-game, no one could hold a candle to them. It was their electric chemistry, the years of want and need they poured into their excellent technique. Plus, they were fun to watch. There was a willingness in their dancing to push boundaries, to entertain and not simply smolder.

Debating whether or not to call James before showing up at his mom's house, she bounded down the steps. Definitely better to call before a random drive by. What if he wasn't home?

Lucy smiled to herself. She'd be fine. His mom would make her tea and she could cuddle with River, which sounded better than any other possible alternative solution.

As she grabbed her coat off the back of the couch, pulling out her phone to text and call a ride share, the front door creaked open like a rusty robot waking from a thousand-year slumber. Lucy's heart danced in her chest, leapfrogging like her middle school gym teacher insisted was good for her. She barely whispered "James" and was mid run, already planning their heartfelt, full firework reunion, when the chatter of her parents stopped her in her tracks.

"Lucy!" Her mother opened her arms wide, enveloping her in the migraine-inducing aroma of her expensive perfume. "We are so happy to see you!"

Closing her eyes, Lucy reminded herself that she was not a deer stuck in the middle of a Pennsylvania highway with an oncoming semi barreling toward her. These were her parents. They loved her. They must have returned early for a reason, a reason she could fathom due to the still-present wake of police intervention in the foyer.

That didn't mean they knew everything, and it would be better to keep it that way.

"Hi, Mom." Lucy returned the hug and stepped away to kiss her dad's cheek. His skin was smooth and he smelled like fresh mint toothpaste. The man never drank coffee after he brushed his teeth in the morning, the better to preserve the minty freshness.

Not for the first time, Lucy wondered how she appeared to these people called her parents. "Hi, Dad. What are you doing here?"

Her mother's kohl-rimmed eyes widened. "Are you kidding? We heard about all the fracas here last night. We've been trying to call you, but you didn't answer, so we came here as soon as we could."

"I'm sorry, Mom, my phone died and I forgot to charge it." She slipped the completely functional and fully-charged phone into the pocket of her leggings, away from prying eyes.

Her father raised an eyebrow. "Why are you wearing your coat? Are you going out?"

"For a walk." She was pretty proud of her parental misdirection skills. Her usual tactic was continual rambling until they interrupted. "It was a really rough night. I didn't get a lot of sleep, so I was reading this article about exercise and how the endorphins help ease your mind and so I thought I'd walk into the village and—"

Her mother set her large, designer purse on the table lining the foyer. "I don't understand why you didn't call us. The police were here? They found a woman hiding in the attic?"

Ah, so that was the news they had heard. "Yeah. Crazy, right?"

"Were you involved?" Her father pinned her with an intense, worried gaze, and her heart sank even lower. Seriously, if there were a cavern at the bottom of her feet, her heart would be stuck in the very back behind walls of lava rock. "You poor thing."

"Nope, I wasn't even here." The lie tasted like acid on her tongue, but she fed it to them anyway.

"Were you at the Team Match?" Her parents exchanged another positively textbook very worried parental glance. "Oh no. After everything that happened. Oh, Lucy, we never should have left you."

Lucy's ears perked up, and she almost forgot to hide it. Anita and Patrick had returned far later from the Team Match than she'd anticipated, but she hadn't really asked what had happened. This was as good an opportunity as any. Then somehow she could sneak out, see James, and they could investigate together.

That would be better, before she suffocated under the mountain of lies she was spewing.

Might as well add one more to the pile. "Yes, yes, I was there and it was awful."

Her mother crushed her against her chest again. "Oh no! I hope that poor woman is all right. To think, running into a ballroom like that! What if she was on drugs? Did she seem like she was on drugs?"

Every investigative nerve in Lucy's body tingled. There had been another woman who had escaped at the ballroom? Her somewhat-random, grief-fueled thought about a trafficking ring suddenly seemed more plausible. "I don't know. I wasn't that close," she said, though her mind was now somewhere far distant, in a place where gears churned through evidence and ideas. What had Mr. Butler been up to? He had to have an accomplice. Maybe while he was at Gryphon House, his accomplice was trying to move the woman at the Crystal Gardens to traffic her. So devious.

"Let's get you something to eat. You can walk later." Her mother steered her toward the kitchen. "Are Patrick and Anita here?"

"No, they had to go to town." She wasn't fully present for the conversation anymore, but this didn't bother her. She was nothing but skilled at dividing her inner thoughts from her parents.

Her mom sat her in a chair and bustled about the kitchen, muttering to herself, while Lucy ruminated. But then something her mom said caught in her ear like a fly in a spiderweb. “Wait, Mom. What was that you said?”

Her mom turned to her, half-filled kettle in hand. “I was just saying we need to ask Mr. Butler where to get some better bread. The one we had in Manchester really didn’t stack up.”

Dread coiled along Lucy’s spine as her mind snapped back into the kitchen and out of investigation mode. “Mr. Butler? You talked to him?”

“Of course.” Her mom set the kettle on the counter, then crossed the room to check Lucy’s temperature with the laying of a hand on her forehead. “We spoke to him this morning on our way back from the city.”

“You spoke to him?” Her breath came in sharp pants like she was having an asthma attack, but she hadn’t had one of those since she was seven years old.

“Why wouldn’t we be able to speak to him? Are you sure you’re all right?” Her mother checked both of Lucy’s temples, her forehead, and even the back of her neck. “Maybe you have a fever. I’ll get the thermometer.”

Lucy barely noticed her leaving. Mr. Butler shouldn’t have been able to answer the phone or talk to her parents about bread. Mr. Butler was supposed to be in jail.

Now more than ever, Lucy desperately needed to talk to James.

Chapter Thirty-Six

Anita's mother clocked her the moment she entered the ballroom. An impressive, nigh Herculean feat given the vast number of people currently crowding the elegant space. Patrick, damn him, made a beeline for Evelyn and Jackson and Alexei, leaving her alone and vulnerable.

"Anita, I'm so glad to see you. It was terrible last night." Her mom wrapped her arms around her body and shivered.

A twinge of guilt curdled in Anita's stomach. "I'm so sorry we got separated, Mom. Are you okay?"

"Of course, of course." She waved her hand in the air, brushing it off, though Anita could still see the grief and fear in her eyes. "That poor woman. Have you heard anything?"

"No, nothing." Lucy would probably be investigating it now. Except, now that she thought about it, Anita hadn't told Lucy what had happened the night before at the ballroom. They'd been too preoccupied with the saga at Gryphon House. Intriguing that both had happened the same night.

"Look, darling, I can't stay today."

"Oh, that's fine." And a massive relief that she did not want to parlay to her mom. "Maybe we can meet for dinner or something."

"That would be lovely." Her mom repeatedly

tucked her curls behind her ear. Her mother was a dreadful poker player. In anticipation of bad news, Anita's jaw clenched. "Listen, darling, there is no easy way to say this, but I want you to know. You should…be prepared. I cannot attend the announcement because I'm going to pick up your father from the train station."

Anita was breathing inside of a vacuum, all of the air pressed from her lungs by a force stronger than gravity.

Her mother approached her, placing a warm hand on her shoulder. "He wants to make this right, Anita. I know this is challenging. But he really wants to make this right."

Dimly, through the wave-like rush of blood in her ears, she registered the sound of the pro/am competitors finishing their heat on the floor to generous applause. Her mother's hand grazed her arm, like fleece on cold flesh. Was she saying something? Anita couldn't hear.

She should definitely have forgotten this entire day and just gone back to bed.

The approach of her teammates' nervous-smiling faces reminded her why she hadn't. "Mom, I've got to go. There's Hanna and Markus and Laurie. They're probably making the announcement soon."

Her mother swiped under her glistening eyes. Great, now she'd made her mom cry. "Of course. You don't even need luck. You are exceptional, my love."

Anita gave her a quick hug, shuffling the new, unwelcome information about her father's impending arrival behind a tall wall inside her brain.

"Anita!" Hanna called behind her.

Time to work. Anita painted on the brightest smile

she could muster with her Rockette-red lips, because sometimes people needed a little glitz to shore them up for the world. "Hanna! Good to see you. This is some bananas shit, right?"

"Tell me about it." Hanna rolled her eyes and kissed both of Anita's cheeks in quick succession. "In all honesty, after everything this week, we've been talking about not returning to the dance festival next year."

That sounded like an exceedingly tempting thought.

Laurie crossed her arms over her chest. She wore a knee-length black lace dress that hugged her curves, with straps criss-crossing her muscular back. "I know who I'm *not* returning with next year."

Anita followed Laurie's gaze across the ballroom to Mikhail, who gesticulated wildly in Lucian Chatelaine's face. Even from this distance, she could see the smoke rising from his ears.

"What's all that about?" Hanna asked.

Laurie harrumphed. "He's pissed because he wants Tom Havens's post on *Dance with Me*, and they won't give it to him. Thank goodness. If I had to work with him every day on the show?" She shuddered violently. "Tom was heinous, but Mikhail's social climber tendencies would wear me out so fucking fast."

Hanna appeared skeptical, which suited her pretty, heart-shaped face. "They're already looking for a new host? He died less than forty-eight hours ago. Super classy."

"Television never stops." Laurie brushed a piece of lint from her shoulder. "I wish they'd pick someone like you two. Or Jackson Alder, but I heard he turned them down flat."

Anita's brain whirred, churning almost too quickly. So maybe this was why Chatelaine wanted to meet today. From the little she knew of him, there was zero chance she wanted that toxicity in her professional life. "Jackson probably doesn't want to work for an asshole."

Laurie nodded her approval and chuffed her shoulder. "Right on, Anita. Completely."

"Besides, he's completely besotted with Evelyn." Hanna gestured toward the happy couple, the faint Danish accent clinging to her voice. Jackson's arm looped tightly around Evelyn's waist, while they all laughed at something Alexei said. Patrick laughed, too, which only served to make Anita long for him. Gossip wasn't her usual forte. "He's one hundred percent moved to Scotland. I doubt he'd relocate to Toronto."

"What exactly is wrong with Toronto?" Laurie smacked Hanna's arm.

"Absolutely nothing! I love it there. Give me some Canada any day. But Evelyn's not leaving her mom and Alexei. Not when they're kicking Standard butt." Hanna sipped from a large, reusable water bottle. "What do you think, Anita?"

She shrugged. The gears still spun in her head, whirling faster than a quickstep. "I don't know if I can speculate."

Laurie nudged her in the side. "Earth to Anita. What's going on inside that sunny blonde head? Come on, speculate wildly with us. It's fun."

A smile tugged at the corner of her mouth, but then she noticed Mikhail storming away from Chatelaine, fists clenched like he was about to punch someone. He was a dickhead, but he wasn't a murderer, was he? He had motive, she supposed, if he wanted the same job. She knew first-hand how single-minded he could be.

When she started to speak, her voice felt ethereal, even to her. "Doesn't it all seem weird? Tom Havens gets murdered and dumped in a peat bog. Women vanishing, then one shows up in the ballroom, bloody and hurt. All this drama about a TV show and the dickhead who runs it. One of the things I've always loved about ballroom is how elegant it is. How structured, how polished. And this entire week has felt like one giant shit show."

Hanna and Laurie clucked beside her. "Well said."

Horace Brixley stepped up to the dais and the DJ played a *bah-bah-bah-bu-bum-bah-dah.* Almost entirely as one, every eye in the ballroom turned to the bandstand, presumably for the announcement. Except Anita. She caught Patrick's gaze and held it. In his eyes, she could see the exact same doubts and questions reflected in her own. They'd been through so much together. Instinct wouldn't let go of its hold on her now. Whatever was going on, Mr. Butler was only a part of it. She had a sense this ran far deeper, and to plumb the depths, she needed to get to Chatelaine.

"Ladies and gentlemen," the announcer said, his words as crisp as his freshly-ironed shirt. "Thank you for coming to this special presentation, where we will announce the winners of last night's Team Match competition!" Applause broke out, but it was far more tepid than Anita or, apparently, Brixley anticipated. He faltered visibly, but then seemed to recover. "Right, good. Well, on to the winners of our Standard Team Match—"

"What happened last night?" someone in the crowd shouted.

"Yeah, what happened?" echoed another.

"Who was that woman?" cried someone else. "Is she all right?"

Brixley clutched the envelope so tightly Anita feared it might disintegrate in his palms, but his voice didn't let on his discomfort. "All in good time," he said frostily. "We don't know much."

"We want answers!" That sounded suspiciously like Alexei to Anita's ears.

"Of course, of course." Brixley sounded almost bored, but his eyes were rimmed with steel. His gaze searched the crowd before landing on Chatelaine, whose face curled into a sneer. Anita didn't know why Brixley even bothered. No help was coming from that quarter. Clearly, Horace decided upon expediency. "Well, the winners of the Standard Team Match are Team Great Britain! Huzzah!"

Evelyn, Alexei, and the remainder of the team didn't move from their spots. Each of them crossed their arms across their chests and stared, stone-faced, at the announcer. The audience seemed divided in their response. Half broke into a confused smattering of applause, while the others did nothing at all.

"Jeez, it's like *The Hunger Games* in here," Laurie murmured.

Brixley's face reddened and he stomped off the dais, handing the cards to a red-haired young woman in a fitted navy-blue skirt suit.

She glanced several times blankly at the cards before ascending the podium. Flop sweat cascaded from her as she turned every which way, trying to find assistance or someone, anyone, else to take charge. But she was a minnow in a sea of sharks. "Um, hello." She had a pleasant Scottish burr to her voice. "I'm Maeve MacReady. Um. Yes. Very good, very good, uh, well done, Great Britain. And the winners of the Latin Team Match are Team Americas! Beautiful, beautiful!" Her voice caught on the last syllable, and she clapped her hands together. White notecards spilled over the dais.

Without speaking, Anita, Laurie, and Hanna all mirrored the British team's stance. Anita's jaw steeled, her teeth clenched so tightly she wondered if she might break something. It wouldn't matter. Answers were far more important at this stage.

Maeve MacReady didn't hesitate. "I'll see what I can find out." She dashed off stage.

Several moments of confused chaos unfurled after that. The DJ startled, played the opening strains to "Stairway from Heaven," then quickly switched to a Strauss waltz, as though that would be more of a stress reliever than Zeppelin. Half the crowd of onlookers and competitors surged toward the dais, as though by sheer force of will they could find answers. The other half dispersed to wherever or whatever it was they were doing.

Anita felt Patrick's reassuring presence behind her, and his warm breath against her neck. "Let's get out of here."

Without speaking, she slid her fingers through his and they wove their way through the crowd, out the back entrance, and into the alley.

Anita pulled Patrick to a stop, her breath heaving in her chest. "What the hell just happened?"

Patrick shook his head. "People are *pissed*. Jackson

said he talked to Chatelaine this morning and there was an angry mob outside the office, demanding answers."

Anita chewed on the inside of her lip. "Do they even have any?"

He shrugged in response. "Jackson didn't know. He said Chatelaine only seemed concerned about finding a replacement host for Tom Havens. But he turned him down."

"Smart."

The back door clanged as more competitors streamed into the alley, clearly staging some sort of walk-out protest.

Anita clenched her fists by her sides, her muscles alive and ready. "We need to find out what's going on. Brixley and Chatelaine seem to be arguing a lot. And did you see Mikhail? He disappears at the worst times."

"Agreed."

"I say we focus first on Chatelaine, since he invited us. Maybe there's something in his office connecting all of this. What's the strategy?" So she wasn't telling Patrick that she desperately needed a distraction from her parents being in Blackstone. She wasn't ready to see her dad. Not by the longest of all possible long shots. If she couldn't dance as a distraction, this was the next best thing.

As Patrick detailed his plan, fire curled up Anita's spine. She was ready. She had taken down criminals before, and she could do it again.

Never underestimate a ballroom dancer.

Chapter Thirty-Seven

Patrick's resolve faded with each step toward Lucian Chatelaine's office, but Anita's not-so-subtle fury pressed him onward. Even if each subsequent step was a little more leaden than the last.

It would have been easier if the Blackstone Police Department hadn't blown them off like their tip was a piece of dirt-streaked gum under their shiny patrol shoes. It would also be easier if Anita would just admit she had wanted to go on this fool's errand because she was avoiding talking to her mom.

His job was to be there and listen. That was all. And, maybe, possibly, subtly encourage her to set a date for their wedding.

They paused outside the entrance to Chatelaine's office building. It was an elegant building of yellowing stone with iron-framed windows filled with sparkling glass. Definitely incongruous in this town of dive bars, off-license shops with bouncers at the doors, and apartment buildings that had seen better days. Like during the Blitz, or the spray-paint fueled and fumed punk rock revolution.

"You're thinking about Sid Vicious, aren't you?" Anita hadn't relinquished his hand, thank goodness and everything holy.

"Can you blame me?" He couldn't even pretend to laugh. Nothing about this situation seemed funny. The instant Lucy had mentioned a trafficking ring, he couldn't shake it from his mind. Now it had grown into an insistent cancer of thought, coursing through his blood and brain, demanding answers.

They stared at the rotating glass doors to enter the building. Inside the marble-fronted foyer, he read signs in metallic letters for the different businesses therein. Barristers, an accounting firm, and there on the wall, Chatelaine Enterprises. Even the script looked sinister, or maybe that was again the kernels of discontent and fear in his chest.

"Are you ready?" he asked. *A.k.a. tell me this is about your dad without telling me this is about your dad.*

"No." Anita squeezed his hand, her jaw tight. "Let's go."

The skies opened as they entered the building, an enormous crack of thunder rippling the earth beneath their feet. Patrick pushed on the revolving door, but a gust of wind behind him refused to allow him entry. He wasn't going to be bested by a simple door. He pushed harder, leaning into it, and when the pressure released, the door spun and he stumbled into the foyer. Anita followed a moment later, her carefully curled locks plastered against her face.

"Talk about portents," she murmured, smoothing the hair from her eyes.

The sharp click of stilettos echoed against the marble floor. "Ms. Goodman. Mr. O'Leary." A lovely young woman with dark-brown skin with bronze undertones and a cascade of rich curls held back by a red headband approached with a tablet in hand. She wore a well-tailored cream-colored skirt suit and crimson heels. "Pleasure. I'm Faye, Mr. Chatelaine's assistant. Follow me, please."

Still clutching Anita's hand like the lifeline it was, Patrick fell into step behind Faye.

"I love your shoes," Anita said without a hint of fear or distraction in her tone. He should emulate her.

"Thank you." Faye smiled warmly at them. "They're my favorite pair."

"They're gorgeous." Anita slipped her hand from Patrick's grasp and followed Faye into the waiting elevator. "We don't know Mr. Chatelaine very well. Have you worked for him long?"

A shade passed across Faye's high cheekbones. "Not long." She pressed the button for the third floor with what Patrick felt was a high degree of angst.

All these lovely women surrounding Chatelaine. Conviction knitted along Patrick's spine. Lucy had been right. There was more going on around here than a messy dance festival and a mysterious murder.

****

When the elevator doors chimed open with a practically medieval gong-like sound, Patrick and Anita followed Faye past a massive oak desk with a dying orchid in a pot on one end. The office was neither as grand nor as large as Patrick had anticipated. In fact, it had all the markers of former glory—empty gilt-edged frames, chipped desk edges indicating cheap plywood construction, dusty fake ficus trees in the corners.

Who was this guy? This office had every aspect of a former gangster trying to make good. Did he really entertain high-powered people here?

When Faye indicated Chatelaine's actual office, it answered Patrick's question. Whatever money there was had been spent here. Thick mahogany furniture with layers of upholstery, his name etched into a gold plate, everything polished and smelling of lemon and pine.

The nervous tingling in Patrick's spine sent lightning-strike-level anxiety rocketing through him. Something was very, very wrong here. Maybe this wasn't just about Anita's relationship with her parents.

If Mikhail really was the guilty party, he couldn't help squeeing a little on the inside. *Focus.*

"Here you are." Faye gestured into the office, a placid smile on her face. "Would you care for anything to drink?"

"No, thank you." Anita was still in people-pleasing mode, and for that, he was immensely grateful. He wasn't certain he'd be able to maintain his composure or hold himself back from making wild accusations. Besides, they were here for fact-finding, not brawling.

Though his muscles twitched, desperate for some sort of action.

As they entered, Lucian Chatelaine stood from behind his massive, euphemism-sized desk. Looking at him, Patrick wouldn't know about the melee at the ballroom. It hadn't touched his perfectly-coiffed hair or the navy-blue pocket square tucked into the breast of his expensive-looking suit.

Though if Patrick looked closer, the suit had all the same flaws as the office. All the appearance of wealth, but with frayed threads at the cuff, the lapel a little too shiny. For the first time, he wondered if Chatelaine had pushed his son on Lucy because maybe there was some sort of business deal behind the scenes. Cassandra Knight did run an extremely successful multinational corporation.

"Welcome!" Chatelaine spread his arms wide, like he was welcoming them into his kingdom. "Did Faye offer you something to drink?"

"Yes, we're fine," Anita said. She folded herself into one of the two large armchairs opposite Chatelaine. Patrick followed her lead.

"Excellent." He clapped his hands together, apparently to signal Faye's dismissal. It only served to make Patrick hate him more. "So you two must know why I've asked to meet with you."

Anita didn't glance at him, her gaze locked forward and mustered into a polite expression. "No. I'm afraid we are a little in the dark here."

"Ah, yes. It has been an unusual festival." The man's expression barely changed. "To illuminate, we here have been very impressed by your performance. Last night's Team Match was quite memorable."

Patrick chewed on that. He could practically see the smoke rising from Anita's ears. Focusing on their performance in the Latin rather than acknowledging the massive elephant in the room? "Who is *we*?"

Chatelaine fixed him with a stare that wouldn't be out of place in the northernmost reaches of Norway. "Pardon?"

Impressive how he packed one word with so much scorn. "You said 'we' have been impressed." Patrick glanced around the otherwise barren office suite. "Who else should be here? Faye? Or is this more of a royal we situation?"

Chatelaine's eyes narrowed slightly. "My partner in *Dance with Me*, Horace Brixley, and I have discussed this situation at length. He does not need to be present in order to give his blessing."

"Blessing about what?" Anita's ballerina-straight posture seemed out of place in the luxurious chair she perched on. "You still haven't told us why we're here."

"Of course. We had thought it would be obvious." Chatelaine pushed some inward button that oozed slimy charm. "Since the passing of Tom Havens, we have an opening for a judge on *Dance with Me*. We would like to discuss the possibility of you two filling that role." Clearly mistaking Patrick and Anita's silence for interest, he continued. "You would have to leave wherever it is you live now. Somewhere in, I don't know, Ohio?"

"Huh." Anita's voice was almost a growl. Sexy and deadly. Patrick fell a little more in love with her because of it. He knew well how much she cared about Lewis, Pennsylvania.

"Excellent. So you would have to move. You might also be asking why we have chosen you, when there are so many qualified candidates."

Patrick was astonished at how many veiled insults Chatelaine packed into this supposed job offer.

The businessman continued blithely. "Your social media presence, your flair, all of this make you two valuable as a couple." Patrick clenched his fists. Any time anyone mentioned another person's value in a monetary or business way, it reeked of deeply seated colonialism. "Of course, you are not our first choice, but that rarely works out in situations such as these. It would be better, too, if you were married. Mr. Havens's reputation…soured some viewers. A married set of judges would bring them back."

Patrick could hear Anita's jaw unclench. It was a

disturbing sort of popping sound, a tight joint snapping open. "So. You want us to leave our business and move to Toronto in order to host your show? Oh, and get married to repair the damage Havens's womanizing did? How exactly would that benefit us?"

Chatelaine's eyes widened, as though he couldn't imagine such a ridiculous question. "It is a very prestigious show, Ms. Goodman."

"Dubious, as the last host was murdered and ended up in a peat bog." Oops. Patrick didn't realize he had spoken this thought aloud until he caught Chatelaine's Arctic stare again.

"What happened to Mr. Havens was…unfortunate. A tragedy." He smiled in the way of snakes, no emotion reaching his eyes. "But he led a dissolute life. I'm certain neither of you will cause such trouble." He tapped his fingers on the desk. "Perhaps next season, consider a well-timed pregnancy announcement. People love a show baby."

Patrick shifted in his seat, mostly to keep himself from launching across the desk and shoving that fucking pocket square down Chatelaine's asshole throat.

"So what would be the terms?" Anita asked. He'd thank her later for redirecting the conversation.

"Yes, of course. We have a new morality clause, but that shouldn't be complicated for you." He leered at her, and it took every force in Patrick's body not to lunge across the desk and throttle the man. That would not give them information. "We offer a competitive salary, but keep in mind, the majority of your compensation would be in sponsorships." He droned on, but Patrick had caught that as well. Did that mean there wouldn't be that much money? He wondered if Mikhail was aware of that, as he had lobbied hard for this exact position. Probably unwise if he had actually murdered Tom Havens.

If Patrick weren't so incensed by everything transpiring around him, he'd gloat a bit more about beating Mikhail and his stupid hair.

"What does that morality clause entail?" Anita chose each word very carefully, closing her mouth around each syllable like she was chewing it.

Chatelaine's gaze narrowed. "We are looking for judges and professionals who embody good, old-fashioned ideals."

Meaning, people who identified as part of the LGTBTQ+ or any other marginalized community would be excluded. Did Laurie Donovan know? Fuck this. He opened his mouth to say it but Anita intervened.

"It's incredible, what you've built." Anita gestured around Chatelaine's office, like she hadn't seen the outside. Patrick tensed, as this was his cue. Why was she bringing it up now? He caught her gaze, but she seemed certain. Fine. He'd play along. It was likely better than to leap across the desk and throttle Chatelaine with his ridiculous posh tie.

"I beg your pardon, but might I use your restroom?" he asked.

Chatelaine, puffed up from Anita's compliment, snapped his gaze between the two of them. "Yes, yes. Down the hall, to the left."

Patrick paused beside Anita, kissed the top of her head, inhaling her grapefruit and hibiscus scent. "Be right back," he whispered.

****

Once out of the office, he checked quickly for Faye, who was nowhere to be found. Initially, he headed like the good rule follower he was toward the bathroom.

Of course, that wasn't the real plan. Ensuring once more that no one else seemed to be in the office, Patrick poked around.

He didn't think there would be any neon signs pointing directly to a folder saying *Trafficking Info Here*! Though that would be convenient. When he and Anita had discussed it, he needed some sort of information, anything that might tell them what could really be going on with the dance festival. A nice smoking gun pointed straight at Mikhail, perhaps.

After a few locked doors, Patrick finally tested one that was open. Whether by fate or Chatelaine's inattention, Patrick didn't care. He wanted nothing more than to get back to Anita.

The room was filled with cardboard boxes haphazardly teetering atop one another. Nothing was labeled.

"How does this guy run a business?" One box was as good as another. He found one that had been folded closed, instead of taped, and pulled it open, revealing stacks of paper. Great. Now he was going to have to sit in the dim light.

Pulling out his flashlight, he knelt beside the box, skimming through the papers one by one. As he did, his heart started pounding in his chest. "Ooh, Chatelaine. You naughty, naughty boy."

Then a black-gloved hand clenched around his mouth, muffling his shocked gasp, and dragged him upright. “Don’t move,” a low voice growled.

Chapter Thirty-Eight

Lucy's phone burned a hole in the back pocket of her jeans. Of all the timing, her parents would show up now.

"Come sit down and tell us how you're doing." Her mom handed her a cup of tea and sat in the living room on one of the stiff leather armchairs, her perfect white suit moving with the fluidity of the ocean. Lucy's heart tugged inside her chest. She would never look like that. No matter how hard she tried. What if James was in trouble? Or his mom? If Mr. Butler wasn't in jail, would he go after his family? And what if James really was some sort of accomplice? Her instincts told her that wasn't true, but maybe she was blinded by her feelings. Feelings which were suddenly very, very real. Falling in love with James was like painting her skin with coziness.

Her dad sat in the armchair opposite her mom, completely oblivious to her inner turmoil, because of course he was. He was checking his phone, scrolling through articles on how to be a better hospital administrator or something. It all felt so futile.

The cup of tea trembled in the saucer she held, the sound rattling through the overly wood-paneled room. "I have to go." Lucy's voice was soft, but her mother tilted her head immediately.

"What do you mean, honey? We just got home. We

were so worried about you, after we heard about last night."

"I'll bet it was all that Barrow fellow." Her dad looked up from his phone and nodded his head sagely.

"No!" Okay, that was maybe a bit too forceful. Lucy set down the cup and saucer on a nearby table before she dropped it and made a total ass of herself. "No. Look, I can't do this."

"Can't do what?" Her mother's face was a mask of confusion. This was probably Lucy's fault, since she hadn't exactly stood up to her parents before. Oops. Live and learn.

"I can't stay here. I need to go check on James and his mom. I need to make sure they're okay." Tears welled up in her eyes, but she swallowed them.

"Why wouldn't they be okay?" Her mom stood and approached her, taking her elbow with one hand. "Honey, what is going on with you?"

Lucy's breathing sped to fast-and-furious mode. She loved her parents, really she did. Even though she hid things from them, it was for their own protection. In their eyes, she was the Lucy they wanted her to be. And yet, it was completely exhausting to keep hiding parts of herself. Just like Anita had said.

Besides, the way her mom looked at her now, it was the same way she had looked at her when she was six and had a nightmare. Her mom would come into her room, rub her back, and sing a Vietnamese lullaby to her. Why hadn't Lucy ever learned it? It suddenly seemed so important to her.

So instead of crying, which honestly felt like an appropriate choice, Lucy flung her arms around her mom and held on tight. Time for the verbal diarrhea, but she would let it flow with truth this time. "I'm in love with James and I'm worried he's hurt. I have zero interest in dancing with Carter Chatelaine. He's a dickhead like his dad." Oops, she should rein in the swearing, but to her mom's credit, she didn't let go of Lucy. Maybe she'd get a one-time pass. "I want to dance with James. He's amazing, Mom. He's so smart and so friendly and I think I screwed it up because I may have accused him of helping his uncle in a sex-trafficking ring." Now her mom did tense, but Lucy held on tightly. She had to get this out. It felt so good to unleash. "I love you guys, but I don't want to be a competitive ballroom dancer forever. There is so much pressure about Blackstone and finding the perfect partner. I just want it to be fun. James is fun, Mom."

Her mom hugged her tightly, and Lucy dug her forehead into the soft silken shoulder of her blouse. "Oh, Lucy, it's okay." Her mom's voice was warm and soothing in her ear. "We love you, honey. We just want you to be happy."

Her dad cleared his throat behind them. "I do have some questions about the trafficking."

Her mom shook her head, then ran her hand down Lucy's straight black hair. "Is there anything else you have to tell us?"

"Um, well, remember when I said I had that internship at the police station and told you I manned the receptionist desk? Um, that wasn't entirely true. I shadowed Sheriff Flaherty the entire time. Oh, and the CSI unit." And had participated in bookings and shakedowns, but she wasn't entirely ready to go into the gory details. Something about her mom's pristine white suit didn't suggest she would welcome a discussion on whether blood spatter analysis was a "real" discipline. "Also, that whole thing about exploring the effects on climate change in peat bogs wasn't true. But I wrote it up anyway, for extra credit." She threw in the last two Magic Parent Words to protect her against everything else she had confessed.

Exhaling deeply, the way she always did when she was thinking about a challenge, her mom stepped back. "Okay. We have a lot to talk about. But I'm glad you told us."

Her dad held up a single finger, his cell phone nowhere in sight for the first time in so long Lucy could barely believe it. "I still have questions about the, uh, trafficking thing."

"Okay." Lucy sniffed, pulling herself back together. "I don't know much, but I can tell you what we think is going on. But first, please, can I go see James? I'm so worried about him."

Her mom nodded. "Of course. Why don't you call him?"

"I tried. I've sent him, like three hundred text messages. He's not answering his phone." Ugh, was that whiny desperation hers? Pass.

Her mom rolled her eyes. "Oh, honey. Pick up the phone and actually dial him. Texting is not the same as a phone call. Way too much gets missed. Your dad and I will find the car keys and we'll drive you wherever you need to go."

Hope soared within her. Okay. This was going to be fine. Her parents were actually on board. Go Anita with the good advice.

Lucy slipped her phone from her pocket, her fingers already sliding over the screen to make the call, when there was a deep gong-like sound that echoed throughout the foyer.

"Who's at the door now?" her dad grumbled, making his way through the front hall and yanking open the heavy front door. "Um, Lucy?"

Lucy turned, the pad of her thumb poised over James's name in her contacts list, and emotions flurried inside of her. "James!" Without caring what her parents thought, or what he was doing there, she dashed across the floor and launched herself into his open, waiting arms. He smelled of chocolate and biscuits. "I'm so sorry. I messed up. I was all confused, and I know—"

James cuddled her closer, resting his cheek against the top of her head. "It's all right, Lucy. I know. That's why we came."

We? Lucy pulled away, but only an inch because being in James's proximity felt pretty much like the best thing ever. Behind him, standing in the open doorway, was his mom holding a portable oxygen concentrator in a nifty little purse and River's leash. The dog barked when she saw Lucy. "River!" Holding James's hand and pulling him with her, she rushed toward the happy pup and descended into a very soothing rub fest.

"It sounds like we have a lot to discuss," her mom said quietly.

****

They didn't really. In the end, Miss Barrow pretty effectively communicated everything with only two sentences. "Lucy, my brother isn't what you think. Yeah, he's a bit of an uptight arse, but he's worked with an international task force for years in South Africa to combat trafficking."

Beside Lucy, her mother tensed. "So there is trafficking? Here, at Gryphon House?" She tsked. "No wonder we got such a good deal. They really should put more disclaimers on the rental website."

Miss Barrow spread her hands wide across the legs of her jeans. "I'm sorry to say it. He took the job here after he wrapped up one in South Africa. He thought he could hide the women here, the ones he managed to get out. That's who the two of you found."

Lucy's mom wrapped a protective arm around her shoulders. Which would be more welcome were Lucy not sitting at a parent-approved distance from James, and the arm felt more like handcuffs. "So he was helping that woman?"

Miss Barrow nodded. Beside her on the rug, River sniffed the air, then laid her soft, fluffy head down on James's knee.

Lucy shook her head. "Wow. Did we mess up his whole operation?"

"Of course not," James replied. He looked as eager as she was to ditch their very loving, involved, and a-little-too-present parents. "We may have forced him to show his hand a little earlier than he had intended. Last night, he was trying to free a woman, the one who was in the little room you found? But he got interrupted, and she escaped."

So that was who the woman had been in the ballroom, the one Anita and Patrick had rescued.

As if reading her thoughts, her mom said, "Where are Anita and Patrick?"

Chapter Thirty-Nine

Even though she had known this was coming, Anita would not have chosen to be alone in a room with Lucian Chatelaine. It wasn't just his overall unearned imperiousness but a not-so-subtle undercurrent of gangster that chilled her.

Still, this was the plan, and she had agreed to it. Though now that it was underway, she wished that they had forced the police to listen to them. If they were home in Lewis, John Flaherty would be there, ready to come to their aid. They had no such friends here.

She raised her hands to tighten her ponytail before remembering that, damn it, she'd left her hair down that morning. Fine. A curl tucked behind her ear would work just as well. Almost.

Chatelaine leered at her. "It is impressive, my empire, is it not?"

Great, a man who loved to expound on all the ways he was superior. She wouldn't need to engage in this conversation at all. It would give Patrick more time to snoop around the office.

Chatelaine stood and rounded the desk, ending with his hip buttressed against the fronting. "I wasn't born into this life, of course. You, as an American, would understand wanting to be a self-made man." Gag. He was probably going to quote Ayn Rand next.

"So how did you get here?" She hoped it sounded

like the interest of someone who might potentially be interested in fame and the trappings of fortune, instead of repulsed.

He grinned, which appeared more lupine than human. “Ingenuity. There are a lot of paths to success, Anita. Not all necessarily…abide by the law.”

Every hair on her body stood to attention. Whether it was his use of her first name or the casual implication that he really was, indeed, a gangster, she couldn’t tell. It wasn’t like any of this was positive information, full of rainbows and fluffy puppies.

Besides, the way he looked at her…no, not looked. Leered. Assessed. Like she was somehow his property.

Flashing red klaxon warning lights sparked in her head. How did she get out of this situation intact and still get more information from him? If only Patrick were here…

Play along. That was good old-fashioned female wisdom. She wouldn’t let on her kickboxing prowess. A man like Chatelaine wouldn’t believe her capable of anything, the dumbass. Mentally, she checked through her body, assessing each and every nerve, tendon, and muscle. If the opportunity arose, she would fight.

Chatelaine sucked his teeth, which was simultaneously gross and clearly meant to be charming. “Do you always abide by the law, Anita?”

Ugh. “I’m a small-town girl and friends with the local sheriff.” Probably good to toss out John’s name, even if he didn’t have jurisdiction across the pond. People would look for her. “It’s better for my business if I follow the rules.”

“Ah, there is a fallacy in your logic.” He waggled a long, tapered finger and Anita stifled her eye roll.

"Businesses are enhanced by skirting the rules. You, Anita...You could be so much, so successful, on the periphery of the law." He reached forward, as though to touch her, but Anita recoiled. Instantly, his face morphed into storm territory. "Is something amiss?"

Her heart pounded so loudly that she wasn't sure she heard him at all. "What are you asking, Mr. Chatelaine?" Better to clarify, particularly when her cell phone was recording this entire conversation. As long as she had set it correctly.

He bent before her, thin lips pulled back to display his chemically whitened teeth. "I'm asking if you know how to play nicely, Anita. A woman like you could make a killing, if you let yourself go a little bit."

"I'm a little slow." She pasted on her dumb-blonde smile. "Spell that out for me."

Instead of speaking, he ran a cold fingertip down the side of her face, and it took every ounce of training that she'd had not to turn her head and bite him. "There are people who would pay a great deal for a woman like you. A champion, a dancer. You're strong and beautiful. Flexible. Oh, yes. You could definitely make a killing. Patrick would never need to know, until you decide to trade up."

It felt like she had just bathed in a shower of awfulness. Bile rose in her throat, but instead of vomiting all over him, she stood instead on shaky legs. Might as well sell the timid blonde thing. "No, thank you."

"No?" He arched an eyebrow, his expression cruel, his muscles tense. "There are other ways to encourage you."

"Like what?" She hoped like hell her phone was

still recording. "There's nothing you could do to convince me to work for you, in any capacity, on any planet in this or any other galaxy."

"Really?" He steepled his fingers together like a sorcerer who'd chosen the dark side. "Are you certain about that?"

Something in his tone stayed Anita's retort. Her body stilled, a rabbit frozen in the glare of a predator.

"Ah, you figured it out." Chatelaine laughed, a soulless, empty chuckle, as he rounded the desk but did not regain his seat. "You have a weakness, and your weakness is a certain brown-haired, lovesick sot. If you refuse, we can always make him disappear. We've done it before. Look at Tom Havens."

The look he gave her spelled out exactly what he had done with his former host. Asshole. At least Mikhail wasn't a murderer.

"No." She clenched her fists at her sides.

"You don't believe me? He has been gone an awfully long time. Maybe we should go find the poor little lost fiancé." There was such threat in his tone, Anita didn't doubt he had a weapon there behind the desk. Likely a gun, because of course it would have to be a firearm. "Honestly, this would be easier without Patrick."

"You will not hurt Patrick."

"I will do what I like." He tossed a hand in the air as though lives were flippant and inconsequential to his overall master plan. "You are something I want. You do not wish to accede willingly, then I have ways to convince you."

"That woman…" She kept her voice breathy, as though she were unsure. "Last night." She kept it vague, couldn't let on about what had happened at Gryphon House. He didn't know she knew.

Chatelaine's eyes narrowed. "Someone tried to help her escape. Don't worry. She'll be dealt with in due time. We have friends on the local constabulary. There is always that convenient scapegoat of the Blackstone ghost."

Of course. Of course, he was using the legend to disappear actual people. Why were some humans so…inhuman?

Also, where the hell was Patrick? He should be back by now.

"So, what? You steal women from the competition and sell them to the highest bidder?"

He yawned. Fucker. "Blackstone hosts all manner of people looking for something. When a young woman wants more and isn't finding it, we find her. We can make her dreams come true."

She'd listened to enough of Patrick's true crime podcasts to know. "What? You drug her, get her addicted to something so she'll play nice with your customers? You're a common pimp."

He tensed. "Careful what you say. I'm a businessman. I connect people and services."

She was done with this conversation. Now she could do what she needed to do to get herself and Patrick out of there, and her recording to the police. "Let me go."

He tsked and withdrew an object from the top drawer of his desk. "I'm afraid I can't let you do that yet." She glanced down and inhaled sharply. Of course he'd have a syringe, filled with who knows what, instead of a gun. Asshole. "Now sit still, and be a good girl. You'll need to get used to that."

Well, shit. She could have handled a gun, but drugs? On the day before her ballroom competition? Absolutely not. No way was she going to sacrifice a single one of her faculties in the presence of this man. He didn't know what she was capable of.

As he approached, she backed toward the door, murmuring and pleading. But she knew what she was looking for. When her butt hit the side of the heavy, well-upholstered chair Patrick had been sitting on, she gripped it between her fingers. "No," she said softly, cowering slightly, bending her knees to incorporate the strength of her legs.

He nodded, his eyes dark and sparkling with violence. "Yes." He lunged for her, syringe in hand, but she was ready for him. She picked up the chair behind her and swung it to the side, knocking into Chatelaine. His body connected with a satisfying *thump* and a groan of deep, internal-bleeding-style pain. She couldn't pity a man who deserved it so little.

He leaned his forearms against the desk, breathing heavily, but he wasn't done either. Rage pushed him through the pain, and he lunged for her, but she stepped neatly to the side before sinking a kick deep into his stomach. There was a sickening squelching sound, like the contents being forced from a water balloon, and she retracted her leg so he wouldn't have time to grab her.

She needn't have bothered. At that moment, the office door swung open, and three people in black tactical gear swarmed into the room, guns up and ready. "Police. Hands up."

Anita did as she was told, hot tears blurring her vision. Where was Patrick? He should be here. If the police had arrived, what had happened to him? “Please,” she said, her voice ragged. “Please, did you find a man outside? Brown hair and blue eyes?”

The leader of the small team, face covered in a black balaclava, held Chatelaine roughly as he cuffed his wrists behind his back. “Ms. Goodman, you could not have fucked up this investigation more thoroughly. Now sit down and let us finally do our jobs.”

The voice was eerily familiar. Anita staggered backward as recognition set into her body. “Mr. Butler?”

The man in tactical gear rolled his eyes. “Finally caught on. Come on, Chatelaine. It’s the station for you, you fucking mobster.” With that, he frog-walked Chatelaine from the office.

The other two team members removed the black hoods covering their faces, and Miranda and Faye grinned at her. “Butler’s gruff. Don’t let it bother you. Nice moves. I’d love to have a chance to plant a facer on that arsehole,” Faye said.

What was actually happening? Her thoughts spun so quickly, she thought she might faint. In lieu of doing this in front of two kickass women, she sank into the armchair.

“Anita?” Patrick popped his head into the open office door, then ran toward her. “Are you okay?”

She launched herself into his arms, nestling into his shoulder and consoling herself with his scent. “What the fuck just happened, Patrick?”

Chapter Forty

In many ways, it was just as it had been the last few times Anita had been center stage in the immediate aftermath of a criminal being carted away, though perhaps with fewer police officers than in her prior experience.

Faye and Miranda supervised, since Butler had taken Chatelaine into custody.

For Anita's part, she stayed close to Patrick, letting his warmth pull her through and give her strength. He was very, very good at that.

"Are you two all right?" Miranda removed her hair from the bun holding it in place and tossed it over her shoulders. In so many ways, this seemed wildly inadequate conversation.

"Sure." Patrick pulled Anita closer. "I mean, hey, it's great that we were here when all this went down. Or whatnot."

Miranda leaned against the desk. "All right, look. I don't know why you two were here, but you're lucky to be alive. Chatelaine doesn't mess about. I've been undercover with him long enough to know that. The man started out in drugs and arms, then moved to people." She shuddered. "How are some men allowed to live?"

"So, these women..." How in the world did she ask such an impossible question?

Nodding, Faye entered and leaned beside Miranda. "Yes. He'd threaten them or bribe them, then hire them out to wealthy clients all over the world." She gestured to Patrick. "Those boxes you found are some of his records. Of all the ridiculous things, the man can't keep electronic records." She scoffed.

"Records. Oh, I recorded our conversation." Anita removed the phone from her pocket and cursed at her lock screen, fully loaded with messages and missed calls. "Oops. When I turned on the recording, I must have somehow turned off my notifications."

Patrick grinned and kissed the side of her head. "I think there are bigger problems."

"You recorded your conversation with Chatelaine?" Miranda repeated, her eyes wider.

Damn it, the missed calls and texts were from Lucy, her mom, and Nigel, all demanding her and Patrick's whereabouts. Of all the ways to let people down. Lucy and Nigel would understand, but Anita had never come clean to her mom about exactly how close she had trod to danger before. What was the right way to enter that conversation? Better to avoid at all costs.

Patrick nudged her, and she snapped out of her wallow. "What?"

"Miranda asked if you could show them the recording."

"Oh." She swallowed, a little too loudly in the otherwise silent room. "Sure." If only she could remember how she'd managed it the first time around. Flailing with the smart phone only served to make her feel un-smart.

"Let me help." Patrick gently extricated the phone from her trembling hands, but she could only see him through tear-blurred vision. He typed in her passcode, swiped through a few screens, then located the recording program he had downloaded to her phone.

The entire conversation sounded far worse on repeat, particularly the section where Chatelaine had threatened her. Her hackles rose again. Had she really been so foolish as to taunt him?

Wrapping her arms around herself, she squeezed tightly, willing warmth into her limbs.

No one spoke for a few long moments after the recording ended.

A cackle rose in Anita's throat, a desperate, crazed sound. "I can't believe I was so foolish." Her voice cracked on the last word, nearly swallowing it, and tears streamed down her face. Not for the first time she silently praised the invention of waterproof mascara.

She expected Patrick's embrace, but not the cool sensation of female fingertips against her chin. When she lifted her gaze, Faye smiled at her softly, her eyes warm and reassuring. "It's all right. You handled yourself well. It isn't the average person who can keep their cool when faced with evil."

Patrick rubbed Anita's back. "You don't know Anita."

With his rhythmic strums against her skin, the adrenaline charging her meltdown ebbed from her body in silver-cool wisps. She shut her eyes, so tight they were ready to bleed.

But she didn't bleed. She hadn't backed down from Chatelaine, and she wouldn't. She couldn't quite imagine competing in the Blackstone Open Latin tomorrow, but she and Patrick had succeeded with far less practice and much worse circumstances.

"How did you suspect Chatelaine?" Faye asked.

Anita cleared her throat. "We didn't. He summoned us. But it all just seemed off. Our student, Lucy, she found a hidden room behind one of the ballroom staircases. She didn't see anyone there, but when that woman escaped into the ballroom last night, I wondered if she had been kept there. All these coincidental issues around Chatelaine and his show. Tom Havens's murder. We thought we might look around, since we were going to be here anyway."

Miranda exchanged a narrow glance with Faye. "We suspected Chatelaine was behind that as well. We've unearthed some records suggesting Havens was a client. If Chatelaine was going to fire him for his bad behavior, Havens was definitely the sort to retaliate. Chatelaine probably hired someone to kill him and dump the body."

Anita shuddered. "Lucy will want to know."

"I already do." The teenager's voice startled her, and Anita whipped around in her chair.

"Lucy! You're all right!"

"I'm fine. You need to answer your damned phone, Anita." Lucy, dressed in jeans and a hoodie, stood beside James in the doorway, a half-smile on her face. "I can't believe you took down the bad guy without me."

"You had all better be going." Miranda crossed her arms over her chest, but her gentle expression belied her tolerance. "We have to gather more evidence. We'll call when we need you to make another official statement. Oh, and good luck tomorrow in the Latin. You two were amazing during the Team Match."

Hah. Anita stood, legs so gelatinous she was

shocked she was upright. But of course she was. Because Patrick had his arm around her waist, supporting her weight with his own.

"Let's get something to eat," he said, kissing the side of her head. She hadn't had a better offer all day.

Chapter Forty-One

A gorgeous light sensation flooded through Patrick's body the moment they stepped outside into the sunshine. The Gothic rainstorm of earlier had faded, leaving behind a rainbow over the beach and amusement park, and the crisp, warm scent of early summer.

"Come on." James squeezed Lucy's hand, and Patrick followed suit. "I know a pub nearby where we can get decent food and no hepatitis."

"Perfect." Lucy bounced alongside him.

Patrick nudged Anita, still a tad paler than usual despite her layers of spray tan. "They're suddenly adorable."

"They were always adorable." She linked her hand through his arm. "So are you."

"Aww, thanks." He rested his cheek on the top of her head. "Busy day."

"Ugh, don't remind me. Just once, I would like to go to a competition without getting into a brawl beforehand."

"Come on, Rhonda Rousey. It's pretty hot, watching you kick a guy's ass."

She shoved him playfully. "I'll kick your ass if you keep that up."

"Promises, promises."

Laughing, she tossed her long hair over her

shoulders. He could definitely get used to this vision of her, free and easy, her cheeks bright with sunshine and the aftereffects of adrenaline.

"What's on your mind?" He took her hand and looped it through the crook of his elbow. *Lucky bastard, thy name is Patrick.*

She shook her head. "Too much. Apparently my dad is coming into town."

"Wow. That's way out of left field."

"No baseball references, please."

Fair. His Phillies fanaticism had no place here on the dodgy side of the northwestern coast of England. Though if anyone could understand Philly sports fans, it would probably be football hooligans. Lot of similarities, there.

Also, sidebars aside, Anita was clearly avoiding the conversation.

"So what's all this about your dad?" *Please please please make up with him so we can schedule the wedding.* Though of course that was a selfish thought. Despite his best efforts, he couldn't squelch the desire. Not that he approved of literally anything Chatelaine had said, but the part about getting married for a show wasn't a terrible idea.

"I think maybe I should learn Farsi." Anita chewed on her bottom lip.

Patrick pulled her to a stop. "Stop deflecting." His therapist had told him to be more direct, so here he was, shooting for the moon. It would just be a long, long, looooong way down. "Tell me what's going on."

She exhaled loudly through her nostrils, dragon style. "You know what he's been like. Nothing I've done in my professional or personal life has ever been good enough for him. I mean, he stopped coming to my competitions when I was fourteen." Tears glistened in her eyes, but she sniffed them away. "Then he screws over my mom, and I'm supposed to do what? Forgive him? One olive branch doesn't repair a relationship."

Okay, maybe his therapist was worth all the extra money he spent on him. He hugged Anita to him, wishing he could suck all the sorrow from her into himself. "No, it doesn't. Sometimes parents mess up and it sucks. We're supposed to look up to them, but they're flawed because they're human. Just like we are." He was definitely blowing this motivational speech. "My point is that you're right. One olive branch doesn't fix anything. But it's an opening. You can't go anywhere in a locked room without any windows, right?"

She looped her arms around his neck, holding on tightly. That was fine with him. He'd be happy to be her life raft for the rest of his days. "You're really making a locked-room reference right now?"

He shrugged. "I can't help it. It's on my mind." He brushed his lips across her smooth, scented curls. "It's a chance, Anita. It's more than what we had yesterday. Maybe there will be more chances in the future. My therapist says, the more we open ourselves to risk in relationships, the more we can get hurt."

She laughed, her body shaking against his. "Wow, that's cheerful."

"I said the same thing. Then he clarified that even though we can get hurt, we also have an opportunity to deepen or heal the relationship."

She paused, her body so still in his arms he only felt the faint rise and fall of her breath. "Okay, maybe your therapist is on to something."

"I think he's pretty smart. We should go. I think we lost James and Lucy. I don't want to go to a hepatitis bar accidentally."

Anita pulled away then and re-looped her hand into Patrick's elbow. For a pleasant few minutes, his words stewed between them. His therapist was far more eloquent.

"Is that what you're trying to do?" She glanced up at him, then down at the street. Likely sidestepping the fallen bachelorette sashes as he was. "With your mom?"

Patrick waited for the anguished clench in his chest, but it didn't come. Maybe he was finally getting better. "Nope. That door has been welded shut, and the key has been mailed to Fiji with no return address, so buh-bye." There was a hint of pain in his words, but overall, he felt far more composed than he usually did around these issues. "I give the canteen money she begs me for to my therapist. It's a much better use."

Anita leaned her cheek against his bicep. So what if he flexed it, just to prove he could? "You're a great guy, Patrick."

"I know. Let's eat."

Chapter Forty-Two

Glitter. Sparkles. Hairspray.

The acrid scent of self-tanner was making Anita nauseous. Or maybe it was the waistband of her dance thong, cutting into her skin.

Either way, she was going to throw up or have a massive heart attack before the second heat of the open professional Latin competition. She was shocked they'd survived the first. Being up late the night before with Mr. Butler interrogating her like an unsexy British procedural detective had not helped her bring her A game.

"Remind me why this is a good idea," she said, twisting the bangles on her wrist.

Patrick kissed the top of her head and squeezed her hand. "Because you're exceptional. You're the best damned dancer out there. You look stunning." He paused. "And I love you."

She supposed that was a good enough reason. It would help if her mother had arrived, as she had promised she would. Marina didn't know about Anita's involvement in the takedown of Lucian Chatelaine's trafficking operation, and by the grace of the ballroom gods, somehow it had escaped the general gossip.

There was time to count her lucky stars once she and Patrick were eliminated from the open Latin. Wait. Strike that. Win. She needed her winner's mojo, not this nagging self-doubt that ate at her like she was worrying about leaving the stove on.

"Anita?" Laurie Donovan, dressed in a hunter green sleeveless jumpsuit, approached them, arms spread wide. "You guys were amazing in the first round."

"At least we found some space," Patrick said. Understatement. If Anita hadn't spent twenty minutes that morning perfecting her manicure, she might have bitten her nails off. Two of the couples dancing beside them had collided mid-samba, hard enough to draw blood. "Let's just say it's a good thing Anita's dress is red." In response, her stomach turned over. There wasn't enough spray tan to cover how blanched she felt. "Hey, Laurie, I'm sorry about Mikhail. Him ditching you like that?"

Laurie rolled her eyes and flicked her hand. "Good riddance. I'm ready to find a new partner after this anyway. What were you two up to yesterday afternoon? You missed all the excitement. Horace Brixley got hauled off in the midst of the pro/am by the police."

Anita's expression froze in place. Great, now she was a deer in the headlights. "Right. Sorry about that. We were practicing for today."

"Good luck." Laurie looped an arm around her shoulders and pulled her close. "Promise me we'll see each other soon, yeah? I told my girlfriend all about you two and she's dying to meet."

A trickle of the warm fuzzies soothed Anita. "Absolutely."

Laurie left them with a wave, and Anita shifted in her strappy golden dance shoes.

Patrick took her hand again and squeezed. "What's

going on?"

"I miss home. I miss our friends, the studio." She bit her lip as the dancers in the last heat finished with deep bows and wild applause.

"Me too. We'll leave soon, okay? This trip has been…a lot."

Another massive understatement. And it seemed like, as usual, her father was nowhere to be found at her dance performance. Tears pricked at the backs of her eyes. Why had she expected anything different? Just because her mom had said he had flown out here and wanted things to change, that didn't mean her dad would actually do it. He had to be the one in charge.

Jackson Alder, who had been recruited to fill the emcee position since Horace Brixley was obviously not available, stepped up to the dais. "Ladies and gentlemen, let's give a big round of applause to all of our competitors." He paused for the whoops and hollers. The open professional Latin always drew a big crowd. Usually it fueled Anita, the excitement and anticipation. Today, though, she just wanted to crawl back to Gryphon House and pull the covers over her head. "On to the next round! The following competitors to the floor, please."

Anita listened with half an ear as Jackson rattled off a list of numbers, none of which were hers and Patrick's. Great. They had flown halfway across the world, set their student up with a new boyfriend, and helped stop a sex-trafficking ring, and now they weren't even going to advance past the first round. It was all so pointless.

Patrick tugged on her hand, looping it through his elbow. "Smile, gorgeous. They called us."

She painted a smile on her face and willed herself to focus. When all else in her life was going to shit, at least she could use Patrick as her anchor and lose herself in the music.

Patrick walked her out onto the dance floor, and the crowd was a sea of nameless faces and flashing lights from camera phones. Anita spun and waved, hoping she didn't look completely inane. She had to get it together. The final couples called were finding space on the floor, and the intro music was ending. It was only the cha-cha, ninety seconds before she would clear the floor and the next heat would go on. Then rumba, samba, Paso, and jive, with time in between for the other heats.

Easy. She'd done this a thousand times. Then the cha-cha music came on, and it was the unmistakable opening sounds of "I Wanna Dance with Somebody." Genuine excitement warmed her muscles. Thank goodness for Whitney Houston. She turned to Patrick and posed, just as they had practiced. "Let's do this."

****

There was a break after the jive for the judges to tally who was going to advance to the quarterfinals. "I need to go to the bathroom," Anita said. Patrick nodded, not turning from his conversation with Hanna and Markus.

Good. She needed a moment to herself. But apparently that was not meant to be. "Anita?" Her mom stood in her path, hands clutching the strap of her vibrantly colored purse.

Anita's already twisted stomach churned. Of course she would have to go to the bathroom now. "Mom?"

Her mom ran toward her and wrapped her arms around her. "We were so worried. Why didn't you tell us what was going on? We tried calling, but you never showed up at the restaurant yesterday."

Oh. Right. She couldn't exactly tell her mom this was because she'd gotten involved in the takedown of Chatelaine's nefarious enterprise. "I'm so sorry, Mom. The day, um, got away from me."

Her mom squeezed her tighter. "No matter. I'm just glad you're okay."

It did not seem, though, that her parents' worry had extended to her father actually showing up at one of her competitions. No matter what her mom had promised. She had gotten far too accustomed to being disappointed by him. "I'm fine. Are you enjoying the performance?"

Her mom's grin could have lit the entire ballroom. "You are amazing, Anita. I thought you were wonderful in the Team Match, but this? You and Patrick are on fire."

"Thanks." It would help if she didn't know that she wasn't exactly at her best at the moment. There was still something off, and if they didn't—or she didn't—pull her head out of her ass, they wouldn't make it past the quarterfinals. Which reminded her. "Mom, I'm really sorry. I have to go to the bathroom and fix my makeup and—"

Her mom's eyes widened. "Oh! But your father wanted to talk to you."

"Dad?" She felt slightly as though she'd just taken a roundhouse kick to the temple. "What do you mean? Dad's here?"

"Hi, honey." His familiar, gruff voice sounded

behind her. Turning felt like moving through molasses, or getting her feet caught in a peat bog. Not that she wanted to think about bog bodies again. She cursed Lucy and Patrick silently.

Her dad looked sheepish; at least he had the decency for that. A thousand conflicting emotions and words rose inside of her. She crossed her arms over her chest, holding them all inside. Whatever. She'd had plenty of practice at this. "So I'm 'honey' now?" Her voice came out sharp and snappy, far more composed than she felt.

His face fell. "I deserve that." He'd gained some weight since the last time she'd seen him, in an extraordinarily awkward family counseling session during his inpatient rehab stay. His cheeks were pale and his blond hair had whitened at the temples. But he was here. That was the thought that kept sparking inside of her. When was the last time he had watched her dance? In the beginning, when she had first started dancing, he had always been there with flowers, even switching his call or work schedules to be present. Somewhere along the way, his disappointment that this had taken a bigger presence in her life than his dreams of medical school for her had gotten in his way.

But here he was now. She hadn't fully believed he would actually show up, despite her mom saying he was in town. A frosted part of her heart melted a tiny amount.

Her dad sighed, hands in the pockets of his tan corduroy pants. Who still wore corduroy, particularly in the late spring? Granted, it had been raining and less than fifty degrees when she'd arrived at the ballroom that morning, but still.

"Let me get this out," he said. Like she was standing in the middle of a stage with the spotlight shining on her, all other thoughts fled Anita's mind. "I know I've messed up. I realize how awful I was, or am, still. But I want you to know how sorry I am. I regret every single minute of every day how badly I fucked up. You and your mom were always meant to be priority number one for me, and I let work and…other bullshit get in the way. I can't let that happen anymore. I miss you. I miss your mom. I miss our house. I miss seeing you smile. I know I haven't been supportive of your dreams, and I am so sorry, but I have to tell you that I was wrong. You followed your own path and you have succeeded." Tears collected at the corner of his blue eyes, so like her own. "I'm so proud of you, Anita. Watching you and Patrick today…you were transcendent. No, you are transcendent. You've worked so hard for this, and I'm in awe of you. You built your own business, and it's a pillar of the community." His voice hitched. "I was wrong to hold it against you, that you didn't go to med school. I just didn't want you to suffer. But I see you're not. You're thriving. And I'm so happy for you. I only hope that someday you'll let me be a part of your life again."

He stopped abruptly, like he was surprised he had said so much. It was undoubtedly far more words than she had ever heard him say to her before, particularly since her senior year of college. Her mom wrapped her arm around Anita, and she could feel Marina's silent sobs.

It was everything she had ever wanted to hear from her dad. Everything she had ever needed to hear. But somehow, it still didn't feel quite right.

"I don't believe you," she said, her voice so soft it was almost drowned out by Jackson's voice through the loudspeaker, saying they would announce the quarterfinalists in five minutes. And that thought—not the quarterfinals announcement, but the realization that she couldn't believe the words her own father said—made her want to burst into tears. Then she would have to re-apply all her makeup, and that only fueled all the rage and indignation she had buried. "I don't believe you." Her voice gained conviction. "You come here, during possibly the biggest and most important moment of my professional career, to tell me you're sorry? I can't handle this kind of emotional turmoil right now. Did you even think how this would feel for me? I don't know if I can go back out there and do what I need to do with all of this roiling inside of me. Why now? Why today, of all days, did you choose to want to be a father?"

When her mom's grip tightened on her, she knew she hadn't just hurt her dad. Which only served to make her feel worse, because of course the universe wouldn't let her have this. It wouldn't reward her with a smooth and easy competition, not when she wanted it the most. "And now you've hurt Mom. Do you know what it is to see that? To see how you wounded her? She was never anything but supportive and kind to you, and you walked all over her."

Her dad nodded repeatedly. "I know. I know, you're right."

Anita shook herself free from this entire situation. "I have to get back to Patrick. I have a job to do."

And she left them standing there in the hallway. She wouldn't cry. Not now. After they announced the quarterfinalists, she wouldn't have much time before she needed to go back on. *Hold it together, Anita. Hold it together*.

Chapter Forty-Three

Patrick bounced on his toes. These dance pants were grabbing his ass like a drunken bridesmaid. Where was Anita? Jackson stood on the dais, envelope in hand, and his beautiful fiancée was nowhere to be found. She wouldn't have gotten kidnapped on the way to the bathroom, right? Had they actually found everyone who was involved in the trafficking ring?

Maybe he did need to cut back on the true crime podcasts.

Then, like the parting of the Red Sea, he saw her. She looked just as gorgeous as she had before she left, bright eyeshadow spreading like wings from the corners of her eyes, the red dress that clung to every delicious curve sparkling in the ballroom lights. Still, he wasn't a fool. Something was wrong.

"What happened?" He took her hand and squeezed. He'd rather kiss her like there was no tomorrow, but that would smear her lipstick and she might hate him for it.

Anita shook her head, her body tensed. "My dad happened."

That was an unexpected turn. "Your dad? I thought you weren't taking his calls."

"I'm not. He's here. With my mom."

That explained her extra-tense posture. If only they had time to discuss this, but at that moment, Jackson cleared his throat. "Ladies and gentlemen, we have your quarterfinalists for the open professional Latin!"

Anita didn't even clap. This was not going to go well. "Are you okay? Do you think you can dance?" he whispered into her ear.

Her eyes narrowed to glinting scepters. "Fuck yes."

He would have to take that for now, because Jackson had called their number, but this discussion could not be over.

****

She danced like she was pissed at the world, and moving was the only thing keeping her afloat. It was all he could do to keep up the pretense that he was supposed to be leading her and not the other way around. It was at least something he had gotten good at over the years, pretending he was anywhere near her league.

They finished the jive with his legs shaking so badly he worried he might have torn something again, but at least he was still standing. After they bowed to raucous applause, he led her off the floor and toward a quiet corner. "Okay. Talk to me."

She tossed her long blonde ponytail, glittering with hair shimmer, over her shoulder. "I don't want to talk about it."

"Come on. Competitions are a marathon, not a sprint, and you were a fucking cheetah out there. Don't get me wrong. It's hot and you were amazing. But I can't keep up with frenetic pixie Anita." He took her face between his palms, careful not to smudge anything, and forced her to look at him. This was better. "It's just us. Me and you. No one else is here right now. Tell me." Technically, this was untrue, as the ballroom was pretty crowded, but hopefully no one was paying attention.

She gulped but didn't break from his gaze. "He just showed up here, today of all days. The one day I don't need any more distractions, and he finally comes to watch us dance? Then he says all of these things, about how sorry he is, and how wrong he was, and how he wants us to be a family again. It's total bullshit."

None of this sounded like bullshit to Patrick, but his therapist kept encouraging him toward active listening.

"I don't get it," she continued, her breath heaving but no tears coming. He always admired her restraint. "Why care now? What is he even thinking? And then, I said something really mean, and it hurt my mom, and now I feel like a giant asshole." She paused and looked at him. "I don't know what to do."

He brushed his fingers over her cheeks. "Sure you do. Even when you feel lost, you always find the right path."

"What would you do?"

That question struck him deep in his psyche. This was something he'd barely scratched the surface of during therapy, not that his counselor didn't ask. But if it would help Anita…He would do anything to help her. "Honestly? My dad left when I was just a kid. And I get why, I do. But he never looked for me, never reached out or sent me a birthday or Christmas card or invited me wherever he went. He just vanished." Idly, he wondered if there were any world where he could have this conversation while not wearing kohl eyeliner, but he had made an early morning decision, and this was the consequence. "I've thought a lot about trying to get in touch with him. I don't expect anything. He needed to move on." He laughed, a coarse, harsh bray, incongruous here amongst all the people in satin and silk and diamanté. Anita, because she was amazing, leaned her forehead against his. "If he ever said even one of those things to me that your dad said to you, my cold, dead heart would break, and I'd run into his arms like a chubby toddler in one of those welcome-home-from-the-Army videos."

"Patrick—"

"I'm sorry. I'm not supposed to tell you what to do. And I'm not trying to, I promise. It's just, if I've learned anything over the last few years, it's that life is about chance and choice and simply showing up. We've made it here, together. We'll keep going, however you want that to look. Whatever you want to do about your dad, I'm here for you. I'll always be here for you. Rain, sleet, broken ankles, handsy assholes, and everything in between."

She leaned her cheek into his palm, resting there, and why did nothing else ever feel quite as good as connecting with her? "Thank you."

"Any time." Though somewhere outside their cozy little bubble, he heard Jackson Alder clearing his throat again. "Except maybe for now, because I think they're going to announce the semifinalists."

Chapter Forty-Four

James wrapped his arm more tightly around Lucy. They had retreated to the quiet of the balcony, where they didn't have to fight for space but could still watch the competition.

"So," Lucy said, resting her head on James's perfectly-sized shoulder. "Your uncle is all MI5?"

He laughed, and it resounded down her spine. "I don't know precisely who he works for. I don't care, either. I'm glad your friends are safe."

"Me too." Plus, they were kicking ass on the dance floor, even if Anita was looking a bit ragey. Something must be going on with her, but it wasn't Lucy's place to ask. Besides, she would far rather spend the little time she had left here with James. There was a sinking feeling in the pit of her stomach, one she wasn't familiar with, and didn't know how to ease.

So she snuggled closer to James and breathed in his soft scent. There were little slivers of River hair all over his dark-gray sweatshirt. What would her life look like tomorrow, once the competition was over and her parents were forcing her to pack for the trip back home? She didn't really want to think about any of that.

"Do you ever want to be that?" James pointed at the quarterfinalists on the floor, a rainbow of glitter and spray tans, all moving around the ballroom with syncopation and rhythm. How judges distinguished between one couple and another in these professional heats, Lucy had no idea, but was inclined to believe it had a lot more to do with politics than anyone admitted. Though Patrick and Anita seemed to be crowd favorites.

"A professional dancer?"

"Yeah. I mean, you're definitely good enough. I don't know if I'm up to snuff."

A warm little kitten of pleasure played with a yarn ball in her stomach. "Are you saying you want to dance with me?"

He kissed the top of her head. "More than dance, if you're up to it. I'd even go tramping through the bogs again with you."

"Aww, that's the most romantic thing anyone has ever said to me." She kissed his cheek, the bristles of his five o'clock shadow tickling her lips.

"I mean it, Luce. I really like you."

The warm little kitten in her stomach started chewing through a mouse toy. "I really like you, too." This was it, wasn't it? The talk, the one where they were going to break up even though they'd barely started dating. Why had it been so much easier to leave every other partner she'd had? Okay, there was only one boyfriend and one dance partner, but still. She mentally ran through her preferred breakup playlist in her brain, starting with Olivia Rodrigo, natch.

When she tilted her head upward, James was smiling at her, his mouth slightly tilted at both corners and his eyes soft. "What's going on in that brain of yours?"

If they were going to have the breakup talk, she might as well wrench herself out of his perfectly Lucysized arms. Ugh, it felt like ripping off a bandage too early. "I'm running through our breakup playlist. I'll start with Olivia Rodrigo, a little Taylor, definitely some Kelly Clarkson—"

He held up his hand, which, for the first time ever, effectively silenced her. Or maybe it was the bemusement creasing all those romcom-style features. "You're a Swiftie? I had no idea."

"That's what you took from that?" She would either run into his arms again or flee to the bathroom. The bathroom sounded appealing.

"Lucy, what are you on about? You're making a breakup playlist already? Is this what you always do, plan the end before we barely begin?"

Okay, yes, but he didn't need to know that. "I don't want to talk about this."

"Talk about what?"

They were getting side eyes from the other viewers up in this balcony, but she could give two flying farts. "This whole where-are-we-going, weird relationship talk thing. I don't want to do it."

"So why are we doing it?"

"Because you brought it up!" That was way too loud. Tone it down, Lucy. She didn't want the entire Crystal Gardens ballroom to know James Barrow was breaking up with her after, like, a day. Even her reputation could barely stomach that.

He shook his head and took her hand, not releasing it even when she tried to pull it away. "Come on. We need to talk about this somewhere quieter."

He dragged her down a hallway lined with photographs of couples in full dance regalia before tucking them into an alcove behind some very dusty, very thick velvet curtains.

"Is this where you're going to murder me?" Lucy asked. "This is a supes murdery corner."

He laughed again. "I'm not—Lucy, come on. Don't you know me better than that by now?"

"I don't know anything about you." Except that she liked him. That he was sweet, and thoughtful, and went out of his way for people, and had an entire shadow network of friends, and had the most amazing dog—

"That's the problem, isn't it? We barely know each other." He wrapped a hand around her waist, pulling her toward him. "But I want to know you. I want to know everything knocking around that giant brain of yours. I want to kiss and fight and explore with you, and find out how you see the world."

"All through emails and sexts?" She did cross her arms over her chest, which was very difficult to do, as there were only about two inches between his chest and hers. Still, it was the point of the gesture.

He tilted his head. "I mean, I'm not ruling out sexting, but does anyone email anymore? I'd have to wade through all the spam from the one time I bought my mum crochet hooks for Christmas."

Unexpected. Damn him. It was the one thing guaranteed to make her laugh. She bumped his shoulder with hers. "Don't make me laugh."

"I like making you laugh." His expression softened. "I know nothing is easy, Lucy. I know we have our differences. But isn't it worth fighting for something that can make you happy?"

But, but, but. She hated those three letters. Unwelcome tears rose up the back of her throat. "You live here." Her voice was too soft, but he caught it nonetheless. She could tell by the generalized relaxation of his shoulders. "I live in Pennsylvania. I'm a senior in high school, and you're off to university next year. I don't even know how to date someone local, let alone long distance."

He moved so he could cup her face between his palms, and good heavens, how had she never known how supported that would feel? His hands were warm and callused and he smelled way too good. How was she even going to survive making a breakup playlist if she could barely manage this?

"Lucy." He caught her gaze, and it wasn't like she could look anywhere else but into those warm eyes of his. She wanted to drown in them, and that was about eight hundred degrees more melodramatic than she was comfortable with. This was going to hurt. She steeled herself. She could do this. She had actually talked to her parents, and that had gone far better than she could have imagined. Maybe she could survive this, too. Anita had weathered enough heartbreak, and look how things had turned out for her. "Lucy, look at me." Right, she was getting broken up with. Focus time.

He leaned forward, pressing his forehead to hers. "Didn't I tell you? I'm going to the University of Pennsylvania. I'll be moving to Philadelphia in two months."

Oh.

She wasn't sure who kissed who but was one thousand percent certain that it didn't matter.

Chapter Forty-Five

This was supposed to be the greatest moment of Anita's life.

She was in the semifinals of the Blackstone open professional Latin competition, further than she had ever gone before, and she was engaged to the best partner and friend she had ever had.

So then why was she still running on rage?

It was all her parents' fault. Well, and Lucian Chatelaine's, but that guy could rot in ballroom hell, with a monster thong-wedgie, being trampled by a thousand pointed stilettos and covered with marabou and eyelash glue.

Patrick squeezed her hand as they waited in the wings to be called. "Are you going to be able to do this?"

"Of course." She was being an asshole. Of course she should have thought about Patrick and his dad. It was one of the very few times he had ever brought it up, and they'd known each other for over a decade.

Aargh. If only someone could tell her what to do. She scanned the ballroom crowd but couldn't see Nigel anywhere. Patrick was right. There was a very particular mindset she needed right now, one where she was utterly convinced she could win this competition. Focus. Clarity.

All she had was muddled red wrath.

Patrick tugged at her hand again. "Are you reflecting on the oddly large number of people now in prison who have reason to dislike us? I mean, it's like a regular Arkham at this point."

Mirth tried to break through the anger but lost the battle miserably.

"All right. Look at me." Patrick spun her to face him and held her hands. "We can do this. Focus on the music. Focus on me. I'm here, Anita. This is the semifinals round at Blackstone. This is the dream. Your dream, our dream. It can be us, only us. Out there, in our personal lives. I mean, I'd love it if we could have Marina, too, because your mom is awesome and mine is in prison, hopefully for as long as humanly possible. But is that what you want?"

She gazed into those eyes that she loved so much. Was it? Did she really want to keep carrying this burden around with her for her entire life? At this rate, it was going to give her kyphosis in her thirties, and that was not helpful for a professional dancer. The clouds cleared from her brain, for the first time in months. This was the right thing to do. "I'm ready. I can do this." He bumped her in the shoulder.

"Hell yes, you can. Let's go."

****

She danced with a freedom and syncopation she hadn't felt in ages. Every time she turned or reached for him, Patrick was there. The entire five dances didn't take long to perform, and by that point in the evening, her feet ached in her shoes like someone had taken a vise to them, but she didn't care. In her bones, she felt it. They were going to get called back into the finals. They were going to win. All these years of striving, and this was her moment.

She was going to shine.

It also helped that the live band was playing music tonight that spoke to her soul, moved through her limbs, and made her feet fly across the floor.

As the audience clapped and whooped and hollered, Anita bowed, unable to hide the grin lighting her up from the inside out.

"You were incredible," Patrick said, even while trying to catch his breath. "I almost hope we don't get into the finals."

"Oh no. Is it your leg? Are you okay?"

"I'm fine. I just need some water."

"You go get water. I have to go do something."

Patrick's eyes glinted but he nodded. "Sally forth, soldier."

She kissed him lightly on the cheek and brushed away the hint of lipstick residue left behind. "I don't understand that reference, but thank you."

She had anticipated scouring the ballroom for her parents. It was crowded enough she could barely tell one face from another. In the end, though, they were sitting in the second row. Anita's anger faded like ice cream on a hot summer's day. To get those seats, they must have been here all day and paid a fortune.

"Anita." Her mom was on her feet first, reaching for her daughter. Gladly, Anita stepped into her arms and indulged in a patented Marina hug. "Darling, I'm so glad we are here to see this."

"I'm so sorry for what I said, Mom." Nope, no tears. Not right now. She had to fix up her makeup anyway before the finals, if and when they got called.

She felt her mom's tears wet her cheek. "It's all

right, my love. We just want you to be happy."

"I am." Anita pulled back from her mom to take in both of her parents. If she squinted just a little in the lights from the overhead chandelier and wall sconces, she could picture them as they had been twenty years ago, standing on the sidelines after her first ballroom competition. "I am happy." She turned to her dad, and the old conflicting emotions rose within her, but she tamped them down. Patrick was right. Forgiveness was a much lighter burden than holding a grudge. "I don't have a lot of time. I have to go fix my makeup before the finals. I just wanted to say, thank you for coming. It really means a lot to me that you showed up here. I'm not sorry that I was angry. I was sad, too. You and Mom, I thought you were unbreakable. Seeing what you went through, it made me doubt a lot of things about myself. But I know what I want." Her dad was nodding, his blond hair falling over his forehead. "And if you're serious, about wanting to try to repair our relationship, then I am very open to that. I miss you. Both." More words bubbled inside her, but they would almost definitely make her start sobbing, and she did not have the time or emotional and physical capacity for that right now.

The frown lines of her dad's forehead softened. "I meant it. Absolutely, one hundred percent. I meant every single word. If I have to spend the rest of my life making it up to the two most important women in my world, then it will be a life worth living."

"Okay." Anita swallowed. Her mom was crying silent happy tears with a tissue in one hand and the other clutching the front of her blouse, over her heart. "Good. I have to go right now, but we will talk. Later."

“Good. Great.” Her dad held out his arms, and Anita hesitated only a moment before stepping into them. How long had it been since her father had hugged her like this? It was awkward, sure, but something about it also felt right. Like it was something she had missed and was only now finding again. “You’re kicking ass out there, Anita. Well done.”

“Thank you.” She kissed her mom’s cheek, and before she could say or do anything else to potentially stop this wave of fortitude, she headed for the green room and some much-needed cosmetic repairs.

Chapter Forty-Six

They stood behind the green room door with the other semifinalist couples, all en masse, waiting for the finals announcements. Hanna Pascal, in a white-and-royal-purple bodysuit bedecked with crystals, waved to Patrick and Anita across the room. She and Markus were definitely getting called to the finals. Not that he had had a lot of time to see their semifinals performance, but from what he had watched earlier in the day, they were killing it and they were well-known to be judge favorites.

None of which made him feel any better. After a bottle and a half of water, and the subsequent necessary trip to the bathroom, his leg wasn't bothering him as much, and his lungs felt like they could actually process oxygen. Twenty more minutes, max. Then he could take Anita out to eat and celebrate. Maybe they could have it be just themselves. Not that he didn't want to spend more time with their friends out here, but they needed some serious one-on-one time after all this tumult.

Some of the competitors nearer the door than he was started murmuring amongst themselves, and a wave of nerves rocketed through him. They must be getting ready for the finals announcements. Six lucky couples, ready to dance their blisters off in the very last round of cha-cha, rumba, samba, Paso, and jive. Would he be one of them?

He didn't particularly care. On one level, his most basic competitive level, of course he wanted to win. Then again, after everything that had happened, all that they had survived that week, somehow winning at Blackstone held slightly less importance to him versus ironing out the details of his future with Anita.

Like, hopefully there would still be one after she talked to her dad. Which he would be able to find out if she ever returned from wherever it was she had disappeared to after the semifinals. Please, please let her not have been kidnapped and trafficked. Things he had only passingly worried about before now felt like a distinct possibility. More fodder for his therapist.

Then, like a phoenix swooping down to save the day, Anita walked through the crowd of competitors, pausing only to greet some of her friends. Whatever she had done, she now looked radiant. The wings of flame rising from her eyes to her temples sparkled with tiny crystals, and her hair shone in the shitty green room light.

She was also smiling and looked far more like herself than she had all day. Excitement curled in his stomach. Anita was back. They were going to win this thing.

"Everything okay?" he asked as he took her hand. Why stand apart when he was better with her?

"Perfect," she replied, gaze straight ahead and fixed on the door to the ballroom.

Jackson's voice sailed through the loudspeakers, and the waiting horde of well-dressed semifinalists ceased all other communication. "Welcome to the finals of Blackstone's open professional Latin competition!"

He paused for the requisite applause, which, to Patrick's ear, was pretty lively. A warm audience was a great audience. "Without further ado, let me introduce the top six couples. First up, Hanna and Markus Pascal, originally from Denmark and now out of New Jersey. Give them a big round of applause!"

Markus twirled Hanna out of the green room and onto the ballroom floor, and Anita edged closer to Patrick. "Hey," she whispered, squeezing his hand.

"Hey yourself." He strained to hear the next couple called, one of the two from South Korea. Totally justified. He had been watching them for years, and their technique was textbook awesome.

Anita bumped her hip against his, drawing his attention back to her, where it should have been anyway. "Do you think people still elope to Gretna Green?"

This was an unexpected turn to the conversation. His mind still half on the announcements—next was a couple from South Africa he didn't know very well but they had a show-stopping rumba routine—but intrigued, he turned to her. "I have absolutely no idea. Probably? I imagine people also show up in period dress. They probably make a lot of money on horse-drawn carriage rides there."

"Hmm."

There was only one spot left. Five couples had already been called. Were his palms sweating? Shit, they were sweating and clammy, but Anita hadn't let go of his hand yet.

"Patrick?"

He turned to her. Why wasn't she more freaked out? There was only one couple left to be called into the goddamn finals and she sounded cool as a cucumber.

When he saw her face, though, the openness and pleasure and sly insinuation behind her expression, all his anxiety fled.

"What are you doing tomorrow?" she asked.

His breathing eased and his resolve firmed. "As long as it's with you, anything."

Out in the ballroom, Jackson Alder's voice rang loud and clear. "And our final couple, from the United States, Anita Goodman and Patrick O'Leary!"

Epilogue

There were far more bagpipes than Patrick had envisioned on his wedding day. Prior to this, he had expected, well, none. There was also an anvil, but hey, when in Scotland. John Flaherty and Will Forbes were going to be so jealous.

He had to hand it to his soon-to-be wife. When Anita had an idea, she ran with it like an Olympic high jumper.

In a few moments, they would step inside the famous Blacksmiths Shop in Gretna Green, a single-story white stone building with black shutters, the door framed with horseshoes, the air smelling of rain and heather and smoke. It was all worth it. When he had seen Anita cross the town square in her dress, her hair falling around her shoulders in waves, carrying a bouquet of white and purple wildflowers, he didn't think anything was more perfect.

"Do you think our friends will be mad at us?" he asked Anita.

"No. We'll plan a big party once we get back. I like that right now it's just us. You and me. The way it's supposed to be."

He kissed her then, not caring about smearing her lipstick or mussing her hair. Just them.

Well, them and Anita's parents. And Lucy and James and her parents, because Lucy would not take no for an answer once she'd figured out where they were going to, so soon after winning at Blackstone. Someone should curb the girl's internet privileges.

Besides. Now he and Anita would go into the shop and stand before a famous anvil while the wedding officiant performed the hand-fasting ceremony. At the end of it all, he would finally be married to the love of his life.

It was a damn good day.

A word about the author…

A lifelong lover of the written word, Natalie used to spend her school recess hours reading Michael Crichton and Jane Austen. Not much has changed, except now she writes stories about smart, kickass women and the people who adore them.

Natalie lives in Los Angeles, where she is married to a man who literally brings life into the world. She is mom to two lovely young munchkins who despise brushing their hair and eat way too much cake. She is unapologetically terrible at taking selfies. www.nataliecrosswrites.com

Thank you for purchasing
this publication of The Wild Rose Press, Inc.

For questions or more information
contact us at
info@thewildrosepress.com.

The Wild Rose Press, Inc.
www.thewildrosepress.com

www.ingramcontent.com/pod-product-compliance
Lightning Source LLC
LaVergne TN
LVHW020539100826
845148LV00010B/1531